GREEN LIVING CAN BE DEADLY

"Dana, where are all the people?" Zennia asked, mirroring my own concerns from earlier.

Before I could say anything, a scream sounded from next door. Then another.

I stared at Zennia, frozen. She snatched up her chef's knife and held it close to her chest.

"What happened?" she asked.

I darted over and ran into Kimmie as she rushed out of the booth. I looked past her through the tent flap and saw Wendy on the pavement, motionless. Her neck was marred by an angry red gash. The wraps lay nearby, tofu and sprouts spilling out onto the pavement.

Kimmie grabbed the front of my polo shirt. "Oh, Dana," she said. Then she fainted.

I caught Kimmie in a haphazard hug, slowing her descent as she crumpled to the ground. I'd never had someone faint on me before, but that paled in comparison to whatever had happened to Wendy in that tent. . . .

Books by Staci McLaughlin

Going Organic Can Kill You

All Natural Murder

Green Living Can Be Deadly

Published by Kensington Publishing Corp.

Green Living Can Be Deadly

Staci McLaughlin

KENSINGTON PUBLISHING CORP.

http://www.kensingtonbooks.com

KENSINGTON BOOKS are published by

Kensington Publishing Corp.
119 West 40th Street
New York, NY 10018

Copyright © 2013 by Staci McLaughlin

All Kensington Titles, Imprints, and Distributed Lines are
available at special quantity discounts for bulk purchases for
sales promotions, premiums, fund-raising, and educational or
institutional use. Special book excerpts or customized print-
ings can also be created to fit specific needs. For details, write
or phone the office of the Kensington special sales manager: Kensington Publishing Corp., 119 West 40th Street,
New York, NY 10018, attn: Special Sales Department, Phone:
1-800-221-2647.

Kensington and the K logo Reg. U.S. Pat & TM Off.

ISBN-13: 978-0-7582-7502-8
ISBN-10: 0-7582-7502-1
First Kensington Mass Market Printing: February 2014

eISBN-13: 978-1-61773-313-0
eISBN-10: 1-61773-313-X
First Kensington Electronic Edition: February 2014

10 9 8 7 6 5 4 3 2 1

Printed in the United States of America

1

A gust of wind blew against the canvas canopy, ripping the pole from Esther's hand and threatening to topple the entire contraption. I scrambled to grab the pole and forced it into the base.

"Got it," I told Esther.

She stepped back and wiped a hand across her brow. "Mercy me, Dana. This setup is harder than I thought."

I glanced around at the nearby stalls along Main Street, where others were struggling to pop up canopies or unfold tables. When I'd first suggested a green-living festival to the Blossom Valley Rejuvenation Committee, which Esther belonged to, I hadn't anticipated the strong winds that occasionally sprang up during fall here in Blossom Valley. Still, even with these temperamental bursts of air and cooler temperatures, the festival would go on, with the O'Connell Organic Farm and Spa right in the middle of the activity.

As owner of the farm, Esther was hoping this festival would draw attention to her bed-and-breakfast and secure her financial future. After a series of murders in the few months since the farm's opening, business had been understandably slow to pick up, but reservations had steadily risen in the last few weeks, allowing us all to breathe a little easier. As the marketing maven for the farm, as well as the backup maid, waitress, and animal catcher, I liked to think my ads and daily blog had helped with business, though it was probably the discounts and proximity to Mendocino that had pulled everyone in. As long as people booked a stay, I didn't care why they were here. Unless it was to murder someone.

I finished securing the canopy and stepped over to the plastic folding table to retrieve a handful of glossy brochures from a cardboard box beneath it. I fanned the stack out as I spoke to Esther. "I can't wait to see how many people show up today."

Esther fiddled with a button on her denim blouse. The embroidered pumpkins and fall leaves fit right in with the spirit of the festival. "Heavens, what if no one comes? The farm will get the blame."

"Relax. This will be a huge success, and then you'll get the credit. We've been advertising it for weeks." I patted her hand, then reached into the box for more brochures.

"You should get the credit, Dana. This was your

idea, and don't think I don't know it. You've saved my bacon more than once."

A cough behind me made my hand jerk. Two brochures skittered off the table and slid to the ground. Gordon, the manager of the farm, had slipped into the booth from the back, dressed in his usual tailored suit and tie, every black hair on his head slicked into place. In one hand, he clutched the clipboard that he carried everywhere.

"Yes," he said. "It's good to see Dana embracing her marketing role. The festival could be the push we need to ensure the farm's success, provided everyone works hard and remembers the goal of attracting more guests to the farm."

Gordon had spent the first few months as spa manager snapping at employees and watching our every move—a reminder that he was in charge, even if Esther really owned the place. In recent weeks, he'd adopted more of a team captain method that involved pep talks—lots of pep talks—though his abrasive personality occasionally showed through. I usually tuned him out, nodding in all the right places while I mentally ran through my list of errands I needed to run after work or what TV shows I wanted to watch that night.

I retrieved the fallen brochures and grabbed a handful of pens with pigs on top from the box under the table. I laid them near the brochures, making sure O'CONNELL ORGANIC FARM AND SPA was clearly visible.

Gordon picked up a pen. "How much did you

squander on these?" He turned to glare at Esther. "Did you approve this purchase?"

Oh, boy, here we go.

Esther snatched the pen from Gordon and practically cradled it in her hand. "These pens are cute as newborn bunnies," Esther said. "When Dana showed me the Web site, I gave her my blessing."

I took the pen from Esther and pushed the pig down. An *oink* squeaked out. "Long after people throw those brochures in the trash, they'll still have these pens. Every time they write with one, they'll think of the spa."

Gordon grunted, which usually meant he agreed, but he didn't want to admit it. "Let's put them away for now. I don't want to run out in the first hour and not have more when the big afternoon crowds show up."

"Don't worry, I bought a ton of these little piggies, but I can save them for later." I pushed the pig to hear one more *oink,* then gathered him up with his other pig pals and dropped them back into the box. You could bet I wouldn't be whipping out the travel mugs until after Gordon left.

He brushed at his suit sleeve, though there wasn't a speck to be seen. "I have to get to the farm, but I'll check back later to see if you need anything from me." He nodded at the brochures. "Keep those stocked. And where's the photo collage?"

"Next on my list." I almost pointed out that I

could have already set it up if Gordon would stop managing me, but then he might launch into another speech about how he was rallying the team for the good of the farm.

"Excellent. Make sure you get that done." He called to Esther, who'd been unpacking a stack of business cards, "Did you want a lift back?"

She straightened up. "Dana, do you need any more help?"

I retrieved the easel from where I'd propped it against the table and popped the legs open. "Now that the canopy and table are set up, I can handle the rest."

She gave me a quick hug. "Thanks again for all your hard work. I can rest easy knowing that you're running the booth."

Gordon placed a hand on Esther's elbow and guided her toward the parking area, clearly in a hurry to get back to work. I finished setting up the giant piece of cardboard, with the two dozen pictures of the farm, rearranged the brochures, and stepped around the table to survey the area from a passerby's point of view.

A little boring. I reentered the enclosure and scooped up a handful of pig pens from the box. The pop of pink instantly livened up the white table. I added half-a-dozen green travel mugs. Much better. Now I was ready for business.

I stood at attention, ready to answer any and all

questions from people wandering by. Only there weren't any people. I glanced at my phone and saw it was five minutes after ten. Where were the crowds? The green-living lovers who would flock here and ooh and aah over all the offerings of an organic farm and spa?

After rearranging the brochures again, I shifted the picture collage to different angles to see if it changed the viewing experience. Nope. Not that any people had wandered by to look at it.

Next door, voices reached me as two women stepped out through the door flap of the tent and stood in the street, talking to someone still inside.

"I'll be sure to contact those customers you mentioned when I get back to the office," the young one said—her spiky blond hair, with black tips, catching my eye. A gust of wind blew past and lifted the filmy split sleeves of her blouse, exposing a large tattoo of a panther on her upper arm.

"And I'll get busy tallying those accounts we were discussing. Give me a call if you get over-whelmed," said the older woman in the business suit. She had a slim, athletic build. Her silver hair, cut into a bob, matched her silver ring, necklace, and bracelet.

The two women headed toward the parking area, and I went back to waiting for my first cus-tomer. After ten minutes of keeping busy doing nothing, I looked down the street. Still, no one in sight.

With nothing else to do, I walked to the tent next door to see if I could figure out what they were advertising. The door flap was tied back, and the banner across the opening declared it was the INVISIBLE PRINTS booth. Miniature wind turbines sat in rows on a table inside. Plastic purple sunglasses, with INVISIBLE PRINTS stamped in yellow lettering on the arms, waited on another table next to a small stand that held brochures. The cover showed a red barn and a field full of pigs, reminding me of the pigs back at Esther's farm. The tag line asked, *What Can You Do with Methane Gas?* I decided not to think about that.

"Come on over and grab a souvenir," someone said. I spotted a woman inside the tent and stepped into the enclosure. She smiled at me as though she practiced that smile in a mirror, and a jolt went through me. I knew the woman from somewhere, but where? I studied her, trying to place where I'd seen her. The bank? The grocery store? She really didn't look like someone from Blossom Valley. Blond and red highlights added depth to her perfectly styled deep brown hair, the large curls cascading down her back. Her makeup looked professionally done, and her business jacket and knee-length skirt reminded me of a top news reporter you might see on CNN.

I glanced down at my khaki pants and navy blue shirt with STAFF stitched on it and reminded myself that I had to wear my uniform for the farm. I couldn't think up an excuse for my barely brushed dishwater-blond hair, which I'd pulled back into a ponytail, as I rushed out of the house this morning. I gave up trying to figure out if I knew this woman and focused on the table. "Cute windmills," I said. "What are they for?"

The woman picked one up and handed it to me. "Wind power is one of the many services Invisible Prints provides. We're a carbon foot-print–offsetting company."

Her words sounded like complete gibberish. "Carbon offset what?"

She chuckled as though I wasn't the first one to ask that question. "Carbon footprint–offsetting company. We help people invest in green-energy projects or sustainable resources to make up for all the energy they use in their homes and fuel they burn while driving or flying. The idea is to replace energy and resources that have been used with new resources, thereby making your carbon foot-print neutral."

"Interesting." I wasn't sure I completely understood everything she'd said, but her company certainly fit in with a green-living festival. I set the windmill back on the table and picked up a brochure from the stand. I stuck it into my back pocket to read later.

"How about you?" she asked. "What business are you with?"

I stepped out of the tent, reached around the pole dividing our booths, and retrieved a brochure of my own to hand her. "I'm with the organic farm and spa here in town. We provide overnight accommodations and meals. The chef uses organic fruits and vegetables grown right on the farm, as well as eggs hatched on site and meat provided by local companies." I held out my right hand. "I'm Dana Lewis, by the way."

We shook.

"Wendy. Wendy Hartford."

As soon as I heard her name, I snapped the last piece into the puzzle. I'd known a Wendy back in school. She'd had a different last name, but this woman looked like the Wendy Clark I'd grown up with. Just as I opened my mouth to mention it, she jumped in.

"Did you graduate from Blossom Valley High, by any chance? I used to go to school with a Dana Lewis."

"I don't believe it." I gave her a hug, memories of the two of us during our middle-school years flitting through my mind. We'd hang out in each other's bedroom for hours, flipping through teen magazines or trying on our mothers' makeup, all the while talking about the future. "What have you been doing these past few years?"

"Oh, this and that. I married the most wonderful

man a few years ago. And I've been with Invisible Prints for two years now. How about you?"

I hesitated. We hadn't talked since high-school graduation, and I was too embarrassed to admit I'd moved back home after a layoff. "I did some marketing down in the Bay Area for a while, but I moved back in with my mom a few months ago after my dad died."

"I'm sorry to hear that."

The sincerity in her voice made my heart squeeze, and I quelled the tears that threatened to rise. "Thanks. I can't believe it's been so long since we've seen each other. We really should have stayed in touch."

"I agree. At least we can make up for that time now."

A man in cargo shorts and a tank top stepped into the tent, the brim of his fisherman's hat brushing the tent flap. "What cute windmills. What do they do?"

Was this an honest-to-goodness festival attendee? I stuck my head out and glanced down the street. Clumps of people stood at various booths. The awaited crowd had arrived.

I headed out of the tent. "Guess I'd better get back to my job."

"We'll catch up later," Wendy said. Her words were the usual thing you'd say when you ran into an old friend, but I found myself looking forward to the idea.

A middle-aged woman in a tie-dyed T-shirt

wandered toward Wendy's tent, and I scurried back to my booth. My hands shook a little in anticipation as I straightened the brochures one last time and made sure the picture display sat straight on the easel.

A woman with long brown hair and wearing an off-the-shoulder peasant dress and cowboy boots walked up to Wendy's tent and peeked in. When she saw Wendy was busy, she turned and went back the other way. Fine, I didn't want to tell her about the farm and spa anyway.

The man in the hat left Wendy's booth and moved over to mine. I spent a few minutes outlining the services of the farm, including the new spa features, such as the pedicures and the facials. He took a pig pen and drifted away. Several people replaced him, keeping me busy for the next twenty minutes.

Once the last person had left, I stretched across the table to survey the crowd. The street had cleared again, leaving only two people. The closer one was an African-American man in tan slacks, a white dress shirt, and a suit jacket the color of a tangerine. He didn't seem to notice me watching as he strode toward Wendy's tent without glancing at the other booths. Behind him came the woman in cowboy boots and peasant dress, who had stopped by earlier. When she saw the man enter the tent, she hesitated a moment, then reversed direction.

I bent down to grab a handful of pig pens to

replace the ones I'd given away. As I straightened up, a loud male voice sounded from next door.

"Wendy, we need to talk."

I felt a flutter of concern. He sounded awfully angry.

I couldn't hear Wendy's response, but the man's next remark came through clearly. "You know exactly why I'm here. I want some answers. Now."

Maybe I should go over there. Make sure Wendy is okay.

I moved toward the gap at the end of the table, but stopped when someone blocked my way.

"Dana, I didn't know you were going to be here."

Forget Wendy. I had my own problem. Her name was Kimmie.

2

Kimmie Wheeler, another former classmate, stood before me, dressed in dark blue skinny jeans, a leopard-print blouse, and a fur-lined jacket. Her boots with the four-inch heels made her tower over my five-foot-five frame, and I had to look up to meet her gaze. Her nostrils were very tidy.

"Kimmie, how nice to see you." For a second, I wondered if there was an impromptu high-school reunion happening at the festival, though I managed to run into Kimmie every couple of weeks. She and her husband lived over in Mendocino and owned a fine-dining restaurant, but her aging mother lived here in town, and Kimmie visited often.

She squinted at the photos on the easel. "You guys have a booth here? How cute. I didn't think your little farm could score a booth."

"Actually, I'm the one who suggested the green-living festival to the rejuvenation committee and helped organize it." I tried to keep the pride out of my voice.

Now Kimmie shifted her squint to me. "You? But I thought this was an important event."

Ugh.

I grabbed a pig pen and hit the top.

Oink.

Kimmie jumped at the noise.

"Here." I handed her the pen.

"Oh, isn't that the cutest thing," she gushed, stuffing the pen into her Louis Vuitton bag.

As she tucked her pen away, I could hear the man still yelling at Wendy next door. "We need to find out what happened."

I heard a murmur in reply, and then, "Don't give me excuses."

"Someone sounds upset," Kimmie whispered gleefully. She shifted closer to the tent and cocked her head so she wouldn't miss a word.

"I don't know what they're arguing about," I said, "but if you have a free minute, you might stop by later. Wendy Hartford is running that booth for some company called Invisible Prints. She went to school with us."

Kimmie clapped her hands together, drawing attention to the enormous diamond sitting upon her overly tan finger. "That's right. She mentioned she'd be here today. I promised I'd stop by and say hi."

I could still hear the angry visitor, and I'm sure Kimmie could, too. "Now might not be the best time."

"Nonsense. Everyone's always happy to see me. I think Wendy could use a friendly face about now." She strode with purpose to the booth next door.

"Hi, Wendy, how are you?" I heard her gush as she barreled into the tent.

The man who'd been yelling at Wendy came into my line of vision as he stepped out. With his mouth set in a firm line, he pointed a finger back into the tent. "This isn't over." He turned and headed past my booth.

I held up a pen. "Pig pen?" He kept walking. Well, not everyone was going to want an oinking pig.

I busied myself with straightening up the booth. Before long, I heard shrieks of laughter and high-pitched chattering coming from Wendy's tent, transporting me back to childhood. After a while, Kimmie emerged from the booth and moved up the street. I watched her retreating back as my thoughts returned to my school days. By senior year, Wendy, Kimmie, and I were running in different circles. What was it that had made us drift apart?

While I tried to remember, Zennia, the spa's health-conscious, daring cook, approached the table with a bag full of vegetables, interrupting my musings. She plunked the bag on the table and extracted several ears of corn, the sleeves of her tunic swinging with the movement. "How's attendance?" she asked.

I saw the street was once more empty. "We had a crowd come through a bit ago, but it's definitely been slow."

Zennia brushed away a strand of black hair, which had fallen loose from her braid. "I'm getting a bad vibe from this festival. The energies in my chakras have been out of balance all morning."

As if backing up her words, a series of dark clouds drifted across the sky at a good clip, thanks to the breeze that continued to swoop through. Rain wasn't due until the first part of next week, and I crossed my fingers that it wouldn't arrive early and interfere with the festival.

Zennia slid a charcoal gray backpack off her shoulders. She rummaged around inside and pulled out a sheathed chef's knife, a small cutting board, and a bag of some sort of mixed lettuce.

"What are you cooking this afternoon?"

"I decided on a nice corn salad, with late-season tomatoes and jalapenos, on top of a bed of greens."

This was the most normal menu item Zennia had ever created for the spa, not including scrambled eggs. Definitely better than those tofu fish sticks. Or the octopus. Or the *natto,* a Japanese fermented soybean dish Zennia had terrified spa guests with a while back. "Save me some leftovers."

Zennia almost dropped her knife, but she

managed to keep her grip. "Don't say such things, or I'll start to think you like my cooking."

I laughed. "Let's not get carried away." I peered closer at the bag. "What kind of lettuce is that?"

She set the knife down and extracted a handful of leaves from the bag. "Mostly, arugula and dandelion greens, with evening primrose root and nettles thrown in."

I held up a leaf and studied the jagged edges. "Are you sure you didn't forget to buy lettuce at the store and just pulled some weeds at the farm before heading over?"

"I'll have you know these greens are top quality. My supplier grows those dandelions in a special greenhouse during the off-season."

"Wait. You paid for *weeds*?"

Zennia playfully slapped my arm. "Oh, stop." She returned the greens to the bag and gestured toward the street. "You can take your lunch break, if you want. I can watch for people while I prepare the salad, and I plan to stay for at least another half hour to hand out samples."

"That'll give me a chance to check out the rest of the festival." I slipped around the table and headed up the street, glancing into Wendy's booth on my way, but it was too dark to see anything clearly. I took a moment to stare down the row of booths that lined the street. I was glad we'd had such a solid start for a first festival.

At the next booth I came to, a man advertised a farming method that used all available land by planting grains between rows of fruit trees. The next booth sold organic skin products. If the woman with the unbelievably smooth and glowing complexion who stood behind the table was an example of someone who used the lotions, I might have to buy some later. Even at twenty-eight, I was starting to notice lines, which didn't used to be there, on my hands and around my eyes. I tried to tell myself my skin was merely dry, but I was starting to suspect the lines were permanent.

As I approached the next booth, I wrinkled my nose and pressed the back of my hand across my mouth. What was that smell?

A hand-lettered sign attached to a pole announced FERTILIZER: $2 A BAG. A grizzled man, wearing a torn plaid shirt, unpacked flimsy plastic bags full of brown lumps and lined them up on the table, condensation visible on the inside of the bags. Flies buzzed around the table, and the man stopped to swat at them with his flyswatter, not that it helped any.

He glanced up at me. "Got here late. My dog had constipation, so I had to wait for him to do his business."

Wait, was he selling his dog's poop as fertilizer? And how did he get approval from the committee?

"Interest you in some of this-here fertilizer?" he asked, holding up a bag, the brown mass straining against the thin plastic.

I shook my head, not wanting to uncover my mouth to speak, and kept walking. I passed booths for organic fudge, solar-power panels, and local honey. Lester Brand, owner of the You Drive a Hard Bargain auto dealership in town, stood by a Chevy Volt, watching for a spark of interest from anyone passing by. I averted my gaze and pretended to study the green-living cleaning products at the booth across the way. Lester could talk for hours about fuel efficiency and cars of the future, not to mention his Civil War–era musket collection.

I spotted Kimmie down at the end of the row, near the food booths. She saw me and waved.

"Dana, I was grabbing a wrap for Wendy," she said as I approached. "Did you want one? It's sautéed tofu, with sprouts and spinach."

"Maybe later, thanks." I'd have to tell Zennia about the wraps. Those were sure to balance her chakras.

Kimmie accepted two wraps from the vendor. "Why don't you come back with me? Wendy was hoping to talk with you more. Did you know she's the owner of Invisible Prints?"

"At twenty-eight?" I couldn't help blurting out. I'd mistakenly assumed she was a lowly employee schlepping the company products at the festival, much like me.

"Amazing, right? And here I've got one of the

most popular restaurants on the West Coast."
She studied me in my STAFF polo shirt. "Don't
worry, your time will come. Some of us are late
bloomers."

"Others peak early and then wither away." I gave
Kimmie a pointed look.

"So true. Thank God I'm not one of them."

Glad she was so sure of herself.

"Come on, let's go see Wendy," I said, heading
back to her booth at the other end of the strip.

Few people wandered the street with us, and I
felt another tickle of worry that this festival would
be a flop. I really wanted Esther's rejuvenation
committee to have one successful event so that
maybe they could expand their membership past
three measly people.

As we approached Wendy's booth, I saw that no
one was at the farm booth sampling Zennia's corn
salad. If I told her about the tofu wraps, it might
distract her from the poor turnout.

"Be right there, Kimmie. I need to talk to Zennia
for a sec."

"Ta-ta for now," she called over her shoulder as
she maneuvered her way into Wendy's booth,
hands full with the wraps. I walked over to where
Zennia stood, arms crossed.

"Dana, where are all the people?" she asked,
mirroring my own concerns from earlier.

Before I could say anything, a scream sounded from next door. Then another.

I stared at Zennia, frozen. She snatched up her chef's knife and held it close to her chest.

"What happened?" she asked.

I darted over and ran into Kimmie as she rushed out of the booth. I looked past her through the tent flap and saw Wendy on the pavement, motionless. Her neck was marred by an angry red gash. The wraps lay nearby, tofu and sprouts spilling out onto the pavement.

Kimmie grabbed the front of my polo shirt. "Oh, Dana," she said. Then she fainted.

3

I caught Kimmie in a haphazard hug, slowing her descent as she crumpled to the ground. I'd never had someone faint on me before, but that paled in comparison to whatever had happened to Wendy in that tent.

I laid Kimmie on the ground and ran inside the enclosure. Up close, I could see the wound on Wendy's neck was huge, the skin clearly gaping around the cut. Near her body, a miniature wind turbine lay on its side, a dark stain on one blade.

Closing my eyes for a half second to gather my wits, I laid my ear on Wendy's chest and listened for a heartbeat, a breath, anything. I heard nothing. Wendy was dead.

I rose unsteadily to my feet and backed out of the tent, trying not to touch anything. My heels bumped into something, and I whirled around to find Kimmie still on the pavement. "Help! Someone help!" I yelled as I knelt down.

A man walking past the booth stopped. "What's going on?" he asked.

"A woman's dead in the tent. You need to call 911."

He patted his pockets. "Phone's in the car." He ran toward the parking lot.

Kimmie moaned, grabbing my attention once more. I ran through all the treatments I'd ever heard for people who had fainted. Wave smelling salts under her nose? Didn't have any. Throw cold water on her? Didn't have any of that, either. Slap her?

I stared at Kimmie as she moaned again and moved one arm. She appeared to be coming around on her own, but maybe she still needed a little help. I bent over and slapped her lightly on one cheek.

Nothing.

I slapped her a little harder, putting more energy behind my swing. This time, her eyes briefly snapped open.

"What are you doing, Dana?" Zennia asked behind me.

I quickly withdrew my hand, aware of how this must look: a dead body, me slapping Kimmie senseless. Talk about awkward.

I turned toward Zennia as she peered through the tent opening.

"Oh no," she breathed.

"Wendy's dead, probably murdered. Someone went to call 911. Maybe you could show the police where we are when they get here?"

Zennia nodded and headed toward the end of the street. I concentrated on waking up Kimmie. I tried to pull her up to a sitting position, but managed to raise her only a few inches before we both collapsed on the pavement.

Her impact with asphalt did the trick. Her eyes opened and stayed that way. She lifted her head slowly. I placed one hand on her back and another on her arm and guided her up to sitting.

"Dana, what happened?" She shook her head as if trying to clear her mind.

I gulped. "I think Wendy's dead," I said for what seemed the millionth time, though I was still having trouble accepting the meaning of the words.

"This is so horrible!" Kimmie wailed. "Who did this to her?" Tears pooled along her lower eyelids.

I patted her back. "I don't know, but the police are on their way. Just relax until they get here."

An older couple wandered over, probably drawn to the sight of us sitting on the ground. Maybe they thought we were participating in a green-living demonstration, showing how the closer you sat to the ground, the less you contributed to global warming. The gray-haired woman lifted the tent flap, spotted Wendy's body, and shrieked.

I struggled to my feet, careful not to look at poor Wendy again. "Please stay back. There's been an accident."

"That don't look like no accident," the man said.

I completely agreed, but now was not the time to offer details. I positioned myself in front of the tent flap so no one could enter the booth. Simultaneously I patted the top of Kimmie's head with my free hand, as though she were a well-behaved Labrador, not a woman bordering on shock.

Three more people stopped before the tent, and I swallowed a curse. *Now* everyone showed up for the festival?

"What's going on?" a man asked. "What happened to that lady?" Guess I wasn't blocking their view as much as I thought.

I could hear sirens in the distance, growing louder. Thank goodness. I spotted a cluster of people down by the food booths and sent up a quick prayer that the authorities would reach Wendy's booth before they did.

If anything, it was a tie.

As the paramedics rushed up on one side, the large group approached from the other.

"Is someone hurt?" a woman in the pack asked.

"What're they doing here?" another said.

I focused on the paramedics, particularly the one holding the medical kit.

"Kimmie here fainted after . . ." I looked into the tent once more. "Well, after she found Wendy."

The paramedic dropped his bag and knelt next to Kimmie, while the other headed inside the tent.

"How are you feeling now?" the paramedic asked Kimmie.

I moved out of the way and sidled over to where Zennia waited behind her table.

She stood with her large bowl of corn salad, several small paper cups lined up before it with samples, which no one was interested in trying. All available customers were too busy watching the paramedics work. I almost tried some so she wouldn't feel slighted, but the idea of eating right now made my stomach roil.

"That poor woman's dead, isn't she?" Zennia said.

I pressed a hand to my face. "I'm almost positive, but the paramedics will make sure."

"And Kimmie?"

"She'll be fine. The shock of finding her old friend must have overwhelmed her for a minute. I know it knocked me back a step."

Zennia looked close to tears. "Was she your friend, too?"

I thought again about our junior-high days, trying on clothes together, gossiping about the latest boy band. "Once upon a time. I haven't seen her in years, not since high school." I felt pressure build behind my eyes.

A hand settled on my shoulder. "Hey, Dana, how's it going?"

A rush of warmth ran through my body as I turned around to greet Jason. We'd been dating on and off since we met at the farm. Lately things had become more serious between us. We'd even had "the talk" about being exclusive and had a standing date every Saturday night, if not more often.

As always, seeing his dimples made me smile, even at a time like this. I hugged him, leaning into his thin, muscular body and relishing the moment of comfort on this cool, dreary afternoon.

He released me and studied my face. His green eyes were filled with concern. "Are you all right?"

"I think so." I suddenly wished I had a chair. Then I noticed the notepad in his hand. "Are you here about the death already?"

"What death? I came to cover the festival."

That made perfect sense, considering Jason was the lead reporter for Blossom Valley's weekly paper, but my muddled brain had all but forgotten about the festival at this point.

Jason glanced around, finally noting the paramedics next door. "What's going on over there? I saw the crowd, but thought the booth had one of those wheels you spin to win free stuff."

"I think there was a murder while I was off touring the rest of the festival."

"Murder," Jason said sharply. "Are you sure?"

I ran a hand through my hair. My stomach twisted at the memory. "I'm not positive, but unless she slashed her own throat, it's a good bet."

Had she taken her own life? That possibility hadn't even occurred to me, and I dismissed it at once. Wendy was a successful businesswoman running her own company. I couldn't picture her committing suicide, especially not in the middle of a festival. Then again, I couldn't picture her being murdered, either, although I didn't really know her anymore.

Jason brushed my hair back from my face. "You must be so upset."

I nodded, unable to say anything more.

He dropped his hand and squeezed his notepad, sneaking a peek back at the crowd. His reporter side was at full alert, ready to ferret out the details.

"Go ahead," I said. "Do your job."

"I'll stay here with her," Zennia said. I'd almost forgotten she was there.

Jason nodded his thanks to her and rubbed my arm. "I won't be long. The cops probably don't know anything yet, not even her name." He turned to go.

"Her name's Wendy."

He swiveled back. "You know her?"

"We went to school together. She's twenty-eight, like me, but with her own company and who knows what kind of fantastic life ahead of her. And now it's all over." I rubbed my forehead. The threat of a headache was creeping in.

Jason jotted something in his notepad. "When did you last see her?"

I thought about how I'd walked straight past her tent when I'd decided to see the other booths. Had she been alive at that point? She hadn't called to me as I went by. Was she already bleeding to death on the cold, hard pavement?

"Dana?" Jason asked, his voice tender.

I rubbed my head again. "Sorry. I talked to her this morning. Then Kimmie showed up here and some guy visited Wendy's booth. In fact, you should find that guy. He was sure mad."

"Do you know what it was about?"

"Was this before I got here?" Zennia asked. "I don't remember that."

"You got here a few minutes later." I closed my eyes, but I came up blank. "With everything that's happened, I don't really remember what I heard," I told Jason.

"Take your time. I need you to tell me anything at all that comes to mind."

"I have a better idea!" someone behind me

boomed. "How about you tell the police everything you know?"

I turned to find Detective Palmer glowering at me. With his arms crossed over his chest, he looked like one unhappy policeman.

Which meant I was about to be unhappy, too.

4

Detective Palmer glanced from me to Jason, then back to me. "Tell me what happened."

I gulped, suddenly nervous, and stared at the diamond pattern on his blue tie. "I don't know. I didn't hear a thing, and I was in my booth the whole time. Well, except when I walked around at lunch." I turned to Zennia. "Did you hear anything? Did you leave the booth at all?"

"For a few minutes. I left the package of napkins in my car, and when I went to get them, I ran into an old friend, who wanted to see the festival. We got to chatting about this new holistic herb she read about, and I'm afraid I lost track of time."

Before I could ask anything else, Detective Palmer took my elbow and directed me toward the parking area. "Let's continue this in my car before you start interviewing all my witnesses. I don't want you messing around in this."

I tried to wave to Jason, but he had his back to me as he busily scribbled in his notepad, all business. Detective Palmer released my elbow and led the way across the street. I trudged behind, trying to ignore all the stares and whispers from the growing crowd, but failing. At least he didn't have a grip on me anymore. People wouldn't mistake me for a felon about to be handcuffed.

He unlocked the passenger side of a blue Ford Taurus and opened the door, motioning me to sit down. Once I was settled in the worn leather seat, he slammed the door and walked around to the driver's side, giving me a few seconds to have a mild panic attack. I managed to get my breathing under control before he opened his door and slid in.

"Now, then," he said, "tell me about finding the body."

In a flash, I saw a chance to escape from the car. "That's where you're mistaken. I didn't find the body. You need to talk to Kimmie." I placed a hand on the inside handle. "Let me get her for you." I pushed the door partway open.

"Hold it." Detective Palmer didn't speak that loudly, but his voice held enough authority that I froze with one foot halfway out of the car. "Shut that. We're not done."

I pulled my leg inside and closed the door, but I kept my fingers wrapped around the handle. I told myself to calm down. Surely, the detective didn't think I was involved in Wendy's death, and I needed to do everything I could to help him.

"If this Kimmie found the body, what part did you play?" Detective Palmer picked up a notebook from the center console.

"Kimmie and I walked to the booth together, but I stopped to tell Zennia about the tofu wraps they were selling at the other end of the street. Before I got the chance, Kimmie started screaming. I ran next door and saw Wendy's body. Then Kimmie fainted. I asked a guy to call 911, and the paramedics showed up. That's it."

"You called her 'Wendy.' You knew the deceased?" He asked the question in a monotone, but the little hairs on my neck prickled all the same.

"A long time ago. We were good friends in middle school and hung out a bit in high school, but I hadn't seen her since graduation."

"Why only a bit?"

"What do you mean?"

"If you were such good friends, why did you only hang out a bit in high school?"

I shrugged. "We ended up on different tracks. Kimmie and Wendy had one lunch period, while I had the other. With no classes together, we eventually drifted apart. I made a new set of friends."

"You sure there wasn't more to it? An argument about a boyfriend, maybe?"

"What are you getting at?" I asked.

Detective Palmer tapped his pen on the notepad. The noise sounded ridiculously loud in the confined space. "Maybe Wendy didn't want to be friends anymore. Maybe you harbored some resentment over that and it resurfaced when you saw her today."

I stared at him. "Are you for real? Who would hold a grudge for ten years? Besides, Wendy was still my friend in high school. We just didn't see each other very often." I shifted in my seat and exhaled loudly through my nose. He couldn't really believe such an absurd theory, could he?

Detective Palmer tapped the notebook with his pen again. I wanted to grab that pen and throw it out of the car, but some law surely existed on the books about throwing an officer's writing utensil away.

"Relax," Detective Palmer said. "I get paid to ask." He flipped to a new page. "Now, then, tell me when you first saw the murder victim today."

My stomach seized. I was almost positive Wendy had been murdered, but to hear Detective Palmer confirm my guess added an extra layer of reality to the situation.

"Well, I think it was around nine-thirty, maybe ten. I got here shortly after nine, set up the table and the photo collage, then waited around for people to show up. No one did, so I figured I'd see what other vendors were offering and hit Wendy's booth first. We recognized each other and started chatting."

I pictured Wendy's smiling face in my mind. The entire morning was taking on a daydream quality, and the details were already bleeding around the edges, much like the wound on Wendy's neck.

I shuddered.

"And then?" Detective Palmer prompted.

"People started coming, so I went back to my booth to promote the farm. Once the crowd thinned out again, I was going to pop back over, but then Kimmie stopped by."

"And that's when she found the body?"

I waved my hand. "No, that was later. First a man showed up and started yelling at Wendy."

Detective Palmer sat up straighter and twisted in his seat, ready to pounce on any information. "Can you describe him?"

I tried to drum up an image of the man as he hustled past my booth, but I found I couldn't recall much. "African-American, probably in his forties, with really short black hair. He was wearing this tangerine jacket and tan slacks."

He scribbled in his notebook. "Did you get a name?"

I squeezed my eyes shut, trying to recall everything I'd overheard, but I hadn't heard much. "No, sorry."

"We'll track him down."

I continued to describe the morning, from Zennia's arrival to running into Kimmie at the food booths. As I talked, I watched as the crowd grew around Wendy's tent. From my vantage point in the parking lot across the street, I couldn't see the paramedics or Kimmie at all. I didn't even know if Kimmie had been transported to the hospital so a doctor could examine her.

One thing I could see, though, was the empty street. Other than the people crowded around the crime scene, no one else walked around or visited the booths. Why look at green-living products when, instead, you could look at dead things and act like you were in the middle of a *Cops* episode?

"What about the festival?" I asked, hating to ask after someone—an old classmate, no less—had been murdered.

"What about it?"

I tugged at a loose thread sticking off my pant seam. "Will you shut it down? I mean, you probably should, but some of these booth operators traveled from Mendocino or all the way from Eureka. It's a pretty big deal for them." And for Esther and me, too.

He tapped the keyboard attached to his computer and read what was on the screen. I had no idea if he was looking up something related to my question or checking the latest weather report.

"Probably not. Once we process the crime scene, it should be business as usual."

As usual as business could be, with a homicide victim in the middle of the festival. In a town as small as Blossom Valley, most people had probably already heard about the murder. The festival would draw mostly looky-loos, not people interested in green products and methods.

Detective Palmer closed his notebook. "That's all for now. If you could point Kimmie out to me, I'll speak to her next."

"Of course." I pushed open the car door and shivered in the chilly air as I stood, regretting my choice to leave my windbreaker back at the farm. I looked at Detective Palmer over the top of his car. "One more thing, I almost forgot. A woman tried to see Wendy a couple of times. When she saw that other people were already talking to her, she left."

The notepad reappeared. "Describe her."

"About my age, long brown hair, flowy dress, with cowboy boots."

"Not much to go on, but maybe we'll get lucky and she'll come back."

I slammed the door. "I'll let you know if I see her again."

As I walked across the parking lot, I spotted Kimmie talking to Zennia at the farm booth and led

Detective Palmer over, glad to see the paramedics hadn't felt the need to take her to the hospital.

"Kimmie, Detective Palmer here needs to ask you about finding Wendy," I said when we reached the table.

I felt Detective Palmer stiffen at my side and wondered if I'd somehow overstepped my bounds. But when I looked at his face, I saw his gaze fixated elsewhere. Namely, on the chef's knife in Zennia's hand.

Uh-oh.

"Ma'am," Detective Palmer said quietly, "would you mind laying your knife down?"

"What?" Zennia dropped the knife on the table, where it *thunked* on the plastic surface. "Oh, my, I was chopping some tomatoes, trying to distract myself from this horrible business."

From his pant pocket, Detective Palmer removed a pair of latex gloves and pulled them on. Once each finger was in place, he took a paper bag from an inside coat pocket and shook it open. He gingerly picked up the knife by the tip of the handle and lowered it into the bag. "I'll take this for analysis."

Zennia had been resting her other hand on the tomato she'd been chopping. At the detective's words, she pressed her hand down. Juice squirted out of the tomato, reminding me of the blood around Wendy's neck. I looked away. I might never eat tomatoes again.

"You can't think I used that knife to . . ." Zennia let the statement trail away. "My soul is in harmony with the world. I would never take a life."

Detective Palmer didn't comment.

"But I thought she was killed with one of those mini turbines," I said. "I saw one next to her body. One of the blades had dark marks like blood on it."

The detective continued his Marcel Marceau routine and remained mute. His face was impassive. Man, he could be annoying.

"Could that little blade really kill someone?" I asked. "Is it even sharp enough?"

He ignored me and addressed Kimmie. "I'm going to put this in my car. Stay here until I get back." He eyed me before looking at Kimmie again. "Better yet, follow me."

Without a word, Kimmie trailed behind the detective like a condemned prisoner walking the green mile. I'd probably looked the exact same way a short while ago.

With my mind whirring, I watched them go. While talking to Wendy, had Kimmie seen or heard anything that would help the police? I turned to Zennia. She appeared to be in a trance of some kind. Was she meditating at this very minute?

"Zennia?"

She snapped to attention. "Sorry, I'm beside myself. How could that detective think my knife was involved in that woman's death? I won't even kill the ants that sneak in my kitchen. I scoop them up and put them outside."

It was true; I'd seen her escort the little critters out. "I'm sure he knows you didn't kill Wendy, but he has to examine any potential weapons. It makes me wonder if that little wind turbine wasn't the murder weapon after all. But then why did it have blood on it?"

"You're not considering investigating another murder, are you?" Zennia asked. She pressed two fingers to each temple as if trying to clear her mind of the image.

"I'm sure the cops will do fine without my help." Besides, it wasn't my problem, unlike the last murder when my sister, Ashlee, had been involved. "But I am a bit curious to know what they're doing next door. Think I'll go check."

I left Zennia with her tomatoes, and nothing to cut them with, and moved to Wendy's booth, where a larger crowd had gathered. The police had set up a temporary blockade, with a semicircle of upside-down buckets and yellow crime-scene tape strung between them. A uniformed officer stood before the opening of the tent, keeping people from seeing what was happening, though that didn't stop the spectators from staring at the tiny gap that still remained. Flashes of light appeared every few seconds from inside the tent. The police photographer must have arrived while I'd been away.

Beside me, a man crunched on a salad he carried in a plastic take-out container. The noise dug into my brain like a drill bit. I tried to tune the sound out as I studied the rest of the faces in the crowd, spotting my mailman, a barista from the Daily Grind coffee shop, and one of my old grade-school teachers. My gaze traveled through the rest of the crowd. On the outer edge of the opposite side, I spotted a tangerine-colored sleeve practically glowing through the clump of people. No way could two people be wearing that color at the festival.

My senses went into hyperdrive as I honed in on the man. The crunch of lettuce sounded exponentially louder. My nose discerned the odor of onions and cucumbers in the salad. The breeze prickled my skin.

A woman walked in front of him and stopped, blocking my view for a second. As she shifted in place, I could just see the back of the man's head as he left the crowd and moved down the street.

He was getting away!

I craned my neck toward the parking area, where Detective Palmer's car sat. From this angle, I couldn't see if anyone was still in the car. I swiveled back toward the man again and saw that he'd turned at the corner of the Prescription for Joy drugstore. As I watched, he disappeared from view.

I took two steps toward where Detective Palmer's car was parked, then reversed course. I didn't have time to find Palmer. The man would be long gone by the time the detective got here, and I was the only one who knew what he looked like. I needed to follow him.

With my sense of self-preservation still trying to steer me toward the detective's car, I pushed it aside and ran toward the drugstore, skirting past the back of the booths on the other side of the street. Around the corner, a narrow dirt path ran between this building and the Get the Scoop ice cream parlor next door. The path was empty. The man was gone.

I trotted down the trail and stopped when I came to the other end of the building. I peeked around the corner. An empty lot with broken glass, cigarette butts, and tufts of weeds waited for me. To my left, a Dumpster sat about halfway down the back side of the drugstore. I detected a faint scratching noise coming from the other side of the metal container.

A stray cat? A giant rat? Or was the man hiding there? Had he seen me follow him? He could easily be crouched down, waiting to strike when I walked by.

Do I dare check it out? He might know something about Wendy's death. Heck, he might even have been involved!

I knew seeking out the source of the noise wasn't the dumbest thing I'd ever done, but I worried that it might end up in the top five. Still, with a rapidly beating heart and quaking legs, I stepped toward the Dumpster . . . and whatever waited on the other side.

5

I trod lightly as I approached the Dumpster, my Vans making the barest of noises on the loose-packed dirt. Rather than walking directly next to the Dumpster, I made a large arc around it. If the man was waiting for me, I wanted a chance to run.

No more than a minute had passed since I'd reached the corner of the building, yet I felt as if I'd been creeping along for an hour. At last, I spotted a foot at the end of the Dumpster. I couldn't remember what shoes the man had been wearing, but he didn't strike me as the dirty-sneaker type. I took another step and saw a leg clad in filthy gray sweatpants.

Definitely not my guy.

I let out the breath I'd been holding and stepped forward with more confidence. A man sat on the other side of the Dumpster, his back to the wall, his feet stretched out. Besides the sweats, he wore a long-sleeved Henley, frayed around the neck, and a worn ski parka, with stuffing oozing from a tear. He was eating a fast-food hamburger. The crinkle of the wrapper must have been the noise I heard.

He caught me watching him and raised his free hand. "Afternoon," he said as he continued chewing.

"Sorry to interrupt your lunch, but did a man run through here a minute ago?"

The man swallowed his bite. "He weren't running, but I did see some guy in a bright coat head thataway." He used the hand holding the hamburger to wave toward the next block. The street was empty, but maybe he hadn't gone far.

"Thanks." I headed across the lot, sidestepping a broken bottle, and reached the sidewalk. As I looked in both directions, I heard a car start up. A maroon BMW emerged from a side street halfway up the block. The mystery man was at the wheel. He hung a left and started to drive away from where I stood.

Too late, I realized I should be getting his license plate number. I sprinted into the street and managed to spy a 7, a B, and a Q before my long-distance vision failed me. Why had he parked all the way back here? There was plenty of parking closer to the festival. Was he hoping to get in and out without being spotted? Then again, he hadn't exactly run to his car and screeched out of the alley. He may not have realized I was even following him. I could have created this entire chase scenario in my head. It wouldn't be the first time.

I headed back to the festival, not bothering to hurry my steps. I still had no idea who the man was and had only a partial description of the car. Not my best hour, but at least I had something for the detective.

The crowd still clustered around Wendy's booth. Next door, Detective Palmer and Kimmie had returned and were talking to Zennia. She nodded in my direction, and Kimmie and Detective Palmer turned and watched me approach.

"Is everything all right?" Zennia asked. "I saw you in the crowd one minute, and then you were gone. With everything that's happened today, I got worried."

"I saw that man again—the one who was yelling at Wendy."

Detective Palmer brushed past Kimmie to stand directly in front of me. "Where is he now?"

"Gone. He parked over on a side street behind the drugstore."

Detective Palmer's face tightened. For a second, I thought he might shoot me. "You should have found me."

I fought my irritation and reminded myself I was talking to a police officer, someone I needed to cooperate with. "I didn't have time to run to your car, then run back to where the man was. As it is, I lost him, but some guy behind the Dumpster helped me out." Detective Palmer raised his eyebrows at that, but I didn't stop to explain. "I did get a look at his car, if that helps. It was a maroon BMW. Looked pretty new."

"Good job, Dana," Kimmie said. "You're almost like a real detective." She actually sounded sincere with that compliment, but maybe I was tired.

If I didn't know better, I'd swear Detective Palmer rolled his eyes.

"Get a look at the plate?" he asked.

"I did." I puffed up a bit, until I remembered that I hadn't exactly seen the whole thing. "It started with a seven, then *B* and *Q*. Or maybe that was an *O*."

The detective pulled out his notebook and wrote down the information, scribbling furiously. "I need to talk to this guy by the Dumpster."

I pointed toward Prescription for Joy. "Great, he's right through that little alleyway between the drugstore and Get the Scoop. I'll go with you." I looked at Detective Palmer's face, in particular, his scowl. "Or not. You go ahead."

He let out a sound that resembled a snort and walked toward the small path between the two stores.

Kimmie clutched my arm. "Can you believe Wendy was murdered? I mean, it must have happened while I was getting lunch. Thank goodness I ran into you. If we hadn't been talking about how you need to do more with your life, I might have come back a few minutes sooner. I could have been the one lying there instead of Wendy."

She paled a bit at that last statement, and I hoped she didn't faint on me again. I couldn't guarantee I'd catch her the second time.

"I'm surprised you're still here, Kimmie. After the shock you've had, and passing out like that, I'd expect you to go home and rest."

Kimmie shook her head. "Wendy was a good friend. I have to make sure the police do everything they can."

"Detective Palmer is an excellent officer."

"That might be, but I want to hang around and see it for myself."

I glanced back at Wendy's tent and saw Jason chatting with one of the EMTs. He spotted Kimmie, broke away, and headed over.

He nodded at me, but he held his hand out to her. "Kimmie, isn't it?"

She ran a hand over her hair flirtatiously and then shook his. "Oh, my, you're with the paper, right?" She leaned in. "I don't know if you're aware of this, but I'm the one who found poor Wendy. She and I were superclose. We're both successful businesswomen and often discussed strategies while we lunched."

Wow, way to lay it on thick. I half expected her to bat her eyelashes.

Jason still hadn't let go of Kimmie's hand and now he brought up his other one and laid it on top. "I knew you were the right person to talk to. Your information could be critical to this interview."

In response to Jason's blatant buttering, Kimmie simpered. She actually simpered. Zennia watched from the other side of the table.

"It's wonderful to be recognized for my value. Let me tell you everything that happened." Kimmie gestured next door. "I stopped at Wendy's stall to bring her lunch. I'm always doing such things for people. When I saw her lying there, I instantly knew something was wrong."

The giant gash on Wendy's neck had probably been a big clue for her.

"I knew I had to stay calm for the sake of the police, so I went and got Dana here for assistance."

I wasn't exactly stunned that Kimmie left out the part where she'd fainted. But then, I probably would have, too.

Kimmie fluffed her artificially colored black hair, ran a finger under each eye for any errant mascara streaks, and then looked around. "Is your photographer here?"

Jason glanced back toward the crime scene. "No, but I'm expecting him any minute."

"I'm surprised he's not already here, since you were planning to cover the festival anyway," I said.

"He got some shots this morning during setup, then left."

Kimmie straightened her jacket collar and

smoothed down her leopard-print blouse. "I assume he'll want to get a picture of me for the article about Wendy. I did find her body after all."

Jason seemed to struggle with his words, no doubt not wanting to offend his star witness. "I can see where that would be one idea. Usually, we use a shot of the victim, perhaps a professional portrait or a photo treasured by the family."

Kimmie stopped futzing with her jacket. "You mean my picture won't be in the paper?"

What was she expecting? Her photo, with a caption that read, *Body finder*?

"Not this time, I'm afraid," Jason said. "Perhaps in a follow-up article."

"Well, I must say I'm disappointed."

Jason held up his hands, as if he sensed she was about to flee and was hoping to stop her. "Let's not forget your name will still be in the article."

Kimmie's shoulders relaxed at the reminder. "Make sure you spell it right. And see if you can slip in that I'm owner of Le Poêlon—not that the restaurant needs it, but a little publicity never hurt."

"I'll do my best," Jason said in a completely unconvincing tone.

Kimmie squinted down the street. "I'm afraid I have to run. I see one of our best customers down there. I should say hi." She turned to me. "Dana, let's chat later. Don't go anywhere."

With a toss of her head, she strode off down

the street. I watched her go, wondering how she remained so steady on such skinny heels. I would have sprained my ankle just trying on those shoes in the store.

"Did she give you anything useful?" I asked.

"Enough to get started." Jason pulled out his phone. "Two o'clock already? That doesn't give me much time to write the story before I'm supposed to meet my parents."

I whipped my head up so fast, my neck made a popping noise. "Your parents? Are they here in Blossom Valley?" I knew his parents lived in Atherton, an upscale small town south of San Francisco, but that's about all I knew. Jason rarely mentioned them.

"They came up for a few days, unannounced. I'll have to set up a dinner so you can meet them." He texted something on his phone, clearly distracted.

"Meet them?" My voice squeaked like the mouse Zennia had rescued from a stray cat last week. I cleared my throat. "I mean, sure, that sounds great."

Jason gave me a sympathetic smile. "Don't worry, they'll love you. If anything, they'll probably pester you about when we're getting married."

My brain froze. Married? Before I could unthaw it, grab Jason, and tell him I was too busy to meet his parents after all, he'd slipped back to the crime scene. I glanced at Zennia, who was straightening the cup samples, and hoped she'd missed that last part. Her giant grin told me she'd heard everything.

"Not a word," I said.

If anyone was going to throw out theories on what the heck Jason meant by his last comment, it was going to be me.

6

Still stuck on the image of me in a wedding dress, I helped Zennia pack up most of her supplies so she could return to the farm and prepare an afternoon snack for the guests. She left the bowl of corn salad and a dozen or so samples on the table.

As she slung a backpack strap over one shoulder, she gestured toward Wendy's booth. "If those people stand there long enough, they'll get hungry."

"I'll keep the cups at the ready," I promised. "I'm stuck here all afternoon."

"Thanks."

Zennia wasn't even out of sight before my mind returned to the visit by Jason's parents. I knew almost nothing about them, and I had to wonder if Jason ever shared information about me with them. What would they think of me? What did they think of Blossom Valley? This rural small town was a far cry from the ritzy digs of Atherton, where a million dollars might buy you a modest three-bedroom house—if it had been gutted in a fire or flooded in a broken-pipe mishap.

Maybe they'd be too busy during their stay to meet me. Maybe they wouldn't want to see me at all and would pooh-pooh Jason's suggestion. I could only hope. Though I saw a future with Jason, meeting his parents added a whole new aspect to our relationship—one I wasn't sure I was ready for yet.

I turned my attention to the crowd. Whenever one person walked off, another immediately took his place. Thank goodness no one was stopping at my booth. I wasn't sure I could muster a smile after all that had happened.

The crowd shifted as a police officer carrying a camera broke through the group and walked away from Wendy's booth. As the people settled back into place, a young woman moved close enough that I could have touched the sleeve of her denim jacket, if I'd been so inclined. As she turned slightly toward me, I realized she was the woman who'd tried to stop by a couple of times to talk to Wendy. Why had she come back? Who was this woman?

Without a better way to start a conversation, I grabbed a sample cup. "Excuse me, miss," I said. "Would you care to try some corn salad?" Maybe it was my hushed tone or my fervent hope that no one else would hear me, but for some reason, I felt like a candidate offering a bribe as a voter stepped up to the booth on Election Day.

She didn't acknowledge that I'd spoken, so I reached across the table and tapped her back. She visibly flinched and whirled around.

"What do you want?" she demanded. She sounded more scared than annoyed, which only increased my interest.

"Sorry," I said. I raised the plastic cup. "I thought you could try some of our organic corn salad while you're standing there."

She laid a hand on her impossibly flat stomach. "I couldn't eat a thing after what's happened."

I set the cup back on the table. "Did you know Wendy?"

"Not in person. I came today to meet her and tell her how much she's helped me."

I moved around the table so I could talk to the woman, without a giant plastic barrier between us. "I'm Dana."

"Lily, Lily Sharp."

Up close, I caught a whiff of some type of lotion, maybe sunscreen. She had little, if any, makeup on. I spied a smattering of freckles across the bridge of her nose. "What did Wendy do for you?"

"I've always been a big believer in taking care of the environment. I recycle, bring my own bags to the store, walk everywhere I can. Then I met Stan."

"Who's Stan?" And what did he have to do with Wendy?

"Stan lives back in Delaware. We met in an online

chat room about global warming and hit it off right away. After we'd talked online for a few months, I decided it was time for the next step." She scratched the back of her hand, and I noticed her flawless French manicure. "I flew out to meet him."

"And he was really a sixty-five-year-old woman with too much time on her hands?" More than one of my friends had been disappointed when they met an online match in person.

She looked momentarily thrown. "What? No. He was exactly as he described himself. Well, maybe a little heavier. And shorter. But we felt an instant deep connection. Now I fly back to see him every few months, whenever I can take time off from my nursing job."

That was all well and good, but had we moved away from talking about Wendy? "Where does Wendy come in?"

"That's what her company, Invisible Prints, does. I pay her a set amount of money for all the miles I fly, wasting all that jet fuel and polluting the atmosphere, and she invests that money in renewable energy and land preservation. Wendy made it possible for me to commit to my true love without ruining the environment."

Was she really balancing out all the fuel emissions she'd generated, or simply throwing money at the problem to appease her guilty conscience? I'd have to wrap my brain around that later.

"So you knew Wendy through her business?" It didn't sound like she knew Wendy well enough to give me any insight into who killed her after all. Not that I was trying to find suspects. I'd let the police handle it as soon as I passed her name along to Detective Palmer.

Lily pulled a tube of ChapStick out of her pocket and applied a coat. "Only from online. That's why I'm here today. Invisible Prints sent out an e-mail to its customers to let us know they'd have a booth at the festival, but every time I tried to meet Wendy, she was talking to someone else." She stared back at the booth next door. Her face was full of sorrow. "Now I'll never get the chance."

"Did you happen to hear what any of these people were saying to Wendy?"

Lily put a hand to her chest. "I'm much too polite to eavesdrop."

I remembered how loudly the guy had been yelling at Wendy. Lily would have had to clap her hands over her ears not to hear something. Had she left as soon as he started talking? Or was she keeping the information to herself? "If you heard anything that could be connected to Wendy's death, you need to tell the police."

Lily pulled the jacket collar closed around her throat. "The police?"

The way she was trying to shrink into that jacket at the mention of the cops, I had to wonder if she was on the FBI's Most Wanted List. Before I could ask her more, I heard a familiar voice behind me.

"Ha, I should have known if someone else got

killed around here, you'd be right in the middle of it."

I turned around to find Ashlee, my younger and far less mature sister, smirking at me. She must be on her lunch break from the veterinary office where she worked.

"I shouldn't have to remind you that the last time I was in the middle of a murder investigation, it was because you got there first," I said.

She stuck her tongue out at me, confirming her level of maturity. "I would have been fine on my own. You wanted a reason to get in the middle."

"Hardly. I was saving your bacon."

"Whatever."

"Look, stop pestering me," I said. "I'm busy talking to Lily. She might know something about Wendy's death."

Ashlee popped her gum. "Who's Lily?"

I gestured to my left. "This nice woman right here."

"Another one of your imaginary friends?"

I checked behind me and saw that Lily was no longer standing there. In fact, she was nowhere in sight, having walked away while Ashlee and I were squabbling. Well, great.

"She's gone," I said to Ashlee. "How'd you hear about the murder already?"

"I was getting a pedicure. The sister of the lady who owns the shop has a booth down here today and said the murder pretty much killed the crowd."

I winced at her choice of words, but she had a point. While the place hadn't exactly been packed before Wendy's death, it had emptied out pretty darn quickly afterward, except for all the gawkers. I looked past Ashlee and saw Kimmie moving toward us.

I couldn't believe she was still here after finding Wendy's body, even if she was keeping an eye on the cops. I'd be wrapped in a blanket on my couch with some hot chocolate and a bottle of aspirin if it had been me, but Kimmie was in a class all her own.

She stopped when she reached us and addressed Ashlee. "I almost didn't recognize you. Did you change your hair?"

Ashlee reached up and stroked a chunk. "A trim. Thought I'd try some bangs."

"Don't worry, that'll grow out in no time." Ashlee opened her mouth for a rebuttal, but Kimmie didn't even slow down. "Mind if I borrow Dana here for a minute? I promise to bring her right back." She grabbed my elbow, and I allowed her to drag me across the street, curious to know why exactly she needed to speak to me with such urgency.

"What's so important that you couldn't talk in front of Ashlee?" I asked. "Did you remember something about Wendy's murder?"

Kimmie shook her head. "No, but I've been thinking since we talked a bit ago. I know you've somehow managed to solve a couple of murders in the last few months."

I raised my hand. "Stop right there. Detective Palmer has already warned me to keep my nose out of this. I know you have your doubts, but the police really can handle Wendy's death. I'd simply be in their way."

"Nonsense. The department's so small, they need all the help they can get. Even you."

I thought back to how I'd already supplied the detective with a partial license plate and description of the man. If Kimmie knew how close she was to the truth, she'd gloat all day. I kept my mouth shut.

Kimmie must have taken my silence as agreement. "The police don't know Wendy like we do. She needs an advocate to make sure they do everything they can to catch her killer."

"Her family will keep the police on track." I knew if I was ever murdered, Mom would pack a bag and move into the police station until they solved the case.

Kimmie took hold of my upper arm. Her fake nails dug into my skin. "That's just it. Her dad died a few years back and her mom passed away last year. She told me that she and her brother weren't speaking anymore, so she really has no one."

"What about her husband?"

"That guy?" Kimmie shook her head. "He can't be counted on. If anything, I'd put him at the top of the suspect list. I never could figure out what Wendy saw in him."

Was Kimmie right? Would no one push the police to find her killer? A lump formed in my throat. I'd grown up with her, been good friends with her, and now she was gone, with so few to mourn her. With a no-good husband and an estranged brother, would she even receive a proper burial?

I felt my concern for Wendy's death replace my resistance at not getting involved. With no one to look out for her, I needed to step up. "I'm not sure how I can help," I said, although I was already generating a few ideas.

Kimmie gripped my arm tighter. "You'll figure it out. I have faith in you."

I knew she was buttering me up like a bowl of popcorn just so I'd help her, but I couldn't stop myself from nodding. "I should at least contact Wendy's brother to offer my condolences." And find out if their rift was worth killing over. "If he says anything interesting, I'll follow up."

Kimmie released my arm and clutched her Louis Vuitton bag. "Great, I'll send you his contact information. I remember Wendy mentioned he lives here in town." She checked her watch again. "Now I've got to get to the restaurant. Send me a status report in a couple of days, and we'll go from there." She walked away.

Status report?

Oh, hell no.

There would be no status report. Kimmie was not my boss. This would end now.

And I would have told her that, too, if she hadn't already reached the parking lot and unlocked her Mercedes. Instead, I watched her zoom out of the lot, tires screeching, and marveled at the situation I'd gotten myself into.

7

I returned to the farm's booth, where Ashlee was flirting with a guy as she showed him various pictures on the easel. As I got closer, she gave him a pig pen and a travel mug, along with her best smile, before he ambled away, clutching his goodies. I noticed he held a strip of paper in his hand, and I had to wonder if one of those goodies was Ashlee's phone number. She handed her digits out like the sample lady passed out potato chips at Costco.

I moved behind the table. "Thanks for watching the booth."

"No problem." She looked toward the parking lot. "Where'd your little friend go?"

"Kimmie? Back to Mendocino."

"Good. Why do you even talk to her? She's such a phony."

"I know she can be annoying," I said, "but she's

had a rough time. She did find Wendy's body after all."

"Tell you what, I'll be nice to her for the rest of the day." Ashlee snapped her gum again. "Since she already left, that should make it a lot easier."

Gee, my sister is the next Florence Nightingale.

George Sturgeon, owner of the Spinning Your Wheels tire shop and leader of the Blossom Valley Rejuvenation Committee, approached the booth. His blue polo shirt and khaki pants looked crisp and new, and his customary crew cut was freshly trimmed. Ashlee and I immediately stopped our banter.

"Ladies," he said, "we're shutting down the festival for the rest of the day so the police can look into that woman's death. We'll start up first thing tomorrow, no later than 0800 hours."

"Think anyone will come after what happened?" I asked.

"Some will come out of curiosity. That'll be our chance to nab them, urge them to take a look at all these booths. I've got some brand-new low-rolling resistance tires that'll help with fuel efficiency to show them."

Well, if that doesn't keep the crowds here, I don't know what will.

"Now, if you ladies will excuse me, I have to let the other booths know." George marched toward the mushroom-dyeing booth across the street. I wasn't sure how you dyed things with mushrooms, but the shirts and sweaters the guy was selling certainly looked remarkable.

"Guess I can pack up," I said.

"I gotta go, too," Ashlee said. "Those feral cats won't spay themselves. But that'd be awesome if they could."

She trotted off toward the parking area. I swept the brochures into a single pile and placed them back into the box. The wind had died down, and I was able to dismantle the booth, including the awning, with little trouble and even less cussing. Vendors at the nearby booths were closing down as well.

I lugged the box of brochures, pens, and travel mugs over to my Honda, opened the trunk, and slid the box in. I slammed the trunk shut and went back for the uneaten corn salad and sample cups. With one last look at Wendy's tent and the diminished group of gawkers, I climbed behind the wheel and motored out of the lot.

Traffic was light on the freeway, and I reached the turnoff for the farm in minutes. Esther had yet to agree to pave the dirt lane. For now, I bounced and jolted along, passing the sign that declared, O'CONNELL ORGANIC FARM AND SPA, before I pulled into my usual parking space near the side path.

I picked up my box of marketing materials, balanced the salad bowl on top, and walked up the path. My shoes crunched the dry, crisp leaves that littered the ground.

All the cabin doors were closed as I walked past, but I heard people talking in the closest one. We'd had a steady stream of guests over the last couple of months, providing us all with a little more job security and Esther with a sense that her farm might make it after all. We'd recently hired Gretchen, a certified masseuse with experience in facials and manicures. These new spa services, combined with the first-ever green-living festival, had guaranteed a full house this weekend.

Of course, Wendy's death would definitely put a damper on the festivities now, at least for me. I'd been so excited to participate in the festival, but now everything had changed. How could I celebrate the new services at the farm when I knew my friend had been murdered?

These thoughts weighed heavy on my mind as I rounded the corner and walked past the pool, catching a whiff of chlorine. With the weather so cool on this fall day, no one was swimming, but a man and a woman sat in the nearby Jacuzzi. Their heads were close together as they murmured to each other. I nodded to them as I crossed the large patio, then cut through the herb garden and in the back door. The kitchen was empty, the only sound the ticking of the rooster clock. Already close to three. I left the salad bowl on the counter next to the wheatgrass machine before heading into the office.

I dumped my box in the corner, the rough cardboard scraping my arms, and pulled Wendy's brochure from my pocket. Once in the desk chair, I took a moment to stare at the photo of the pigs and wonder if Wendy had thought up this particular project. She'd been so young. What could have happened that someone would want her dead?

With a sigh, I wiggled the mouse to activate the computer monitor and opened a browser, inputting the Web address that was listed on the Invisible Prints brochure.

Photos of lush rain forests and rushing streams filled the screen. A picture of wind turbines reminded me of the miniature models Wendy had handed out at the festival, and I shook my head. She'd been alive a few hours ago. What had happened between the time we'd talked and when Kimmie found her body? If I hadn't seen her body myself, I still might not believe it.

I clicked on the "About Invisible Prints" link and scanned the brief bio. Wendy had started the company two years ago after visiting Brazil and seeing how portions of the rain forest were still being decimated. Upon her return, she'd found investors and opened for business. The "Carbon Offset" page described how Invisible Prints worked and provided a calculator to see how much energy you wasted each day through various activities.

The premise was a little complicated, and I wondered how successful the company was. Since Wendy had been manning her own booth at the festival, instead of having an assistant do it, I had to assume the company wasn't yet at Fortune 500 status.

I clicked the "Contact Us" link and saw that the company headquarters was based in Mendocino. Maybe I'd stop by on one of my days off and see what my old classmate had built for herself.

A cough from the doorway interrupted my planning.

"Why aren't you at the festival? Who's passing out the pig pens?" Gordon demanded.

My hands froze on the keyboard. Gordon didn't have a link to the town's gossip network. He hadn't heard about Wendy's death.

"They shut the festival down early," I said, stalling for time.

"Shut it down? On whose authority? I want names. We spent weeks getting ready for this."

I wasn't sure who this "we" was that Gordon mentioned, considering Gordon didn't belong to the rejuvenation committee. Along with my help, they'd done all the planning, organizing, and ordering, but I let his comment slide. We had bigger problems.

"The police closed the festival early for an investigation." I wasn't sure how to couch what had happened, so I didn't bother. Gordon could handle bad news. "The woman in the booth next to us was murdered."

Gordon's face reddened. "Murdered? How? When?" He viciously twisted his pinkie ring. "Tell me, please, that you weren't involved this time."

When I'd first started working here, Gordon's menacing attitude would have frazzled my nerves and had me shaking. Now that I knew his hard exterior was mostly for show, my hackles rose at the implication in that statement. "I don't go around finding bodies all the time, Gordon."

"Thank God. I know you helping solve those murders a few months ago hasn't exactly hurt business here at the farm, maybe even increased it, but pretty soon, people are going to see it more as a circus act. We have to protect the reputation of this place."

"Don't worry." I made a mental note to make sure Jason wasn't planning to include my name in any articles.

"So that's it? One dead body, and the festival is over?"

How many bodies did he want? "It'll reopen first thing tomorrow morning. The police should be done with their investigation by then."

Gordon rubbed his hands together. "I bet we get an even bigger crowd. People will come down to see where this woman was killed. Right next to our booth, you said? That might work in our favor."

I cringed at his insensitivity, but he didn't notice. George had said pretty much the same thing, but not with that calculating smile. "You know, I was best friends with this woman back in school. She was a wonderful person who didn't deserve to be murdered."

"I'm sorry. I didn't realize you knew her." Gordon straightened his tie. "Still, make sure you're at the festival before it opens tomorrow. People will show up early now. In fact, you need a team member to assist you. Maybe I'll send Zennia." Without waiting for an answer, he walked out the door.

I said a silent thanks that he hadn't volunteered himself to help run the booth before I returned to the Invisible Prints Web site. I clicked on a few more links, but I'd probably found out about all I could from the site. I checked my e-mail and found a message from Kimmie with Wendy's address, as well as that of her brother Kurt. She also let me know she'd attached a status report form I should use, but I didn't open the file. I jotted down both addresses for later reference and tried to get my mind back on my day job.

I spent the remainder of the afternoon, what was left of it anyway, fleshing out a brochure I'd been working on about our new massage offerings and trying not to think about Wendy and who might have killed her.

After an hour, I gave up and clocked out early. Kurt lived here in town, and I was ready to talk to him. I could only hope the police had already notified him about Wendy's death. I'd hate to be the one to break the news to him, even if they hadn't been getting along.

I put on my windbreaker and made a quick side trip out back to see Wilbur and the other pigs in their pen. I tried to check on them at least once a day, though it wasn't technically part of my job. I just liked the pigs.

As usual, most rooted around, looking for random scraps of food, while two slept on their sides. I patted Wilbur's pink-and-brown back for a moment before I headed down the vegetable path to my car. The temperature still hovered around the mid-sixties, but the wind had a bite. I pulled my windbreaker tighter as I unlocked the door and slipped inside.

According to Kimmie's e-mail, Kurt lived on Honeysuckle Street, in the older part of town. I jetted down the freeway, exited at Main Street, made a few turns, and slowed to a crawl as I turned onto Honeysuckle. Most of the curb numbers were too faded to read, so I inched along and tried to find house numbers on the mailboxes or porches. The address Kimmie provided belonged to a two-story house, which had a newer coat of paint and a large garage in back down a long driveway. The lawn was a couple inches too tall, and overgrown bushes blocked most of the windows. Apparently, Kurt wasn't a fan of gardening.

As I started to pull to the curb, I spotted a blue Taurus in front of me and groaned. Oh no. If that was Detective Palmer's car, how would I explain my presence? That I was offering condolences to a brother I barely remembered of a woman I hadn't seen in ten years? Maybe I'd wait a few minutes.

I flipped a U, parked on the opposite side of the street, and sat in my car, watching the street activity, or lack of it. A butterfly fluttered around the lawn, a cat wandered across the street, and the occasional early-autumn leaf blew by. Even with the cool weather, the interior of the car was starting to warm up. I opened the door and inhaled the outside air. If that was the detective's car, what was taking him so long? Was he merely notifying Kurt about Wendy's death, or was he questioning him about any enemies Wendy might have had? Either way, he should be done by now.

After another minute, I got out of the car, crossed the street, and stepped onto the sidewalk. From where I stood, I could see a line of windows running down the side of the house and the garage at the far end of the driveway. Maybe I could take a peek in one of the windows to see if the detective was wrapping things up. Otherwise, I'd go home and come back later in the evening.

I walked partway down the driveway and stopped at the first window, peeking through the bush, which I hoped would block me from anyone inside the house. The first room appeared to be the living room, with a couch, a recliner, and a large-screen TV. No one was there. The next window was small and high, and probably belonged to a bathroom. I was leaning forward to peer through the glass of the third window when someone behind me said, "What are you doing?"

With a shriek, I shot forward, throwing my arms out as I hit the bush and bounced back. I whirled around.

Detective Palmer stood before me. There was a grim set to his mouth. "Care to explain why you're spying on the people in this house?"

Blood rushed to my face. I straightened out my jacket and brushed off a leaf clinging to one sleeve. "I came to offer my condolences."

Detective Palmer reached up and plucked a twig from my hair. "Ever tried knocking?"

"I didn't want to intrude during such a terrible time, so I was looking in the windows to make sure he was up for company." Man, what a lame story.

"So you think having a giant face pop up in the window is less intrusive than ringing the doorbell?"

I ignored the fact that he had called my face "giant," considering the position he'd caught me in. Instead, I wondered if I could get him to share anything with me. "How did Kurt take the news of his sister's death?"

Detective Palmer pulled a stick of gum from his jacket pocket, offered it to me, and stuck it in his mouth when I declined. "About as well as anyone else in that position."

"Think he'd be willing to talk to me?"

"That depends. Are you really here for condolences, or to snoop around in Ms. Hartford's death?"

Ha! Like I'd ever admit I'm snooping. "Condolences, of course. I have no plans to get in the way of your investigation." I might have added too much sugar to the sweetness in my tone, because Detective Palmer started chewing his gum hard enough that I worried he'd dislocate his jaw.

"You'd better mean that," he said. "Stay out of my investigation."

I held up my hands. "Whatever you say. Now excuse me while I see Kurt." I headed back toward the front of the house.

"Where are you going?" Detective Palmer called after me.

I pointed up the driveway. "To ring the bell."

He jerked his head in the opposite direction. "Kurt lives back there."

"In the garage?" Based on the appearance of the outside of the garage, I'd assumed it housed old car parts, broken furniture, and rusty yard equipment.

"Yep." He walked past me, probably headed for his car. "Remember what I said about meddling."

I resisted the urge to say something smart-alecky. I was already embarrassed enough that he'd discovered me peeping in a stranger's windows.

Instead, I waited until he'd reached the street before I walked to the garage. The main door was shut, so I went around the corner of the building. The side door was slightly ajar. I knocked on the jamb and waited. No response. I knocked again.

Was Kurt inside grieving? Should I really interrupt such a moment just because I fancied myself a bit of a detective? Maybe I should go.

A man appeared at the door, eliminating that possibility. He wasn't much older than I was, but he already had a receding hairline, with an unshaved face. I hadn't seen Kurt since middle school when Wendy and I used to trail after him on his way to the store for candy. If it wasn't for the same upturned nose that Wendy had, I couldn't have picked him out of a lineup.

Looking past him, I glimpsed a cement floor with a battered and worn plaid couch, a lawn chair, and an upside-down wine barrel, with a can of Budweiser on it. Not exactly the Ritz-Carlton.

"I know you?" he asked.

My palms suddenly felt clammy. "You probably don't remember me after all these years. I'm, I mean was, a friend of your sister's. Wendy," I added, which seemed unnecessary, since he probably knew his own sister's name. "I wanted to tell you how sorry I am about your loss."

"Thanks, but I don't need your sympathy." His face closed up. "Wendy's death was no loss to me."

I gaped at him. Did he really believe his sister's death was no big deal? What exactly had happened between those two?

8

My face must have broadcast my shock at his statement, because Kurt immediately said, "Hey, don't get me wrong. She was my sister and all, but I can guarantee she brought it on herself."

Handling death wasn't my forte to begin with, and I struggled to think of an appropriate response. "I'm sure news of her death is hard to process under these circumstances."

He shook his head. "God knows I've wished Wendy dead a hundred times, but someone actually went and did it." I couldn't tell if he was disgusted or impressed.

I hoped Ashlee would be more upset than this if I died. Then again, she'd probably be delighted to plan my funeral. I pictured ice sculptures, wreaths of black roses, and a chocolate fountain.

Kurt placed a hand on the inside doorknob as though he was getting ready to pull the door shut.

"When was the last time you talked to Wendy?" I blurted out before he could slam it in my face.

He glared at me. "What's it to you?"

Ack. This conversation is not going the way I envisioned.

Despite their estrangement, I'd expected a weeping, distraught guy who would want to talk about his murdered sister and provide details about who might want her dead. Instead, Kurt looked about as open to talking as a seasoned Mob boss waiting for his lawyer to show up during a police interrogation.

"I thought if you'd seen each other recently, it would provide you with more closure than if it had been a long time."

Kurt smirked. "Wendy's dead. That's all the closure I need." He crossed his arms. At least he'd taken his hand off the knob. "I don't know why you women are always talking about *needing closure*. It's exactly what my wife said when she left me."

Time to backtrack. I didn't want him getting bogged down by his ex-wife.

"Sorry to hear about that." I scratched my arm. My skin was itching with anxiety. "Anyway, I at least wanted to stop by and offer you my sympathy. I actually saw poor Wendy this morning at the green-living festival. I hadn't seen her in years, and right when we get the chance to reunite, this tragedy happens."

He snorted. "Advertising that company of hers? Selling her carbon-footprint garbage to a bunch of rich folks who want to feel better about their private jets and wild-animal fur rugs? All a bunch of hooey if you ask me, but then Wendy's specialty always was conning people into giving her their money."

The bitterness in his words made my stomach turn. "What do you mean?"

"You were friends with her. You must remember how she could sweet-talk anyone into doing anything for her. How do you think she graduated high school? Talked all the nerds into doing her homework."

My school memories had been somewhat hazy before. Now that he mentioned it, I recalled that Wendy always had a knack for getting people to help her on science fair projects, class reports, and homework, especially math homework. Wendy stank at math. And when she'd won the student class president election by a landslide, there'd been murmurs of ballot tampering.

"Still, starting your own company at such a young age is pretty impressive," I said.

"Not really." He shrugged dismissively. "Anyone can throw up a PowerPoint presentation, promise all sorts of ways to make money, and someone'll help you out. I'm sure her little house of cards would have come crashing down soon enough when those people didn't get any of their money back."

Hmm. Definitely an angle worth pursuing. Maybe I should tell Detective Palmer about this.

A ringtone sounded from the pocket of Kurt's

pants. He pulled out a cell phone and glanced at the screen.

"I gotta get that."

"Sure. Sorry to have bothered you."

He shut the door without a good-bye.

I walked down the driveway and back to my car. As I slid behind the wheel, I looked back at the main house and saw an old man shuffle out and stoop to pick up the newspaper off the porch. I considered getting out and talking to him, but then thought better of it. Kurt wasn't the most open guy in the world, so it was unlikely he regularly shared personal details with his landlord, if that's who the man was. Time to call it a day.

I drove home in a funk. How sad that Kurt wasn't even sorry his sister was dead. What rift was so severe that he'd react to Wendy's death in such a callous manner? Was it somehow related to money? Was that why he'd mentioned Wendy conning people? Maybe Kimmie could fill me in, since she and Wendy had stayed in touch, just so long as she didn't ask for a status report in exchange.

At home, I parked on the street in front of the single-story house where I'd grown up. Every few years, Mom would pay to have the house painted, but always the same light blue with white trim. I passed the brick planter full of African daisies and entered the house, where the scent of spices and tomato sauce greeted me in the front hall. I went straight to the kitchen. Mom stood before the clean white stove, stirring the contents of a large pot. The green-and-white-striped kitchen towel was tucked into the waistband of her half apron.

"What smells so good?" I asked. Mom had been on a brown-rice-and-chicken kick ever since my father had died of a heart attack two years earlier. Because of her years of serving chicken-fried steak with mashed potatoes, and macaroni and cheese, too, she'd felt partly responsible for his death. She had vowed to improve her own eating so she'd be around for us girls a lot longer. Her healthy cooking, along with Zennia's concoctions, left me craving fast-food burgers and sugary snacks on an almost hourly basis.

She ran a hand through her gray curls, then patted a few back into place. "I found a recipe for fish stew in one of my magazines and decided to give it a try. Other than having too much salt, the dish is quite healthy."

"I'm glad to see you're trying new things." *And, thank goodness, we get a night off from chicken!*

Mom lowered the heat on the burner, popped a lid on the pot, and washed her hands at the sink. "Sue Ellen called a while ago," she said over her shoulder. "She said someone had an accident at the festival. Did you hear anything about that?"

Sue Ellen was Blossom Valley's central hub for all things gossip related. I was surprised she hadn't heard yet that Wendy had been murdered. I took a deep breath and waited until Mom had turned off the water. "Worse than an accident, I'm afraid. The woman in the booth next to me was murdered."

Mom whirled around, gripping a hand towel. "Oh no! How awful. Do the police know who did it?"

"I don't think so. The victim was Wendy Hartford. Do you remember Wendy? Her maiden name was Clark. She used to come over here after school all the time."

Mom set down the towel and came over to pull me close. "Of course I remember her. Such a sweet girl. How are you handling it?"

I relaxed into Mom's hug. She smelled of spices and Dove soap. "I'm all right. But poor Wendy."

Giving me one last pat, she went back to the stove and lifted the lid to stir the stew. "Is that the end of the festival, then?"

"They closed early for the afternoon, but it'll start up again in the morning. Who knows if anyone will show up once the early-bird vultures get done gawking at the crime scene?"

"I know you put a lot of effort into this festival. I'm sorry this happened."

"Thanks. We'll see if the rest of the weekend can be salvaged."

I heard the front door open. Mom pulled a loaf of French bread out of a bag on the counter. "That must be your sister. I'd better get the bread warmed up."

Ashlee bounced into the kitchen. Her ponytail

was swinging behind her. Clumps of white fur were clearly visible on her navy blue vet smock.

"Dana, tell me everything that happened after I left the festival."

I gave her a questioning look. "You were there when George announced we were closing early. I packed up and left."

Her eyes widened in disbelief. "That's it? You didn't talk to all the people who had booths there? You didn't ask who might have wanted Wendy dead?"

Mom placed a hot pad on the table, her signal that the stew was almost ready. I removed three bowls from a cupboard and then opened the silverware drawer to grab the spoons.

"Ashlee," Mom said, "the police should be handling that. I don't want Dana involved in another murder. It's too dangerous."

I shivered as I thought about my close call from a few months ago, when I'd been chased by a killer. "Don't worry. I'm not getting involved in the investigation." I paused for a beat. "Although Kimmie and I were talking, and we thought it might be nice if we helped the police a tiny bit."

"Dana!" Mom snapped. The sheer intensity of her voice forced me back a step. I clutched the spoons to my chest.

Ashlee gave me a smug look. "I knew you couldn't keep your nose out of it. You always make fun of me for gossiping, but you're a total meddler."

I raised my right hand, spoons and all. "I swear

I'm trying to stay out of it." I lowered my arm. "Only, Kimmie mentioned that Wendy's parents are dead and she's estranged from her brother and her husband might be the one who killed her. It doesn't seem right that she's dead and no one's going to miss her."

Mom slammed the pot of fish stew on the table, causing a wave of tomato broth to slosh over the side. "That doesn't mean you need to help. The police will find the killer."

"I'm sure they will," I said to soothe Mom before she spilled the entire meal. "I just thought people might be more open to talking to me than to the police." That plan had failed spectacularly with Kurt, but I didn't mention that.

Mom grabbed a sponge and dabbed at the table. "Nonsense. I want you to give up this idea right now."

The teen rebel in me—the one that still lurked beneath the surface and reared its head anytime Mom tried to tell me what time to be home from a date—popped up once more. "I'll think about it" was all I said. Not exactly a hard-nosed response, but it was enough to make Mom press her lips together and stop talking.

She sat down at the table and carefully unfolded her napkin, smoothing it in her lap. I followed her lead, and we all sat in a strained silence until Ashlee mentioned a cute guy who had come into the vet office that day with his sick turtle. That reminded her of her favorite coffee guy at the Daily

Grind, the one who always knew her order and got the temperature just right. He reminded her of the guy who was running a green-cleaning booth at the festival and gave Ashlee free samples. Mentioning the festival brought us right back to the murder.

"The poor guy was so distracted by Wendy's death that he didn't even ask for my number," Ashlee said.

"Maybe he didn't want it," I said, but she swiped that idea away with a wave of her hand.

"Seriously, Dana. We had something going. You don't give someone fifteen samples of bamboo dust rags for no reason."

I speared a scallop. "He probably couldn't find anyone else to give the samples to."

"Whatever. I'm going to stop by again tomorrow and see if he's there. Give him another chance."

"That's very generous of you."

Ashlee snarled at me.

Mom cleared her throat, and Ashlee focused on her dinner.

"I remember when you used to bring Wendy over after school," Mom said. "Such a smart girl, and so outgoing."

"Yeah, she was friends with everyone," I said. "Always a class leader or president of the clubs she joined."

Mom sipped her water. "I'd heard she'd started her own company. It's really no surprise, since she always had such strong leadership skills."

Apparently, Mom had been keeping tabs on Wendy. I wondered what she knew about my other high-school friends. "When she won the class president election, I'm not sure the other guy got a single vote," I said.

Ashlee snorted.

I lowered my spoon. "What?"

"She didn't win the election. She rigged it."

This time, I set my spoon all the way down in my stew. "How do you know?"

"Because my friend Brittany helped her do it. Traded that for a spot on the cheerleading squad."

"Are you kidding me?" Guess those rumors about ballot tampering had been true.

"Have you ever watched Brittany walk?" Ashlee asked. "I mean, I love her to death, but she's a klutz. No way could she make the squad without Wendy's help, so they made a little deal."

Mom laid a hand on the table and leaned toward Ashlee. "You didn't help, did you?"

"Of course not," Ashlee said. "She told me about it later when we were sneaking some booze from her dad's liquor cabinet."

Mom looked aghast, while I stifled a smile.

"Not that I drank any," Ashlee added quickly.

Mom opened her mouth as if to say something, then sighed. "Somehow I don't think any of that is connected to her death."

"Probably not," I agreed. "But it lends credence

to her brother's remark that her company might not be on the up-and-up."

"When did you talk to her brother?" Mom asked.

Oops. Busted. "I stopped by after work to offer my condolences."

Mom sighed again, as though her children made her impossibly tired. "I told you. I don't want you involved in another murder, Dana. I don't even want you talking about the case with Jason, like you always seem to do."

"Don't worry. Jason's parents are in town, so he'll probably be too busy to see me."

"Ooh, his parents," Ashlee said in a singsong voice.

I pointed at her. "Don't start. What are your plans this weekend?"

"I've got a date tomorrow night, of course."

"And Lane's supposed to take me to that new restaurant in Santa Rosa," Mom said.

I'd initially been troubled when Mom started dating a few months ago, with Dad's death still a presence in our lives. But Lane had proven to be a decent guy, and I'd grudgingly accepted the situation.

I finished the rest of my stew and helped with the dishes before settling down to watch TV. All the while, I was wondering how I could possibly look into Wendy's death without Mom catching on. I didn't like to deceive her, but I didn't want to worry her, either.

Sometimes living at home had its drawbacks, and now was one of those times. I'd just have to be crafty about it and hope I didn't get caught.

9

Early the next morning, I ran out to the farm to retrieve my box of brochures and pig pens and assured Gordon I didn't need any extra help running the booth. Though I did start to second-guess myself when I arrived at the festival and saw the crowds. It wasn't even eight yet and swarms of people were already showing up. I hurriedly set up the folding table and awning, but everyone headed straight for Wendy's booth and clustered around the entrance. The crime scene tape was gone, but no one stepped inside the tent.

"So that's where it happened," an older woman said.

"Is that a bloodstain?" a man asked as he pointed to the pavement and what, in all likelihood, was actually an oil stain.

I tuned them out as I arranged my brochures, popped the photo collage on the easel, and laid out my pens. Then I stood at attention and waited to bestow the benefits of the O'Connell Farm and Spa on any interested attendees, occasionally calling out to the crowd and offering them brochures.

People wandered past, most ignoring me as they examined the scene of the crime. A handful slowed to scan my brochures, and three even took pens, but no one talked to me.

When the next woman moved in to grab a pen, I spoke up. "While you're here, let me tell you about our new spa services," I said. My voice sounded as perky as those home-shopping network hosts'.

The woman avoided my gaze as she drew her hand back and eased into the flow of traffic, moving past. She must be under the mistaken impression that pig pens bite. Or else I did. I readied my smile for the next person who came close enough, but no one did. They moved past as though they were at the zoo and the dead person's booth was the star white-tiger exhibit. I should start charging for each peek. I'd make a fortune for the farm.

After the next twenty people didn't as much as glance in my direction, I let my smile droop and dug my cell phone out of my pocket to check the time. *Thirty minutes? I've only been here thirty minutes? Egads, this day will go on forever!*

Maybe I'd talk to some of the other booth owners,

ask if they had seen anything yesterday. If I'd heard that man yelling at Wendy, surely the guy on the other side of her booth had, too.

I stepped from behind the table, moved around the people at Wendy's tent, and approached the booth on the other side. Behind a folding table, a solar panel stood on end, propped up on some type of stand. The table itself held glossy postcards and little pots with plastic flowers that waved in the sunlight. A stack of visors with the company's name printed on top sat to one side.

The man behind the table beamed at me, exposing crooked teeth. One of his front ones was the same color as the cappuccino I'd purchased on my way to work this morning. "Good morning, ma'am. I appreciate you stopping by today. Are you interested in installing solar panels on your roof?" He spoke so fast, his words tripped over one another.

Do I sound this desperate? No wonder the woman left.

"Sorry, I run the booth two down. I was wondering how business is this morning for you."

His smile winked out, replaced by a scowl. "Not great. This damn murder has everyone distracted. No one can talk about anything else."

"It's big news. Were you working yesterday when it happened?"

"No, I must have been on my lunch break. But I was here all morning before that." He watched a couple making their way down the street, and I leaned in to draw his attention back to me.

"Then you must have heard the argument between Wendy and that man."

"Sure, anyone within fifty feet couldn't help but hear," he said.

"I heard part of it myself, but couldn't figure out what they were fighting about. Any ideas?"

He straightened up and looked me over. "Hold up now. Did you say you were part of the festival or part of the police department?"

I really need to be more subtle with my questions. People are so darn suspicious these days. I put a hand to my heart to prove how trustworthy I was. "Festival. In fact, I helped organize this event, and I hate to see all that effort go to waste." My answer didn't really explain why I was asking questions, but he immediately nodded.

"Boy, I hear you on that." He held up a pot, with the flower merrily bobbing. "I spent a ton on these knickknacks, and now no one wants them."

"We're in the same boat, except I'm stuck with pens that oink."

He gave me a funny look, but I didn't bother to explain.

"So, did you hear what they were arguing about?" I asked again.

"Some. The guy who was yelling kept asking where the money had gone."

My skin prickled. "Money? What money?"

"How should I know? He asked what the lady running the booth had done with it. That's about all I heard."

This information certainly held promise and once more supported Kurt's comments. He'd said Wendy had a knack for deceiving people into giving her their money. Had this guy been a customer of Invisible Prints who felt swindled, or had this been a personal matter?

"Guess I'd better get back to my booth," I said. "Thanks for the info."

"You betcha. And if you get any customers, send 'em my way when you're done."

I offered my hand and he shook it. "Deal," I said. His mention of customers added a little speed to my step, but I was wasting the effort. No one waited at the table, and no brochures or pens were gone.

With no customers in sight, I walked across the street to the mushroom-dyeing booth. Clotheslines were strung across three sides of the booth. Sweaters and T-shirts colored various shades of yellow, green, and red hung from the lines. Price tags were pinned to their fronts. The table held more shirts, folded, and a basket full of scarves, along with stacks of flyers and coupons.

I'd briefly met Jim during the initial planning stages for the festival. In his thirties, he was tan and buff. Right now, he looked about as bored as I felt as he sat on a stool near the silent cash register.

He raised a flyswatter. "Want to borrow this to beat the crowd back? I see you're about as swamped as I am."

I shook my head. "This has to get better before the day's over. Right?"

Jim ran a hand through his blond hair. "That's why I haven't packed up yet."

I gestured toward a T-shirt covered in rusty red and orange swirls. "Beautiful colors on that shirt. How does this mushroom dyeing work?"

He practically bounced off the stool, clearly glad to have an audience. "Different types of mushrooms create different colors. The woods near Mendocino have a variety of species that I collect. I toss each one into a pot with a few other ingredients, add the shirt, and—voila—the colors leach out of the mushrooms and dye the cloth."

"That's so creative. I've never seen anything like that before." I picked up a coupon for a mushroom-foraging class and stuffed it into my back pocket. Might be an unusual way to spend a Sunday afternoon.

Jim adjusted the scarves. "Most people haven't." He glanced around as if afraid of eavesdroppers, but the closest person was over at Wendy's booth. "You get questioned by the police yet?"

Here I was wondering how to circle around to

the murder, but he'd done all the work for me. "Right after it happened. Were you here? I don't remember seeing you."

Jim refolded a T-shirt, which had looked a little crooked. "The crowd was so small, I went and sat in my truck to make some business calls. By the time I got back, the cops had already shown up."

"So you didn't see anything?" I asked. Wendy's booth had been surrounded by people, yet we'd all stepped away at that crucial time. Part of the killer's plan, or was it a lucky coincidence?

"Earlier I saw a man stop by and get into it with Wendy. I couldn't hear what they were saying, but you could tell he was yelling. Too bad they were inside that tent—I couldn't see much." He slapped his hand on a stack of coupons as a gust of wind blew through.

I handed him a thermos, which sat on the table, so he could weigh down the coupons. "What happened next?"

"Some good-looking lady in a leopard-print shirt showed up, and the guy left."

He must have been admiring Kimmie. I'd known it was a long shot that Jim would have heard anything all the way across the street, but I still felt a sigh of disappointment escape my lips. "Too bad you couldn't hear. That argument might be tied to her murder."

He flashed a row of perfectly white teeth at a

woman walking by, but she didn't stop. He focused on me again. "That's what the cops said, too. I told them they need to talk to that lady who was standing right outside Wendy's booth while those two were yelling. She must have heard the entire thing."

I felt like I'd swallowed a shot of espresso as my pulse sped up. Had someone else overheard the argument? "Can you describe her?"

"Real pretty. Like a cowgirl, with those boots."

My initial excitement died away. This wasn't a new witness after all. "That must be Lily, one of Invisible Prints' customers. She really wanted to meet Wendy yesterday."

"She looked awful upset when she ran off. Whatever she overheard, it wasn't pretty."

I needed to talk to Lily again. Maybe she'd come back to the festival today, although I couldn't imagine why. Her one reason for visiting was now lying in the morgue. I shivered at the image.

Jim noticed. "That wind is chilly, isn't it? One of my mushroom sweaters would keep you warm."

"Thanks, but I've got my jacket in my booth. Speaking of which, guess I'd better get back, in case someone shows up."

I walked across the street, feeling the stirrings of resentment at the group of spectators. If they weren't interested in the festival, they should clear out, instead of offering up false hope. I had better things to do than try to lure over people who only wanted to tell their friends they'd seen a real-live murder site. I slapped my hand on the table when I reached it. The action created a loud *pop*.

A couple of people looked over, and I snatched up a brochure.

"Have you heard about all the new features at the spa?" I asked.

They both shook their heads and moved away. *Maybe that's how I can get rid of all the looky-loos. Pester them with brochures. I'd get the space cleared in ten minutes.*

Up the street, a woman carrying a bouquet of flowers headed toward Wendy's booth. Finally there was someone who cared about Wendy, not just a busybody who wanted to see where she'd died.

As she walked closer, I got a better look at her face, partly obscured by the sprig of baby's breath. The woman was Lily, Wendy's devoted customer.

My gloom instantly lifted.

Now we are getting somewhere.

She approached Wendy's booth and stopped in the spot where I'd put the crime scene tape earlier. Several people wanted to draw near, but the good-natured looky-loos stayed milling around and staring at where Wendy had been killed. Lily, on the other hand, was expected as a handful of people visiting her booth. She just dabbled at her spot as if to imply she wanted to have been dealing out a booth to interested buyers.

"Did you have a joy vacation to bring flowers?"

She held the handful of the hydrangea, and I noticed the soft line of the hydrangea. Wendy

10

Feeling slightly guilty that I hadn't brought flowers myself, I paced the small confines of the booth as I waited for Lily to make her way down the street. With her long, billowing skirt and bouquet of flowers, she was a throwback to the sixties.

She approached the tent and laid the bouquet on the pavement next to the open flap. Conversation ceased as people watched. I'd swear a few had the good grace to look guilty for standing around and staring at where Wendy had been killed. Two or three even drifted away. Lily extracted a handkerchief from within her long sleeve and dabbed at her eyes. I waited until she turned around to leave before darting out of my booth to intercept her.

"Lily. What a lovely gesture to bring flowers."

She held the handkerchief to her chest, and I noticed she'd torn one of her fingernails. "Wendy touched my life at an important time, and I want the world to know that she'll be missed."

"She would have loved knowing she made such a difference." I remembered how in high school, Wendy had basked in all the attention and accolades of being head cheerleader and student class president.

"I can't believe I got so close to her yesterday, yet we never spoke."

I inched toward my own booth, hoping to draw Lily away from the remaining bystanders. "Say, I know I already asked you this, but I could really use your help. I need to know what Wendy and that man were fighting about, in case it will help find Wendy's killer. Someone mentioned they saw you standing right outside the tent during the argument, so you must have heard at least part of the conversation."

Lily twisted the handkerchief in her hands until her knuckles turned white. Something had definitely affected her. "I don't feel it's my place to say."

"You of all people must want to bring Wendy's killer to justice. You can't keep valuable information to yourself. Think of Wendy." I felt a smidge guilty for using such cheap tactics, but only a smidge. She could be a key witness.

Color sprang into her cheeks. "Of course I'll

help any way I can. But that fight was a big misunderstanding."

"What kind of misunderstanding?"

She opened her mouth, then pressed the handkerchief to her lips, reminding me of a damsel in an old Western film who'd just seen the town preacher kissing a dance hall girl. "I couldn't possibly repeat all those terrible things. Wendy would have cleared everything up—I know she would have. And now she'll never get the chance." She burst into tears, and everyone turned to stare.

I gave brief consideration to crawling under my table, but there was no tablecloth to hide me from the accusing glares, so I dismissed the idea. Instead, I took her hand in mine. "Look, Lily, I didn't mean to upset you."

She sniffled. "It's not your fault. I still can't believe she's gone." She pulled her hand away. The tears were already welling up again, so she ran her handkerchief under her nose. She looked ready to collapse.

I checked around for a chair, but I saw none. "Do you need to sit down?" I gestured toward the parking lot. "My car is right over there in the parking lot. It's the red Honda."

She glanced at my car, but she shook her head. "I need to be alone for a while."

"But you still haven't told me what you heard yesterday," I said.

She didn't answer. Instead, she walked off down the street, shoulders slumped. I wanted to follow her, but I had a spa to promote. I returned to the booth and noticed the crowd next door had continued to thin. A few minutes later, the last of the spectators in front of Wendy's booth departed. The space was empty, much like the rest of the street. I could see a handful of people milling about way at the other end, but who knew if they'd ever make it down my way?

While I waited for more people, I studied the shops across the way behind the tables and canopies. The going-out-of-business sales weren't as frequent as they had been in past months, but most of the stores were still struggling. Now that autumn had arrived, the Get the Scoop ice cream parlor had started offering hot coffee drinks and cookies to entice customers. The Raining Cats and Dogs pet supply store seemed to have their dog food half off at least every other week.

Looking down the street again, I could see that this festival wouldn't be bringing in extra business, considering there were still no people. I restacked the brochures and then fanned them back out again. I tested each pig pen to make sure they were oinking correctly. I nudged each table leg with my Vans to make sure I'd set the table up properly. When I spotted Zennia heading my way, I almost cheered. "Zennia, you're here. It's so nice to have some company."

She heaved a Crock-Pot onto the table. "I'm afraid I can't stay. I have to get back and finish preparing lunch for the guests. But I was hoping you'd have time to set up these samples for the attendees. The cups and spoons are in my backpack." She set the pack on the ground.

"More corn salad?"

"No. I wanted a power pack of vitamins and minerals, so I'm trying a new recipe with cabbage, broccoli, and tofu, with a little calamari thrown in to remind people how close we are to the ocean."

I felt my nose scrunch up in an automatic reflex. "Did you say cabbage *and* broccoli?"

"Try not to make that face when people ask about it," Zennia said.

"Sorry. I'll smile as though I won the lottery."

"Good, now I've got to run."

She retrieved her keys from the backpack on the ground, gave me a quick hug, and hurried to her car.

I lifted the Crock-Pot lid, caught a whiff, and slammed the lid back down, afraid one of the calamari might crawl out.

I unzipped the backpack to pull out the cups Zennia had mentioned, not that anyone would try a sample. As I straightened up, I found Kimmie standing on the other side of the table. In a tailored, knee-length sheath dress, with her hair pulled back in a sleek bun, she could be a topnotch fashionista.

"Dana," she said in a tone that told me I'd probably prefer to eat the cabbage concoction than hear whatever she was about to say, "I have been waiting and waiting for your status report, but it hasn't arrived. Didn't you get my e-mail with the form attached?"

"Yes, I got it, but I don't think a status report is going to work for me." Especially since I wasn't her employee, though she seemed to be confused on that point.

Kimmie put a hand to her throat and tapped her foot. I got the idea not many people refused her demands.

"But why not? We need to be organized. We need to keep track of everything you're doing."

"First of all, I'm not doing much, simply talking to people. I think I can keep that straight."

Kimmie tilted her head at me. "Are you sure?"

"Yes." I lifted the top off the Crock-Pot, swinging the lid in an upward motion to make sure the stench would blow in Kimmie's direction. "Calamari casserole?"

She wrinkled her nose and stepped back. "Oh, yuck, stop." She fanned a hand in front of her face. "I'm on my way to see my mother right now, so I can't stay, but let's get together tomorrow to talk about everything you've been doing."

"With all my work here at the festival, I'm not sure I can squeeze in a meeting."

"Can't you please make time? I really want to know what you've found out about Wendy. You could stop by the restaurant at nine, before I open for brunch, and then be on your way."

I'd never had the chance to try Le Poêlon, Kimmie's upscale restaurant. Besides being out of my price range, reservations were booked out months at a time. Would I actually get to try all that fantastic food Kimmie was always bragging about? My head filled with visions of eggs Benedict, with Dungeness crab, and crêpes stuffed with mascarpone cheese and topped with strawberries. That alone would make the drive over to the coast worth the effort.

"I suppose I could make that work," I said, trying to imply I was doing her the favor. "I was already scheduled to take tomorrow morning off."

"Perfect. See you then. And don't be late. I have things to do and can't waste time waiting for you."

With that, Kimmie spun around on her spiky heels and strode away.

I watched her go and wondered why I'd agreed to help her. Tomorrow's breakfast had better be the best meal of my life.

11

Maybe it was the warmer weather once noon rolled around, maybe it was because Saturday TV was usually so bad, but the afternoon brought a steady stream of attendees to the festival. These were real attendees, too, not just people wanting to see where Wendy was murdered. I spent two hours spouting the virtues of the farm and spa and the benefits of all that fresh air. I couldn't get anyone to try Zennia's cabbage-and-broccoli creation, but who could blame them?

Eventually interest in the farm waned as fewer people stopped. I wondered how I could draw in more folks.

"I'll give a free, state-of-the-art oinking pen to anyone brave enough to try this delicious secret recipe," I said on impulse to a clump of people walking past.

The group slowed as one. "Aren't the pens free, anyway?" a man in a bowling-style shirt asked.

I cupped my fingers around the dozen or so remaining pens and dragged them closer to me. "Nope. Only the most courageous of souls shall have the honor of a pig pen bestowed upon them."

"What's in it?" he asked.

"All sorts of nutritious goodies. A little cabbage, a little tofu . . ." I stopped before I listed the broccoli and calamari.

The man grimaced. For a moment, I thought my ploy had failed. Then his friend piped up, "I'm game."

I hastily popped the lid off the Crock-Pot and scooped a spoonful into a cup before he could chicken out. The man stared at the contents as though he was about to eat a live scorpion. I could see him take a deep breath before putting the cup to his lips and throwing his head back. He chewed for a moment and swallowed. The group watched his every move, me included.

"You know," he said to no one in particular, "it's not half bad."

I felt the muscles in my shoulders relax. "See, everyone, the O'Connell Organic Farm and Spa offers healthy and delicious meals." I plucked a pen off the table. "Here's your reward."

The man chuckled and stuck the pen inside his shirt pocket. I surveyed the rest of the group. "Who's next?"

Three more people tried samples, each commenting that it was tastier than they'd anticipated. As they moved away, a new surge of attendees appeared. Before I knew it, five o'clock rolled around, the official ending time for the festival.

I couldn't help humming as I packed up the few remaining brochures, two pens, and the other items that littered the table. The festival had gone from an absolute failure to something bordering on success, and we still had one more day.

"Great turnout this afternoon," Jim called as he unclipped his mushroom-dyed shirts from the line and placed them in a plastic bin.

"Can't wait to see what tomorrow brings," I hollered back.

I lugged the Crock-Pot to my car, set it on the floor on the passenger side, and went back to retrieve everything else. If I hurried, I could return the supplies to the farm so they'd be available for Gordon in the morning. After that, I needed to race home to shower and change. I had a date with Jason.

The house was silent as I unlocked the door and walked inside. Ashlee and Mom must have already left for their dates. I took a moment to relish the silence, something in short supply with three people living here, especially when one was as chatty as Ashlee. Before I relaxed too much, I headed for the bathroom, where I took a quick shower, fiddled with my hair, and applied a touch of makeup. That done, I turned to the contents of my closet and donned a pair of skinny jeans, a thin sweater, and black ankle boots. I returned to the bathroom for a final mirror check.

As I applied one more coat of mascara, the doorbell rang. Jason waited on the porch in fresh-pressed chinos and a crisp white dress shirt under a leather jacket. His reddish brown hair was still damp.

"How's my favorite girl?" he asked, offering me his smile that heated up my insides.

"Even better, now that you're here," I said. "Let me grab my purse." I retrieved it from the kitchen table, where I'd left it, and joined him, pulling the door closed and locking it behind me.

Jason put an arm around my waist as we walked down the path. He opened the car door for me when we reached his silver Volvo, the car of choice for safety-minded drivers, according to Jason. I'd been secretly amused when he'd first explained the reason for his purchase, but I'd grown to appreciate his practical nature.

I slid into the seat and buckled up while Jason did the same.

He started the car and pulled away from the curb. "Did the festival go better today? I didn't hear about any more murders."

"One's more than enough. But the afternoon was phenomenal. I even got people to try one of Zennia's dishes."

"No small feat. Did you have to pay them?"

I put a finger to my lips. "Hmm . . . does bribing

them with a free pen count? But don't tell Zennia. She takes such pride in her cooking."

Jason made a zipping motion across his mouth. "My lips are sealed, especially when it comes to Zennia's cooking."

"Mine, too." I watched the buildings pass by as we turned off Main Street, drove down Second, and pulled into the lot at Table for Two. Since this was the sole restaurant in town with actual table-cloths and a wine list, we'd become regulars here over the last few months. My mouth watered as I mentally pictured a buttery platter of shrimp scampi with garlic bread.

The restaurant was half full, but I knew it'd fill up by the time we were done. The waitress led us to a table in the corner, away from the kitchen and through traffic. She handed us our menus and left.

I set my menu to the side and rested my arms on the table.

"Tell me about the murder," I said.

Jason grinned. "Couldn't even wait for us to order, huh?"

"Give me one thing. Call it an appetizer of sorts."

"A tidbit of info, huh?" He closed his menu and laid it down as well. "I've found out that Wendy and her brother had a strained relationship."

"Kimmie mentioned that. Any idea why?"

Jason tapped his chin. "I may have used my investigative reporting skills to find out."

I reached across the table and grabbed his hand. "And?"

Jason shook his head. "That's the appetizer you wanted."

"*What?*" I practically yelled, then lowered my voice as a diner at the next table looked over. "You can't just leave me hanging like that."

He leaned back and crossed his arms. "I'll tell you more in a minute."

Before I could plead my case, the waitress returned with a basket of rolls, and we placed our orders. As soon as she departed, I pointed at Jason. "Okay, now tell me."

He gave a fake cough and patted his throat. "I'm parched. I couldn't possibly talk until after our drinks arrive."

I thought about chucking a roll at him, but I didn't want to give him the satisfaction of seeing me act like a two-year-old. Instead, I pulled the roll apart and slapped some butter on one half, using more force than necessary. Jason watched me with a bemused expression, occasionally waggling his eyebrows at me. Who did he think he was, Groucho Marx? I didn't find him nearly as funny at the moment.

"Fine, don't tell me," I muttered. "But don't expect me to share with you, either."

One eyebrow shot up. "And what do you know?"

Practically nothing, but I wouldn't admit that to him. "I'll see how good your information is first."

I finished the half of the roll as Jason brushed

at imaginary crumbs on the tablecloth. The waitress brought an iced tea for me and a glass of red wine for Jason. I tore the wrapper off my straw and took a long sip. Jason picked up my wrapper, rolled it in a tiny ball, and set it near his glass before sipping his own drink.

"Is your throat still dry?" I asked, offering a smile along with my words.

Jason smacked his lips together. "Much better. I wouldn't have left you in suspense much longer anyway. I just like the way your nose gets red when you're angry. Makes you adorable."

"Forget about my nose and tell me what you found out about Wendy and her brother."

"They had a falling-out over money."

Money again. What had Wendy been doing to have so many arguments over money?

"What happened?" I asked.

"Their mom died a while back. She'd always said she'd split everything evenly between the two, but she changed her will shortly before her death. Wendy got the bulk of the estate, while Kurt got a few sports memorabilia and knickknacks, which had belonged to their father. He wasn't happy."

"Kurt's not the first guy to get cut out of a will, but shouldn't he be mad at his mom? Why blame Wendy?"

"He said when his mom was diagnosed with cancer last year, Wendy swooped right in to care for her and started planting the idea that she de-served all the money. Kurt's almost positive she conned their mom into changing her will while their mother was under medication. The fact that the will was handwritten made him even more suspicious."

I moved my elbows off the table as the waitress arrived with our meal. She set the platter of scampi before me, and I inhaled the pungent smell of garlic intermingled with the sweet aroma of warm butter and white wine. She gave Jason his T-bone steak and baked potato. We took a moment to get settled.

When we both had forks in hand, I said, "That's a pretty serious accusation. Did he do anything about it?"

"He wanted to contest it, but first he dug around on his own and found the neighbor who witnessed the signing of the new will. She said their mom was alert and didn't appear to be under the influence of drugs. Kurt decided he stood a good chance of losing and couldn't really afford a lawyer anyway, so he let it drop. But he still believes Wendy pressured their mom."

I pierced a shrimp with my fork. "When people know the end is near, they sometimes reevaluate things. Wendy's mom could have decided that Wendy deserved the money, even though Kurt needed the money more."

"I'll say Kurt needs cash. You should see where he's living."

"Yeah, someone's converted garage doesn't exactly scream, 'I'm rich,'" I agreed.

Jason stopped cutting his steak and set his knife down. "How do you know where he lives?"

Oops, I haven't mentioned my trip to Kurt's place yet, have I? "I, um, wanted to offer him my condolences."

"I didn't realize you knew Kurt."

"Not well. I used to see him all the time when I'd go over to Wendy's house to hang out. It's been years, but visiting him seemed like the right thing to do."

Jason picked up his knife and resumed cutting. "Good. For a second there, I thought you were going to meddle in Wendy's death."

I clenched my teeth as his words instantly put me on the defensive. "I haven't done too shabbily when it comes to solving murders."

"You've also managed to almost get killed twice. Look, I don't want anything to happen to you. I care too much."

His concern gave me the warm fuzzies, and I momentarily got lost in the idea of how much our relationship had advanced in a few short months. We'd gone from adversaries to friends to . . . what?

Jason was staring at me, and my warm feelings vanished as I thought about his remarks and overprotective attitude. "I've learned from past mistakes, thank you. I won't put myself in any danger this time."

He set his knife on the plate. His face was an unhealthy pink on its way to red. "So you are investigating. Dana, you swore you'd never do it again."

Who was he, my mother? "If I want to help solve the murder of one of my closest childhood friends, I will." I didn't add that if my job at the farm didn't pan out, I'd already considered becoming a professional sleuth. I really was pretty good at it.

Jason shoved a bite of steak into his mouth and chewed hard enough that he could have chewed through the bone if he wanted. "We'd better talk about something else."

"Fine. How's the visit with your parents going?"

He gulped his wine. "This topic might not be any better."

My earlier irritation vanished. "It can't be that bad. I mean, how much time could you possibly be spending with them, anyway? You probably spent all day writing about Wendy's murder, and now you're here with me." That hadn't struck me as odd before, but now I had to wonder why he wasn't having dinner with his parents. He could see me any old time, but they were only here for a short while.

"We have an interesting relationship."

This was one of the rare times Jason was talking

about his family. I didn't want to press too hard, but I couldn't help asking, "How so?"

"I come from a long line of overachievers: doctors, lawyers, rocket scientists. I mean that literally. My uncle Keith is a scientist at NASA." He drank more wine before continuing. "When it became obvious that my parents expected me to follow the family line and be a big-money earner rather than pick a career I was interested in, I moved out on my own and put myself through school to get my journalism degree."

Going against your parents' wishes took a lot of guts, and I gave Jason mental props for it. "Surely, your parents just want you to be happy."

Jason grinned wryly. "They'd rather I be rich *and* happy. They're starting to come to terms with my career choice, but mostly we avoid the topic altogether." He wiped his mouth with his napkin. "I'd still love for you to meet them, though. I almost brought them along tonight, but they'd already made plans with friends in the area."

The shrimp in my belly started swimming around, creating waves of unease. "Another time, then." I tossed the words out like they meant nothing, but even I heard the nerves in my voice.

Jason didn't seem to notice. "Great, I'll set something up."

I stared at the remains of my scampi. If they thought a career in journalism was too lowly, how

116 Staci McLaughlin

would they feel about a marketing maven who also slopped out the pigsty and collected chicken eggs? Especially one who still lived with her mom?

I tried to block all these questions out with a bite of rice. Thinking about Wendy's murder suddenly held more appeal.

12

We finished our meal and saw the latest comedy down at the theater. By the time the movie let out, the temperature had dropped to an uncomfortably chilly level. We hurried to the car and were back at my house in minutes. The porch light was on, meaning Mom had already returned from her dinner with Lane. Jason killed the engine, and we sat in companionable silence for a moment.

"You working the festival tomorrow?" Jason asked.

"In the afternoon. I'm stopping by Kimmie's restaurant in the morning. She's really upset about Wendy's death and wants to talk about it." I almost asked Jason about Wendy's husband, but then he'd get on my case again about investigating. I wanted to end the evening on good terms.

"That's nice of you to lend an ear," he said.

"Really, I want to try some of this food she's always bragging about. It can't be that good, can it?"

Jason threw up his hands. "I wouldn't know. I've never been able to get reservations."

"Use those newspaper connections. Tell her you want to do a review."

"Tried that. But when your restaurant's already been covered by every major Bay Area paper, a small-town weekly doesn't get you in the door."

I touched his arm. "Come with me. Kimmie won't mind."

"Wish I could, but I'm supposed to take my parents sightseeing in the morning."

I almost laughed. "Sightseeing in Blossom Valley? What are you going to show them?"

Jason shrugged. "The bowling alley? The tractor collection at the fairgrounds? I have no idea yet."

"Good luck with that." I patted my stomach. "And I'll give you a full report on the delectable eggs Benedict I'm planning to eat." I reached for the door handle. "For now, I'd better go in."

"I'll walk you up."

We strolled to the door, fingers linked, and stood on the porch for a moment. The porch light glinted off Jason's reddish brown goatee as he leaned in for a kiss. I closed my eyes. Before our lips met, the front door opened.

"I thought I heard a car door," Mom said. "How was your evening?"

"Great, Mom," I said, trying to stifle my irritation

as I pulled back from Jason. This wasn't the first kiss she'd interrupted. "And yours?"

"Marvelous. Lane took me to the most wonderful restaurant. You two should try it some time." She turned to Jason. "Would you care to come in? Have some coffee?"

He gave Mom a half bow. "Thank you, Mrs. Lewis, but I'll pass this time. I have an early day tomorrow."

"Next time, then," Mom said.

I opened the screen door, but I twisted back to face Jason, my gaze lingering on his lips. "Good night."

"I'll call you," he said, and then he walked down the path.

I followed Mom into the house, realizing once more that I really needed more privacy.

The next morning saw the start of another cool fall day. I donned black slacks and a cream-colored blouse, adding a simple faux-pearl necklace and earrings. I even whipped out my curling iron and spent more than the usual two minutes on my hair. Knowing Le Poêlon was one of the most popular dining spots in the area gave it more weight than when I ate at the Breaking Bread Diner, Blossom Valley's homey cafe.

Mom was already up and reading the paper when I entered the kitchen. While we chatted, I nibbled a piece of toast to quell the hunger pangs, then retrieved my purse and headed out. I skirted the downtown, which was blocked off for the festival, and merged on the freeway behind a motor home.

Several cars headed west along with me, although the traffic would reverse once afternoon arrived and weekenders left the coast. I pressed the gas pedal down to push my Civic up a long hill. As I coasted down the other side, the road transformed into a series of twists and turns. Redwoods sprang up on either side, making me feel like a Lilliputian in a land of giants.

I flipped on my headlights against the deepening gloom and followed the motor home toward the coast. After thirty more minutes, I crested another hill and could see the ocean off in the distance, a layer of clouds hovering above it. Good thing I'd thrown a sweater in the backseat. A few minutes later, the tang of salty air reached me through the car vents.

At the junction, the motor home swung a left, and I headed right. Following the highway along the coastline, I drove past cypress trees bent so low they almost touched the ground, years of steady wind twisting their trunks.

I neared the edge of town and pulled into the parking lot for Kimmie's restaurant. The redwood walls blended in with the natural surroundings, as if the place belonged there. An oversized cast-iron skillet, with the name of the restaurant imprinted on it, hung near the door. I knew I was in the right place, but what I didn't know was whether Kimmie had forgotten our meeting. My Honda was the only car in the lot. The inside of the restaurant looked dark and closed up.

Still, I locked the car and walked to the front door. I rapped on the glass, then cupped my hands around my face, and peered in. Through the gloom, I could see a figure heading toward the door. I drew my head back.

A moment later, I heard the lock turn, and Kimmie swung the door open. Looking at her pencil skirt and skintight blouse, I wondered how she moved around without feeling like she was trapped in saran wrap all day.

"Oh, good, you're on time," she said. "Let's get this done."

Wow, such gratitude. "Don't worry, the drive wasn't too much trouble," I commented.

"What?" Kimmie patted her hair, where it was pulled into a bun. "Oh, right, good to hear." She held the door open wider and I stepped inside.

"I wasn't sure anyone was here, since there are no cars in the lot."

Kimmie shut the door, blocking out the ocean breeze. "I make the workers park on the street so they're not taking up customer spots. I do the same, so they know I don't think I'm special." She gestured to the closest table. "Let's sit here so we won't be disturbed."

Now that I was inside, I could see the kitchen through the pass-through window across the room. Chefs worked under the bright lights, the stainless-steel ovens gleaming. The constant sound of pans clattering and people talking was faint but audible. Must be prepping for brunch. A whiff of frying onions drifted out. My stomach growled in return.

"Coffee?" Kimmie asked.

I was thinking more along the lines of a full entree, hash browns and bacon included, but Kimmie probably wanted to talk about Wendy first. "Coffee sounds great."

Kimmie waved toward the side of the room. "There's a pot over behind the bar."

I retrieved a generic white mug from a shelf under the bar, filled it with coffee, and returned to the table. Kimmie waited, drumming her finger-nails on the polished wood surface.

"Let's get started," she said.

"Yes, let's." I sat down and wrapped both hands around the mug, savoring the warmth. "What can you tell me about Wendy's husband?"

"Preston?" Kimmie lifted one side of her lip to let me know exactly what she thought about Wendy's husband. "Like I said, he may have been the one to kill Wendy. I'm positive that he's wanted out of the marriage for a while now." She tapped her finger on the table. "Make a note to talk to him."

Bossy, bossy. "Since you already know him, it'd be a big help if you talked to him instead."

"Oh, no, I'm much too busy here."

I ripped the top off a sugar packet and dumped the contents in my coffee. "Well, Kimmie, I'm busy, too. If we're going to figure out who killed Wendy, I'm going to need your cooperation."

Kimmie traced one finger along the grain in the table wood. "All right, if you must know, Preston and I don't really get along. He's got this crazy idea that I don't like him."

"Do you?"

"No, but I'm quite good at hiding that from people." She rotated the diamond ring on her finger until the stone sat exactly on top. "It's one of my best skills."

For a half second, I wondered if she actually liked anyone or spent all her time pretending, but then I realized I didn't care all that much. "Okay, I'll talk to the husband." It was probably better if I did it anyway. Who knew if I'd get accurate information from Kimmie? "Now, then, about her brother. I found out that Wendy might have cheated him out of his share of their mother's inheritance. Do you know anything about that?"

A shout came from the kitchen, and Kimmie leapt to her feet. "That didn't sound good. I'll be right back." She darted across the room.

While I waited for her to return, I sipped my coffee and studied the dining area. With her restaurant so close to the ocean, Kimmie had chosen a nautical theme for the décor. She'd festooned the walls with paintings of clipper ships and schooners, all tastefully done in muted grays and browns. As I drained the last of my cup's contents, Kimmie sat back down.

"Everything okay?" I asked.

"Fine. One of the cooks burned his hand, but he'll be okay."

Ouch. "Should he go to the hospital?"

"Oh, it's not that serious. Besides, his shift's almost over. He can go then." She patted her bun. "Now, what were we talking about?"

"Wendy, and her mother's inheritance."

"Right. Kurt's bitter because he didn't get his share, or what he considered his share, I should say. He really had no claim on that money."

I pressed the point, not willing to dismiss Kurt's complaints as readily as Kimmie. "He believed his mom had promised half to him."

"She might have. But that must have been before she got sick. Wendy's the one who visited her every day, took her to all her doctor's appointments, worked with the hospital to make sure she got the right care."

I momentarily wondered what would happen if Mom ever got sick. How would we take care of her? How could we afford it? I squeezed my mug and focused back on Kimmie. "And where was Kurt while Wendy was helping out?"

She shrugged. "At home, I guess. Wendy said he only visited twice that entire year. He was having trouble with his marriage, so he used that as an excuse. But, obviously, Wendy's mom saw through that, because she changed her will a couple of months before she died. Wendy earned that money, but Kurt didn't see it that way."

"Wow, you sure know a lot about what happened."

Kimmie's mouth drooped at the corners. "Wendy was very upset and told me about it."

Wendy used to confide in me about her troubles. I felt another stab of regret that we'd lost touch. "Do you think he killed Wendy over the inheritance?"

"He was furious about it, stopped talking to her as soon as probate closed, but he's always been a weak man. I can't imagine him doing anything physical."

I wasn't ready to cross his name off my list just yet. Sometimes the person you least expected turned out to be the killer. I'd already found that out myself. Still, I sensed that Kimmie didn't have any more information about Kurt. "What about Preston? Anything I should know before I talk to him?"

"There's another weak man in Wendy's life. He doesn't even work. What kind of man is that?"

"Do they have kids? Is he a stay-at-home dad?"

"Nope. He sits at home all day and does God knows what. I would have kicked the bum out a long time ago."

Remembering Wendy at the festival with her polished appearance and enthusiastic attitude, I

had a hard time matching her up with the couch
potato Kimmie was describing. I was suddenly
more interested in meeting Preston.

Kimmie glanced at her diamond-encrusted
watch. She wore enough diamonds to start her
own jewelry store. "Sorry to cut this short, but are
we about done? I need to talk to the wait staff
before we open."

"That's it for now. I'll talk to Preston, and then
I might stop by Invisible Prints for a quick look at
the operation. They're here in town, right?"

"Well, technically, they're outside of town, a
little ways down the highway. You can't miss the
billboard."

So I was looking for a giant billboard for a company that promised to help restore the beauty of
nature. I wondered if Wendy had thought about
the irony, or if she was solely interested in drawing
in customers.

I rose, and Kimmie followed suit.

She walked behind the bar, bent down, and
straightened up with a cluster of keys in her hand.
She sorted through them for a moment before
putting them back. "I'd lend you my spare key to
Invisible Prints, but I left it on my key ring at
home. Oh, well, I'm sure someone will be there."

"Why do you have a spare key?"

"Wendy and I got together on an almost weekly
basis to talk about our businesses. She was usually
upstairs in her office when I'd stop by, so it was

easier to give me a key to let myself in. She has . . . well, had one for here as well."

She walked me the few feet to the door and held it open, ever the conscientious hostess. A blast of ocean air swept in, and I crossed my arms over my chest, wishing I'd brought the sweater with me instead of leaving it in the car.

"Let me know if you find out anything you think might help," I said as I stepped outside.

"And you make sure to start sending me those status reports so we can be synced up at all times."

I turned around to tell her she might as well give up on this status report idea, but she'd already shut the door. At that moment, I realized I hadn't gotten breakfast, either. So much for those hash browns and eggs. I could only hope the day got better from here.

13

Wendy had lived in a two-story yellow Craftsman home in a quiet neighborhood in Mendocino, where the yards were full of flowers and shrubs, and the houses were set far apart. A dark blue Lexus sat in the driveway, giving me hope that Preston would be home.

I walked up the path, with a border of driftwood on one side and a birdbath on the other. I rang the bell and heard a chime from inside, followed by footsteps. The door opened, and a man in sweatpants peered out at me. Based on the stubble sprouting from his chin, he hadn't shaved this morning and maybe not yesterday, either. He ran a hand over his short brown hair, drawing attention to a hole in the armpit of his Henley shirt.

"Yes?"

I suddenly wished I had a casserole to offer. "Preston?"

"That's me. And you are?"

"I'm Dana Lewis. I was a friend of your wife's. I wanted to offer my condolences and see how you're doing during this difficult time."

He gave me a closer look. "You were a friend of Wendy's? I don't remember ever meeting you."

"I knew her back in high school. But I ran into her at the festival the day . . . ," I trailed off, pausing, not wanting to mention her murder. "The day before yesterday," I concluded.

Preston's smile was wistful. "You knew Wendy in high school? I'd love to hear about it."

This guy was not the picture of a husband who was unhappy in a marriage. I had to wonder if Kimmie had made up the story because she didn't like him.

"Do you have time now?" What better way to get into the house? I'd found that the inside of a house could tell you a lot about a person.

He stepped aside so I could enter. I'd expected more resistance, considering we'd never met, but his wan face and the exhausted look to his eyes made me think he welcomed any kind of distraction right about now.

The front entryway had large mirrors on opposite walls, with mahogany tables under each. A copper umbrella stand sat near the archway to the living room. It was the last bit of color I'd see as I walked in, because the living room was all white: white carpet, white sofa and chairs, and clear glass tables. The paintings on the walls had gray trees and cloudy skies, which didn't add the least bit of color.

Preston hit a switch on the wall. I blinked in the sudden glare as light from the overhead fixture bounced off the glass. "Wendy loved this room," he said. "She thought it looked so pure and clean."

He sat on one of the white cloth chairs. I settled on the leather sofa, suddenly worried I had dirt on my pants, which could transfer to the flawless surface.

Preston frowned at his sweats. "Sorry, I'm a mess. I wasn't expecting visitors this morning."

"My fault for not calling first. I happened to be in the area." I shifted my weight and crossed my legs. "How long were you and Wendy married?"

"Four years. Seemed like forever when we celebrated our anniversary back in July. But now that she's gone, we really had no time at all together."

I nodded in commiseration as I thought of my dad. Since he'd been around my whole life, I always felt we'd have all the time in the world. Once he was gone, I realized our time had been far too short.

I cleared my throat as I shook free from the memories. "Did you two have children?" Kimmie had already said they didn't, but what did Kimmie know?

"Not yet," Preston said, "although I wanted to start a family right away." The muscles in his face tensed, hardening his appearance. "Wendy was focused on her career. She figured we had years before we had to worry about kids. Guess she was wrong."

What did someone say to that?

Preston ran a hand over his face. When he looked back up, the small smile had returned. "Tell me about Wendy when she was a child."

I uncrossed my legs and scooted closer to the sofa's edge. "She was always the most popular girl in class. She had so many friends and belonged to all the clubs."

"That's Wendy. She lit up every room."

She really had. I felt myself matching his smile as I remembered how much fun she'd been. Then I remembered she was dead, and that wiped the smile off my face. "That's why her death is so shocking. Can you think of any reason someone would kill her?"

Preston looked at his hands. The nails were trimmed, and the skin was smooth. "No one. I already told the police that Wendy's business was doing great. She had lots of friends." He glanced up, the sadness on his face replaced by concern. "There was that one man who stopped by the house on Friday morning."

I leaned closer. "What man?"

"I didn't catch his name, but he came by really early, demanding to talk to Wendy. When I told him she'd already left for the green-living festival, he raced out of here."

I had only seen one guy who'd been angry with

Wendy on Friday morning. "Was he driving a maroon BMW?"

Preston jerked in surprise. "Yes. Do you know him?"

"No, but I saw him talking to Wendy at the festival. Well, yelling at her, really. Something related to money. Do you know anything about that?"

He rubbed at a stain on his sweats. "Money? Wendy and I certainly weren't having money troubles, and she never mentioned any problems with the company. I can't imagine what he was talking about."

I stared out the window at a sparrow hopping on the backyard fence. His twitchy movements reflected my own feelings of anxiety. I was supposedly here to offer condolences, and yet I needed to know if Preston had wanted a divorce. How could I possibly ask such a question?

Preston rose from his chair. "Well, it was nice talking to you." Definitely an exit line, and I hadn't worked up a way to ask about a potential split.

I stood as well, my mind whirring. We faced each other across the white carpeting. "Yes, thanks for inviting me in. And again, I'm so sorry for your loss. You two obviously had a wonderful marriage." I hesitated. "Right?"

Preston gave me a curious look. "Yes, everything was fine." Was that because they'd really had a good marriage, or was it because his marital problems had ended with Wendy's death?

"Well, er, great. And again, I'm sorry." I crossed

the room, stepped into the entryway, and opened the front door. I looked back, but Preston was by the window now, looking out at the backyard. I let myself out.

I couldn't quite get a handle on Preston. He'd been reserved and thoughtful, but not exactly crushed that his wife had just died. Perhaps he was the type who kept a tight grip on his emotions. Or maybe he really wasn't broken up over Wendy's death. Either way, I wanted to know more about Preston.

I got back into the car and crossed the highway back to downtown Mendocino, making a stop at Moody's for a blueberry muffin and vanilla latte. Once I'd finished eating and brushed the crumbs off my clothes, I started the car and merged onto Highway 1. As I cruised down the road, I could see the ocean off to my right, waves crashing over rocks along the shoreline, seagulls coasting on the air currents.

After a few miles, I spotted the billboard Kimmie had mentioned. Invisible Prints touted solar- and wind-energy projects, as well as refor-estation. I waited for a logging truck to thunder past on the highway and swung a left into the driveway.

Invisible Prints was housed in what might have been a onetime vacation home. The two-story affair had windows all along the side that faced the ocean, providing what must be spectacular views. The wood shingles on the walls looked worn and faded from the constantly damp weather, but the front yard sported a sprightly array of ice plants and mosses and an area of river rock, where little white flowers peeked out between the stones.

I parked in the small lot at the end of the short driveway, near two other cars, and walked to the front door. The sense that this was someone's home was so strong that I almost rang the bell. Then I reminded myself I was at a place of business and turned the knob instead. The door was unlocked. Guess the company was still open, in spite of Wendy's death. I stepped inside.

The entire downstairs was one open room, and I could see all four walls from where I stood. Three-foot-high partitions created a series of cubicles in the back half of the room. From the looks of it, Wendy had about eight employees. Not too shabby for a young businesswoman.

To my immediate right, a brown suede sofa, a glass coffee table, and a wooden brown chair were grouped together over an area rug to create the atmosphere of a lobby. A side table next to the sofa held a series of small wooden figurines, African in nature. A coordinating stone statue sat in the center of the coffee table. The carved face stared at me.

To my left, a staircase led to a partial second story. The rest was open space, which allowed for the vaulted ceilings in the front and the high windows, which looked out on the ocean. Past the staircase, a long counter ran along the side of the room. A young woman, with spiky blond hair with black tips, stood behind the counter, making notes in an appointment book. I couldn't be certain, but I was pretty sure I'd seen her at Wendy's booth the first morning of the festival. Maybe she'd been there to help set up.

She caught sight of me. "I'm sorry, but we're closed today."

I crossed the room. "I figured as much, but I wanted to stop by anyway. I was friends with Wendy. She was so proud of Invisible Prints that I had to see the company myself." I gestured to the room at large as if we stood in the Taj Mahal, rather than a single-family residence converted into office space.

"Wendy was certainly enthusiastic, wasn't she?" The girl held out her hand, exposing bright red nail polish with skull decals. "I'm Drew."

We shook. "Dana. Pleased to meet you. Did you work for Wendy long?"

"Only a couple of months. I really needed a job, and this place was hiring."

She failed to mention a love of environmental affairs, and I got the impression that she was here strictly for the paycheck. "How was business going? Did you guys have a lot of customers?"

Drew tilted her head, exposing a tattoo of a cross on her neck. "Enough to keep us busy, but Wendy was always trying to find more."

I pointed toward the cubes in the back. "Seems like you've got a good-sized staff here."

Her cheeks reddened. "Oh, well, those cubes aren't actually in use."

"What do you mean? Do the other employees work from home?"

Drew cast her gaze down. "There are no other employees. Except for the vice president, of course."

"Invisible Prints is made up of three people?" I asked, the surprise clear in my voice.

"Well, three's all we've needed so far," Drew said. "Wendy dealt with the sales and working with people. Helen handles the back office stuff and controls the accounts. I answer the phones and welcome the clients. Wendy talked about hiring more salespeople, but she hadn't bothered yet."

"I thought I heard someone," a woman said from the top of the stairs. I looked up and saw the other woman who'd helped Wendy unpack for the festival. Once again, she wore a dark-colored business suit with sensible flats. Her silver pageboy swished as she descended the stairs.

She held out her hand as soon as her feet touched the bottom step. "I'm Helen Goldstein, vice president here at Invisible Prints."

"Dana Lewis. I was a friend of Wendy's." Every time I repeated that, I wondered if someone would accuse me of being a fraud, but only Preston had questioned why he'd never met me. Everyone else took my presence at face value.

"We're closed, but is there something I can help you with today?" Helen asked.

"Not really. I wanted to stop by to see Wendy's company. I'd never had the chance to visit before." Mainly because I didn't know it existed.

"I was telling her how the three of us ran the whole company," Drew chimed in. "We really didn't need anyone else."

Helen gave Drew a frosty smile. "Yes, but that's not generally something we talk about in front of customers. We were planning to expand, once the business took off, which is why we have the cubicles set up."

"Wendy said it was so . . . ," Drew started to say, but Helen cut her off.

"That'll be all, Drew. I'll let you finish what you were doing, while Dana and I chat in my office."

Drew strolled back behind the counter, her attitude bordering on insolent. She reached down into a box and came up with a handful of miniature windmills. The image immediately brought back memories of Wendy's body, with the windmill lying nearby, but I blinked them away and followed Helen upstairs. A long hallway with two doors ran the length of the upstairs. The right side of the hallway was open, except for a waist-high railing. I slowed my steps to enjoy the view of the ocean from this high up before following Helen past the first closed door and on to the second.

The inside of the room held a heavy oak desk, with a high-backed leather executive chair behind it. A small, plain guest chair sat in front of the desk. The walls were covered with degrees and citations. Clearly, Helen knew what she was doing, or at least she had the diplomas to appear so. I wondered if Wendy had that many.

I perched on the edge of the guest chair, wondering why Helen had invited me up.

She settled into the executive chair, looking so comfortable that I suspected the chair had been built to custom fit her. "That's better. Now we can talk without any prying ears." She tilted her head. "So, you were a friend of Wendy's?"

"Yes, although we lost touch for a while." I didn't mention how long that "while" was. "I saw her again at the green-living festival, and was impressed with how she'd started her own company at such a young age."

Helen picked up a pen and tapped the tip on the desk. "Yes, she certainly had a gift."

"What will happen with the company now?"

A look of annoyance flitted across Helen's face, but she instantly masked it. "I'm looking into that. Wendy owned the company, although she got monetary backing to start it. It may depend on whether she had a will and what that document specified. I really need to talk to my attorney, as well as hers, to see where things stand. Preston might have additional information." Helen's computer made a *ping*. "Excuse me a moment." She clicked her mouse and read something on the monitor.

I looked around the office. My gaze lingered on the shelves along one wall. One was full of what appeared to be African artifacts, with various art pieces and sculptures, like the ones downstairs. Helen must have helped decorate the lobby area. The other shelf held row upon row of trophies for softball, swimming, bowling, and more. The word "overachiever" popped into my head as I studied the shiny gold figures. Isn't that how Jason had described his family?

Helen finished her work and clasped her hands on the desk in front of her. "Sorry about that. I'm twice as busy, with Wendy gone."

"I'm sure all your customers are wondering about the fate of the company now."

Helen leaned back in her chair and crossed her legs. "Yes, I especially miss Wendy at these moments. She was a genius at dealing with individuals."

"I met one of your customers at the festival. Lily Sharp. She adores what you guys are doing."

Helen nodded. "Superb. I always like to hear about satisfied customers."

I felt we'd wasted enough time skirting around the issue. "Any idea who killed Wendy?"

The bluntness of the question didn't seem to surprise her.

"No, Wendy was a sweetheart. Everyone loved her."

Well, not everyone. "What about her brother? Did she ever mention him?"

Helen raised her eyebrows. "I didn't realize she

even had a brother. We didn't talk much about our personal lives. We were too busy getting this company off the ground."

Loud voices drifted up from below. Helen frowned and stood. Her leather cushion creaked as she moved. "I'd better check on that."

I followed her out and down the stairs. At the bottom, Drew stood with a man in a pin-striped gray suit and orange tie. I immediately recognized him as the one who had shouted at Wendy in her booth, then disappeared when I'd tried to follow him.

Based on the scowl frozen on his face, he was still upset about something. Would I finally discover what he'd been yelling about the day Wendy died? Was it reason enough to kill?

14

The man glared at Helen and me as we stepped off the stairs. I saw a look of relief flash across Drew's face as we joined them. "Helen," she said. "I was telling Mr. Stevens that we're still straightening out company business after Wendy's unexpected death."

"What's to straighten out?" Mr. Stevens demanded. "Either you have my money or you don't."

I was already fixated on what he was saying, but my ears perked up even higher when he mentioned money.

"Perhaps you'd care to step up to my office, Marvin," Helen soothed, gesturing toward the stairs.

"No. We can talk right here, in front of your cohorts."

He must have thought I worked here. Far be it from me to correct him.

"I gave this company two million dollars,"

he said. "And now I find out you're a bunch of phonies."

I gulped. Two million dollars?

He pulled a glossy picture from his inside jacket pocket and waved it at Helen. I recognized it as the brochure from Wendy's booth, the one that had pigs standing in a field. "I drove by this place. And do you know what's there? Nothing but dirt. Not even a farm."

I glanced at Drew. I'd swear there was a smirk on her lips. She saw me looking, and the expression disappeared.

"Perhaps you went to the wrong address," Helen suggested.

Marvin's face reddened. "I'm not an idiot, although apparently Wendy thought I was when she fleeced me out of my money. I already have my lawyers working on this, so you can expect to hear from them." He threw the brochure on the floor, turned on his shiny wingtip shoes, and strode out.

We all watched as he marched across the parking lot, yanked open the door to his BMW, keys already in hand, and peeled out of the lot.

Helen slowly bent and retrieved the brochure from the floor, smoothing it out and placing it on the nearby counter.

"Helen, is what he said true?" Drew asked. If I didn't know better, I'd swear she was almost excited by the news. Why would Marvin's accusation make her happy?

Helen waved her hand. "I'm sure this is a misunderstanding. Return to your work, and I'll take care of everything."

Drew drifted back behind the counter.

"I'm terribly sorry you had to witness that," Helen said to me. "I certainly appreciate everything Marvin has done for us, but he's been quite difficult to work with, and I'm afraid we haven't heard the last from him."

I smiled in what I hoped was a sympathetic manner. "You'll get everything straightened out."

"Of course we will. Now, if you'll excuse me, I have other matters to attend to." She headed for the stairs, leaving me alone with Drew, which is exactly where I wanted to be.

I sidled over to where Drew was jotting something on a tablet, but waited to speak until Helen had disappeared into her office. As soon as she was out of sight, I placed my elbows on the counter and leaned forward. "Think there's any truth to what Marvin said?" I asked.

Drew set her pen down and glanced upstairs at Helen's open door. "I don't know, but I'm definitely going to keep my ears open around here."

I almost asked her if she'd let me know what she found out, but that might clue her in that I wasn't here merely to admire Wendy's business. Instead, I asked, "What were you going to tell me about the cubicles when Helen interrupted you?"

Drew lowered her voice. "I really shouldn't say. Helen hates it when I bad-mouth the company. I can't risk her overhearing me. I still need this job."

I didn't push her. I knew what it was like to need a job.

"I didn't realize you were still here," Helen said.

I looked up to find her coming down the stairs. As before, her expression was pleasant yet reserved, reminding me of *The Stepford Wives*. "I was just leaving."

"Good-bye, then."

"See ya," Drew added. "Can't guarantee we'll have this much excitement on your next visit, but you're always welcome to come back."

Helen shot her an angry look. "Drew, someone from the festival called. Now that the police are done with the booth, you'll need to go over there and pack up everything. I'm too busy to get over there today."

Drew mumbled something I couldn't hear as I walked out the door.

I left the building and climbed into my car. The clock on the dash said 11:15, and I was due at the festival by noon. Good thing I'd had a late breakfast, since I wouldn't have time to stop for lunch.

I got back on the highway and zoomed down the coastline, at least for the first mile or so. After that, I caught up with a line of motor homes and semis on the two-lane highway, guaranteeing a slow drive back to Blossom Valley.

I willed myself to relax as I puttered along behind a Winnebago, going forty in the fifty-five-mile-an-hour zone. The driver refused to use a single turnout, and I flinched every time the numbers on the dashboard clock changed.

By the time I hit the wider stretch of freeway that led away from the redwoods and back to civilization, it was already noon. I still had to get to the center of town. I sped down the highway, took the off-ramp for downtown, and parked in the first slot I found. I hopped out, locked the car, and trotted to the farm's booth. On this side of the hill, the sun was shining. A light, gentle breeze ruffled my hair, a noticeable difference from the coolness of the coast.

At the booth, Gordon paced behind the table, glancing at his watch and thrusting brochures at anyone who veered toward the table. One look at Gordon's pinched face and most people gave him a wide berth.

"Gordon, sorry I'm late," I said. I knew that even though it was only by five minutes, he'd treat it as though it were thirty.

He stopped pacing, but couldn't resist checking his watch a final time. "I have a million things to do at the farm. I can't be handing out brochures to people who don't want them."

"I wanted to offer my condolences to Wendy's husband this morning, and I ran into traffic on my way back from the coast."

"I keep forgetting you knew her," Gordon said, the wrinkles in his forehead smoothing out.

"That's fine, then. You being a few minutes late didn't hurt me."

My mouth almost dropped open. The old Gordon would have spent the next ten minutes lecturing me on professionalism and then threatened to dock my pay. I couldn't help but wonder what else I could get out of if I used Wendy's death as an excuse. As soon as the thought went through my head, I felt the cold clutch of shame squeeze my gut as I realized I was trying to benefit from my friend's passing.

"I don't want to keep you any longer," I said. "I can take over now."

"Fine." Gordon picked up his ever-present clipboard, counted the pens and brochures resting on the table, then jotted a note on the top sheet. He took one last look around the booth, then walked toward the parking lot.

Once he left, I poked through the boxes under the table. If the dwindling supply of travel mugs was any indication, Gordon had seen some brisk business this morning. Or he'd gotten frustrated when no one stopped and simply threw the cups at people as they walked by.

For the next hour, I handed out pamphlets and chatted with visitors as a small but steady stream of people trickled past. Combined with Saturday's big turnout, most people would consider the festival to be a modest success. I'd wager that there'd even be talk of another festival next year. Score a win for the Blossom Valley Rejuvenation Committee.

As I handed out the last pig pen, Ashlee approached my booth in black leggings and a long pink sweater with Uggs. She brushed her blond hair out of her face as she stopped before me.

"Hey, sis," she said, sipping a mocha frappe, which I recognized from the Get the Scoop ice cream parlor, "stumble over any more dead bodies lately?"

"Not unless I kill you right now."

"You need a chill pill. And here I was going to share all the gossip I overheard around the festival this morning."

I stopped pulling the remaining travel mugs out of the box. "Any of it related to Wendy's death?"

"Gee, I don't know if I should tell you now. You did just threaten to kill me and all."

"*Ashlee.*" My tone held a warning that I might still make good on that threat.

"Oh, relax, I'm screwing with you." She poked at her drink with her straw. "I heard that Wendy's husband wanted out of the marriage, but she wouldn't let him."

Here was a second person who thought Wendy's marriage was in trouble. Maybe Kimmie was a more reliable source than I'd given her credit for.

"I don't think you can keep people in a marriage against their will. If he wanted to leave, he could."

"True, but then he'd have to give up his easy life."

"Whom did you hear this from?"

"You know that cute guy who runs the green-cleaning booth? The one who didn't ask me for my number the other day? His sister knows Wendy's husband and she stopped by his booth a while ago. At least he said she was his sister, although he sure wasn't kissing her like a sister."

I skipped right over Ashlee's romantic naiveté. "Did she say anything else?"

"Something about how dumb Wendy's husband was for quitting his high-paying job at a social-networking company."

She sucked on her straw. It emitted a loud rumbling sound as she hit a patch of air bubbles. She shook the cup, tried one more sip, then walked over to a nearby trash can and dropped the cup in.

"No idea why he quit?" I asked when she returned.

"Nope."

A couple drifted past, studying the collage of photos on the easel. I handed them a brochure, then turned back to Ashlee. "Did his sister say anything else?"

"Not much. Some snotty comment about how no one in that family can stay married."

"Was she talking about Wendy's brother? Kurt mentioned that his wife had left him."

Ashlee popped a stick of gum into her mouth, the citrus scent drifting across the table to where I stood. "Yep. Oh, and get this. His wife left him after he didn't inherit anything from his mom. Pretty cold, huh?"

Pretty cold, indeed. And if this little rumor was true, that gave Kurt one more reason to despise Wendy. He already blamed her for his not inheriting any of his mom's money. If his wife left him because of that, he'd hold Wendy responsible for his failed marriage as well. Would those two blows fuel his bitterness enough that he killed her?

Ashlee waved a hand in front of my face. "Earth to Dana. Your boyfriend's here." She leaned in close. "And I think he brought his parental units."

My heart stopped for a beat. Then it started hammering as my eyes scanned the crowd down the street. Ashlee was right. Here came Jason in jeans and a green button-up shirt, which I knew would match his eyes. He was flanked by a well-dressed couple. The woman wore a cream linen pantsuit and a wide-brimmed hat, while the man wore tan slacks and a navy blue blazer.

At least I was wearing my black slacks and cream-colored blouse from my visit with Kimmie, rather than my usual khakis. I glanced down and noticed a series of creases from when I'd been wearing my seat belt earlier. I was still trying to smooth out the wrinkles, when Jason and his parents reached the table. Out of the corner of my eye, I could see Ashlee grinning at me as she stood to one side like a spectator at a pro-wrestling event. Glad to see she was being so supportive.

"Dana, I was hoping you'd be working the booth now," Jason said. "I want you to meet my parents, William and Nadine Forrester."

I stuck out my hand, shaking his mom's hand first. "Mr. and Mrs. Forrester, what a pleasure." And I meant it, even if my insides were shaking like one of those miniature poodles.

"Please call me Nadine. Jason has told me so many wonderful things about you. I couldn't wait to meet you." She offered me a smile, which immediately untied some of the knots in my muscles.

"I'm still planning to take you all out to dinner," Jason told me. "I haven't forgotten."

His mom rubbed his back. "Oh, honey, you're so busy writing about this murder that I don't want to take your attention away from your work." She turned to me, with her emerald teardrop earrings sparkling in the sun. "Jason tells me you have quite the knack for solving crimes in this town."

I blushed at the unexpected compliment. Jason might harass me about investigating, because he didn't want me in danger, but deep down, he thought I wasn't half bad.

"I bet you're as smart as that guy on *The Mentalist*," Jason's dad said.

Ashlee snapped her gum. "Oh, she's mental, all right."

I bit back a smart retort. I didn't want Jason's parents to see us bicker. Instead, I pointed at Ashlee. "This is my sister, Ashlee."

Nods of greeting were exchanged all around.

Jason's mom said, "Dana, maybe you should solve this murder, and then Jason would know how to finish his news article."

I chuckled along with everyone else. Little did she know, I was already working on that very thing.

"Jason tells me you do marketing at an organic farm and spa," she continued. "That must be interesting."

"Yes, I'm really enjoying it right now, although I don't see it as a long-term career." *I don't know what possessed me to say that. Aren't I happy with my job?*

"Oh? What's your long-range plan?" she asked.

I didn't want to admit that I didn't have one, so I hedged my answer. "I'm not quite sure. I like my job, but I'd prefer to concentrate solely on marketing again. That's what I did when I worked at a software company down in San Jose. Right now, the owner of the farm has me doing a variety of projects, not all of which are related to marketing." Jason's parents looked at me as if waiting for more, only I didn't have anything else to say.

"It's wonderful that you and your sister live in the same town," Mrs. Forrester said. "I was so hoping that Jason and his brother would be that close. But then, Jason, well, he forged his own way in life. Of course we're proud of him, but it's unfortunate that he moved so far away."

Ashlee stepped closer, wedging herself into the conversation. "Dana moved away for a while, but she moved back, just like I knew she would.

She missed me way too much when she lived in the Bay Area."

Lord, where did she come up with these things? "Our father passed away, and I wanted to move home to help out my mom."

"Plus, you got laid off from that fancy job of yours," Ashlee said.

Ugh. "Right, thanks for reminding me."

"Oh, so you live with your mother?" Mrs. Forrester asked.

Did I sense a hint of disapproval in her voice, or were my heightened nerves making me extra sensitive?

"Me too," Ashlee said.

I wished she'd go find something else to do, but I knew this interaction was the best entertainment Ashlee had seen all day. She wasn't going anywhere.

"Well, doesn't that sound cozy," Jason's mom said.

I detected a trace of distaste again, definitely more obvious. "Not for long," I said on the spur of the moment. Ashlee gave me a look implying she questioned my sanity.

"What do you mean?" Jason asked.

My brain was screaming for me to shut up, knowing I was about to say something stupid, but everyone was staring at me now, and my mouth kept moving. "Ashlee and I were talking last night, and we've reached a decision."

"What decision is that?" Mr. Forrester asked.

Ashlee was watching me with raised eyebrows now, no doubt wondering what I was talking about. "Yes, Dana, please tell them all about *our* decision."

"We're going to rent an apartment," I said. "We're moving in together." Too late, I slapped a hand over my mouth.

Oh, God, what have I done?

15

There was a brief pause after my announcement, or maybe time in my world had momentarily stopped. Then Mrs. Forrester nodded. "How fun. My sister and I roomed together back in college. Some of the best years of my life."

"But you refuse to talk to Aunt Karen now," Jason said.

"Hush, that was later," his mom said, an icy edge to her tone.

I dared a peek at Ashlee. Her cheeks had to hurt from the size of that grin. She was loving every minute of this.

Jason studied me, a quizzical look on his face. "I had no idea you were even considering such a big decision."

That made two of us.

"Mom has been doing better in recent months, and, really, it's time that I got back out on my own." I wasn't sure if leaving my mom's house for an apartment with my sister *really* counted as being on my own, but it was a move in the right direction.

"Mom's even started dating again," Ashlee said.

A small group of retirees wandered by the table, then shifted closer to study the pictures of the farm. I handed each a brochure, along with a travel mug. "I'd love to tell you about all the great offerings at the farm. Really, I should call it 'the spa,' because we have so many new options," I said to them.

Jason stepped aside to make room for the group. "We'll let you get back to work," he told me. "I'll call you later."

"Nice meeting you," I said to Mr. and Mrs. Forrester. Mr. Forrester shook my hand. Mrs. Forrester patted my arm and smiled before they both followed Jason away from the table. I turned back to the group and went into my spiel about the massages and facials we now offered, while Ashlee stood to one side and chomped on her gum.

After the group left, Ashlee entered the booth so I couldn't possibly ignore her. "Were you serious about moving in together?"

"Absolutely not. I said that so Jason's mom wouldn't think I was a total loser."

"Come on, Dana, it's not a bad idea. We're both a little old to be living at home."

She didn't need to tell me that. "But what about Mom?"

"What about her?" she asked. "I was as freaked out as you when Dad first died, but she's got a boyfriend now. Like you said, she's doing way better."

At the mention of Dad's death, I clutched the St. Christopher medal he'd given me years ago that I now wore every day. Was Ashlee right? Had Mom moved on? Did she not need us anymore? "I'll think about it. We need to talk to Mom first."

She clasped her hands together. "Imagine how fun it'd be. We could throw parties. We could have guys over anytime we wanted."

That's exactly what I was afraid of. "Relax. We're not turning our apartment into a drive-thru dating service for every new boy toy you meet." Although I had to admit, the words "our apartment" had sounded so natural when I said them.

"And you could have Jason over and make out with him all night long. I wouldn't mind."

The idea of getting cozy with Jason while Ashlee puttered around the apartment wasn't a huge selling point. "Who says 'make out' anymore? Are we back in high school?" I gave her a little shove. "Now, get out of here so I can work."

Ashlee winked at me. "Sure thing, roomie." She sauntered away, probably headed for the cleaning products booth, so she could tell her latest love interest about her impending make-out apartment. Maybe he'd bring his "sister" along.

I tried to block all thoughts of moving in with Ashlee from my mind, but with the dwindling afternoon crowd, I had extra time on my hands. Really, would it be so bad to live with her? Judging by the condition of her room, she wouldn't be the neatest roommate, but at least I knew exactly what to expect. I didn't have to worry about getting stuck with a roommate who was always late with the rent or stole my clothes.

The bigger question was whether I should even move out. When I'd first returned home several months ago, Mom had been an emotional wreck, staying inside and mourning my dad all day. Was Mom ready for another big change already?

My cell phone buzzed in my pocket, saving me from reaching a decision. I pulled out the phone and looked at the screen: Kimmie.

"Hello?" I said, handing a brochure to a woman as she passed the booth.

"Dana, it's Kimmie. I don't have time to talk, but I wanted to let you know that Preston has scheduled Wendy's memorial service for Tuesday morning."

"That soon?" I asked. For some reason, I'd thought they might keep her body until the police had wrapped up their investigation.

"Everyone keeps asking about a service, so Preston set something up."

"I'll see if I can get the time off. I'd love to talk to the attendees. Maybe you could help me."

Kimmie sighed. "I'll try to make it, although it's really not the best time for me. I don't think Preston took into consideration that some people have to work for a living."

As usual, Kimmie was all about Kimmie. "He's

probably distracted by the fact that his wife was murdered," I said.

"I suppose. I just wish he'd think about other people."

I changed the subject before I launched into a lecture about grief and compassion. "Say, Kimmie, did you ever hear about the people who funded Invisible Prints to help get it started? Did Wendy ever say what she did with that money?" A man moved close to the table, so I gave him one of the few remaining pig pens.

"Funny you ask. I heard some rumors last week that the company wasn't investing the money the way the venture capitalists had expected. I asked Wendy about the rumors, but she laughed them off. She said people were always trying to undermine the success of companies run by women."

I twisted toward the back of the booth so people walking by wouldn't overhear me. "I learned today that a man invested two million dollars in the company, and he seemed to think the money had simply disappeared."

"Two million? That's quite a bit, even for me. But you know how fussy people get when they loan out money. They want every penny accounted for," Kimmie said, sounding distracted. I could hear noises in the background.

"But don't you think that could be related to Wendy's murder?" I pressed.

"I don't know, and I can't worry about it right now. I have to go."

Gee, sorry your friend's murder is interfering with your life. "Fine, I'll see you on Tuesday."

Kimmie hung up without saying good-bye.

I shoved my phone back into my pocket and tidied up the knickknacks on the table. For the next couple of hours, I watched fewer and fewer people walk by. By late afternoon, the crowd had grown sparse, which was just as well since I'd already handed out my last pig pen and had only one travel mug left.

When five o'clock arrived, I broke down the booth for the final time, made a few trips to load everything into the trunk of my car, and drove home. Ashlee's bright red Camaro wasn't in the driveway, so I took the coveted spot, and was sure I'd hear about it later.

Inside the house, Mom sat in the threadbare recliner that Dad had loved, watching a cooking show. A dark spot on her red turtleneck showed where she'd missed her mouth while eating from the open carton of hummus and the pile of chips, which sat on a plate in her lap. I dropped onto the couch, glad to rest my feet after a day of standing.

Mom muted the sound on the television and set the remote on the chair arm. "How was the festival's last day?"

"Great. We had a nice turnout."

"I'm glad. Were people still talking about the murder?"

"Not that I heard. And no one really stopped at her booth, either." At least during the few hours

I'd been there. No need to mention the fact that I'd spent the morning in Mendocino. "Say, Mom, you usually hear about what's going on around town. What are people saying about Wendy?"

Mom leaned over the arm of the recliner. "I try to avoid hearing all the scuttlebutt, but you know how Sue Ellen is always pestering me. She called not two hours ago to tell me that someone's conducting a surprise inspection at Invisible Prints tomorrow."

Had Marvin made good on his threats? He certainly worked fast. "It can't be much of a surprise if Sue Ellen has already heard about it."

"She knows a lot of people. Some are even important."

"Did she say who ordered the inspection?" If Marvin had requested the audit, he must be fairly positive that Wendy had stolen his money. And two million dollars was no pocket change. Had he become so furious that he'd killed Wendy in her booth when Wendy denied the accusations?

"You know how tight-lipped Sue Ellen can be about names," Mom said, breaking into my musings. "That's why people tell her so much. That's one of the reasons I don't want you looking into Wendy's death. In a town this size, word will get out. It could put you in danger."

I stared at my toes as though they were as fascinating as a painting at the Museum of Modern Art, all so I wouldn't have to meet Mom's gaze.

One look at my face, and she'd know what I'd been up to.

"By the way," Mom said, "you and your sister are on your own for dinner tonight. Lane's taking me out again."

"You're sure seeing a lot of him lately."

"He's a nice man, and we have a lot of fun."

I considered the picture of Dad on the mantel, his warm, open face reminding me of all the times we'd played catch in the yard or gone hiking together.

Mom caught me looking. "Your father will always have a place in my heart. Lane can't replace that."

"I know." And I did. "I've noticed that you seem a lot happier these days."

Maybe moving out was a possibility after all.

"I won't lie—those first few months were tough. Before I met Lane, I felt like I'd been sleepwalking through the days. He helped wake me up."

Before I could respond, the front door flew open, banging against the wall. Ashlee bounded into the room, her blond hair flying behind her.

"You're in my parking spot," she said to me before turning to Mom. "Did Dana tell you the big news?"

I jumped in before she could say anything else. "That's not your spot, and I was just about to."

"What big news?" Mom asked. "Does it have to do with Jason?"

I didn't even want to know what big news

Mom thought might involve Jason. "No," I said, "but Ashlee and I did want to talk with you about something else." I tried to think of a way to ease into the idea that both her children would be packing up at the same time, leaving her with an empty house.

"We're moving out," Ashlee said.

So much for breaking the news gently.

Mom pulled her head back. "What? Where are you going?"

"Don't know yet, but Dana told Jason today that she and I are getting our own apartment."

"Hang on a second," I said. My sister was such a peach, putting all the blame on me.

"Did you say that, Dana?" Mom asked. "I didn't realize you were unhappy here."

Pack the bags. I was going on a guilt trip. "Of course I'm not unhappy. I love it here. And that's why I'm not going anywhere."

Ashlee threw herself onto the couch next to me. "Dana, you promised," she said, her voice rising an octave.

Oh, great, now I was taking two guilt trips. "I said I'd think about it. And I did. I decided now's not a good time."

"Is it because of me?" Mom asked. "I certainly don't want to keep you girls here."

I held up my hands, not sure which person I was trying to appease. "Look, I met Jason's parents today, and stress got the better of me. I told them that Ashlee and I were getting an apartment, but I didn't really mean it."

"Dana," Ashlee whined, "I've already told my friends we're getting a place. They want to know when the housewarming party is."

"First off, even if we share an apartment, there will be no parties. Second, we're not sharing an apartment."

Mom stood up, stopping Ashlee from whatever she was about to say. "I think you two should do it."

I jerked my head around. "Mom, you don't mean that," I said. "It's too soon."

Mom took both my hands in hers. "Dana, I'm ready for you two to move out. Sometimes I want to have Lane over without my daughters hanging around."

I gawked at her as Ashlee snickered.

"Gee, sorry we're cramping your style, Mom," I said, a bit hurt that she saw Ashlee and me as some sort of third-wheel combo.

"You girls need your privacy, too."

Ashlee smacked my shoulder. "See? It's settled. I'll start looking for a place."

I studied Mom's face, trying to decide if she was putting up a front or she really wanted us out. Her face was free of worry, her smile open. Maybe I was the one who needed to move on from Dad's death.

I pressed my palms together for a moment. Then I slowly relaxed my muscles, letting all the tension out. "Okay. Let's do it."

Ashlee clapped her hands and jumped up.

"Sit down," I told her. "We're not moving tonight."

"I know, but I need to start looking up places online. See if I can find out how many single guys live there, and which place has a hot tub."

I let out a groan and laid my head on the couch. Whether or not I was ready to come to grips with it, I was moving in with my sister. Maybe if things didn't work out, I could go live with Wilbur and the other pigs.

16

I tossed and turned all night, dreaming of Ashlee taking over the bathroom counter space with her makeup, curling irons, and hair care products. We'd definitely need to look for an apartment with two bathrooms. I was still grappling with the idea that we were really moving in together as I rose from the bed and headed into the bathroom for my morning shower.

After I toweled off, I pulled on my khakis and navy blue polo shirt, scarfed down my sugarless oatmeal, and drove to the farm. The sky was mostly clear this morning, with low-hanging clouds hovering above the mountains in the distance. I parked my Honda in its usual spot and headed down the path.

I passed the pool, where a handful of pine needles floated on the water's surface. Two guests sat at the big picnic table on the patio, poking at their yogurt and making faces at each other. I already knew the yogurt was made from tofu rather than milk. Perhaps the guests had realized it, too.

Seeing them reminded me that other people might be eating in the dining room. I didn't want to interrupt their meal, so I detoured through the herb garden. I detected the scent of cilantro and the fainter smell of parsley as my shoes crunched across the pea gravel. I entered the back door to the kitchen, where Zennia was washing dishes.

"Morning," I said, popping the lid off the Tupperware container on the counter and spooning out a handful of granola. I tossed a cluster into my mouth, savoring the honey and cinnamon flavors.

Zennia dried a bowl with the dish towel. "Are you back to your regular schedule, now that the festival is over?"

"For the most part. After I post today's blog, I was going to sample the new spa services we offer. Do a little research so my descriptions will be accurate in the ads and write-ups."

"Oh, lovely. I've been meaning to try the cactus massage myself."

I took more granola. "What is that?" And why did it sound so scary?

Zennia rinsed off a plate and began drying it. "You get a massage with cactus paddles."

Sounded like a form of torture, not a relaxing spa treatment. "I was going to start with a facial."

"I've heard the massage will remove toxins from your body, and you know a healthy body leads to a healthy mind."

"Then I should save it. Give myself something to look forward to."

Zennia laughed. I went down the hall to the office and sat before the computer. The machine was slow to boot up, and my mind wandered while I waited. My gaze fell on the Invisible Prints brochure I'd left on the desk, and I thought about Wendy's death and what I could accomplish at the memorial service tomorrow. I didn't know how many people would be attending or if I'd have a chance to talk to Preston and Kurt again. Was it even appropriate to talk to either one at the service? Or should I leave them to their grief? Not that Kurt was exactly grieving.

I also wondered if Detective Palmer would be there. On television, the detectives always attended funerals to see if the killer was watching from a hidden vantage point or standing among the crowd. If the detective showed up, I needed to tell him what I'd learned about Kurt and the missing money at Invisible Prints without broadcasting the fact that I was snooping in his investigation.

The computer finished booting, and I checked Facebook and my e-mail account before I typed up the day's blog. I'd been pushing the green-living festival all week. Now that the weekend was over, I needed to return to healthy-living advice. Today's topic covered sodium intake and foods to avoid, such as bacon and canned soups. I posted the blog and took a few minutes to answer comments from a previous post.

That done, I headed toward the new spa area back past the cabins. When Esther and Gordon had first decided to expand the farm's spa services, Esther had pictured a state-of-the-art facility with mud rooms and redwood saunas. But once she and Gordon had gone over the budget and list of required permits, she'd settled on a giant tent, like ones I occasionally saw attached to restaurants, along with a much shorter list of services. To promote the spa, I'd started weekly giveaways on the Web site. Every person who left an e-mail address was entered into a drawing to win a free facial or massage. Based on the number of entries, people were definitely interested in everything the farm offered.

I reached the tent and poked my head in. Most of the sections were partitioned off, but I didn't want to interrupt anyone's treatment. The small foyer was empty, and I moved over to the massage area. Gretchen, our latest hire, stood next to a massage table, folding towels and humming. As she moved, the light from a floor lamp bounced off her gold eyebrow ring. Her jet-black pixie cut and dark eyeliner were a sharp contrast to her pale skin.

Gordon had almost refused to hire Gretchen because of her edgy appearance. As usual, he was worried about the spa's reputation and didn't want the townspeople talking about the strange new hires at the spa. But she had valuable experience and impeccable references, so he'd eventually agreed to hire her on a trial basis. Based on all the positive customer feedback, she'd be around awhile.

Gretchen looked up and smiled at me as she set the towel on the stack. "Hey, Dana, what's up?"

"I was hoping you had time this morning to help me out. I'll be promoting the spa services in upcoming blogs and ads, and I wanted to try some of the offerings myself."

"How about the cactus massage? Most places don't have that."

I shuddered. *Why are Gretchen and Zennia trying to cause me pain?* "I thought I'd start with a facial. Everyone expects that at a spa."

Gretchen placed the towels on a side table. "Good enough." She tapped the now-empty massage table. "Go ahead and take off your shoes and lie down."

I sat on the table, untied and removed my Vans, and lay back, watching as Gretchen pushed a button on a CD player in the corner. Soothing instrumental sounds filled the space.

"Now, then, let's take a look." She peered at my face, reminding me of a trip to the dentist. "Do you have a regular cleansing routine?"

We chatted for a moment about what products I used. Then she grabbed a nearby bottle.

"First I'm going to remove any makeup you're currently wearing, along with residual oils and dirt," she said as she squeezed cream into her hand and smeared it on my face. After a moment, she wiped the cream off with a warm, wet towel and then shook a clear liquid onto a cotton ball. She swiped that across my face while I stared at the white canvas ceiling.

Gretchen scrutinized my face again and frowned. Not a good sign. "Have you been under a lot of stress lately?"

Are you telling me I look old and tired? "A bit. I don't know if you heard about the woman killed at the festival, but she was an old classmate of mine. I'm going to her memorial service tomorrow."

"Oh yes, that poor woman. I'm sorry about your friend." She twisted around and lifted the lid of a container. She pulled out a towel and wrapped it around my face, leaving the space around my nose open. Her voice was somewhat muffled by the hot, damp terry cloth that was partially covering my ears, but I could still hear her next words. "It's tragic how she was killed while she and her husband were making such wonderful plans."

My hands flew up to the towel and I tugged at the cloth until my mouth and eyes were exposed. "What are you talking about?"

"My friend who works at an adoption agency in Santa Rosa mentioned that the woman's husband had recently filled out the paperwork."

I pulled the towel lower. "Wendy and her husband were going to adopt?"

Gretchen pressed her lips together and rearranged the towel on my face. I willed myself not to yank it off. "Please, Gretchen, I need to know."

"I shouldn't have said anything. They have rules about confidentiality."

Which her friend apparently ignored. "I promise not to say anything. Just tell me if the Hartfords were trying to adopt a child."

"That's what my friend said."

Poor Wendy, slain before she could start a family. Preston hadn't mentioned that they'd even been trying. Had Wendy chosen to adopt because pregnancy and recovery would take her away from her job for too long? "How sad. I can't imagine Preston will still try to adopt, now that Wendy's gone."

Gretchen lifted the towel off my face and dropped it into a basket. I blinked at the sudden exposure to the cool air.

"I don't know about that," she said. "My friend said the husband was the one who was so gung ho about adopting. She hadn't actually met the wife yet, but she recognized her name in the papers. Said it was the first time in her ten years of working at the agency that she'd only dealt with the husband. Usually the women are the ones pushing it."

"Well, Preston didn't work, so perhaps he had more time to take care of the initial forms and interviews." I lay still as Gretchen squeezed cream from a different bottle into her hand before slathering a layer on my face. The faint scent of lavender filled my nostrils as she worked the cream in, giving my face a mini massage and limiting further conversation.

When she was finished, she wiped her hands on a new towel. I wondered how many she went through in an average day. "That's the basic facial," she said. "We also offer more thorough deep cleanings, and you can request a shoulder massage while your face is steaming."

"I'll be sure to mention that in my blog." I sat up and hopped off the table. "Thanks for the trial. I'll probably be back in a day or two for something else."

"Don't forget the cactus massage."

"Who would forget that?" I slipped on my shoes while Gretchen tidied up her work space. I left the spa tent and followed the path past the chicken coop. Berta, the largest and loudest hen, clucked at me as I went by. I wondered if she noticed my newly smooth and relaxed face.

I slowed as I approached Wilbur and his pals in their sty and stopped to lean on the rail. The pigs were snuffling around, looking for any remnants they might have missed from their breakfast hours earlier.

"I get it now," I said to Wilbur.

He stopped sniffing and stared at me, with his nostrils flaring.

"That facial was great. And I'll bet a mud bath feels even better. No wonder you spend so much time lying in it."

Wilbur snorted and went back to rooting. I

returned to the house. The kitchen was empty, and I headed straight to the office to write about my spa experience before I forgot any details. I spent the rest of the day helping Zennia with lunch service, fine-tuning an ad, and drafting tomorrow's blog. By the time five o'clock rolled around, I was more than ready to finish the day.

I needed to get home and dig through my closet for some black clothes. First thing in the morning, I had a memorial service to attend. With any luck, I'd get some details about this adoption.

17

The next morning, I was finishing my last bite of whole wheat toast, with natural peanut butter, when Ashlee entered the kitchen, dressed in pajama shorts and a T-shirt.

"I'm not used to seeing you in the mornings," I said.

"I heard you farting around out here and it woke me up." Ashlee was such a lady in the morning.

"I didn't realize my chewing was so loud."

She plopped herself into a chair and stretched out her legs. "Before you took off for work, I wanted to tell you about the apartments I found online. I've narrowed our choices down to two."

"It's only been a day," I said. "What's the rush?"

Ashlee glanced down the hall toward Mom's bedroom, but the door was closed. "You haven't been living here as long as I have. You worked in the Bay Area all those years, with your own apartment, doing whatever you wanted."

Snatching a napkin from the holder, I wiped my mouth. "You could have gotten your own place, too."

"I was going to. I'd even saved up enough for the deposit."

My eyebrows rose. I'd never heard a word about Ashlee planning to move out. "When was this?"

She paused. "Right before Dad died. Once he was gone, I didn't know what was going on anymore, so I decided not to move. I couldn't leave Mom all alone."

I felt the familiar guilt rise up. While Ashlee had stood by Mom, I'd stayed in San Jose, grieving on my own, too shaken up to handle anyone else's needs. Tears clouded my vision. I blinked to clear them away. I'd come home eventually, and now Mom was better. That's what mattered.

"Once I moved back home, you could have taken off," I said. "Surely, one of your girlfriends would share an apartment with you."

Ashlee picked at a nail. "Living with you is better. All my girlfriends are hot. We'd always be fighting over some guy. I don't have to worry about that with you."

"Gee, thanks. Good to know I'm completely unattractive to men."

"That's not what I meant. But you have Jason. And even if you didn't, you're not the type to steal someone else's guy."

Wow, my sister is complimenting my character! It

was almost too much to comprehend so early in the morning. "Thanks" was all I could think to say.

Ashlee straightened up in the chair. "So let me tell you about the first place."

I rose from the table. "It'll have to wait. I have to drive to Mendocino for Wendy's memorial service."

"That explains why you're still here. And the outfit."

I'd donned a simple black dress and blazer for the service, though I was already itching to get out of my nylons.

"We'll talk tonight," I said. I carried my plate to the sink, rinsed off the crumbs, and set it in the dishwasher. After brushing my hair one last time, I got into the car. I hadn't attended a funeral since my father passed away. My peanut butter breakfast sat heavy in my stomach. I vowed to focus on Wendy's death, and not my dad's.

The drive over the hill was a repeat of the trip on Sunday, full of towering trees and dark roads. When the ocean came into view, the dreary weather made the sky and water appear to be one solid gray mass. I exited the highway and parked in the small lot for the Presbyterian church. A handful of cars occupied spaces. I had expected a bigger crowd, but maybe people were running late.

The inside of the church was silent. I signed the guest book at a small table and took a program from the stack sitting next to the book. The front had a professional shot of Wendy, which I recognized from the Invisible Prints Web site. Underneath,

Wendy's name and the dates of her birth and death were listed. I flipped the program open to read a poem about the life of a butterfly. I stuck the paper in my purse and moved into the main part of the church, where a few people sat in pews.

The stained-glass windows looked bleak with no sun today, and the muted interior of the church matched the somber mood of the event. I spotted Helen, Drew, and Preston in pews in the first two rows. Drew was busily thumbing on her phone, while Helen and Preston stared straight ahead. I didn't recognize the two ladies sitting in the next row, but I was glad they'd shown up to pay their respects. I dug my own phone from my pocket and saw that it was two minutes to ten. Was Kurt coming, or was he really going to skip his own sister's memorial service?

I slid into a pew near the back and studied the altar. Two large photos of Wendy—one from her high-school graduation and the other from her wedding—sat on easels near the pulpit. A large wreath of red and pink roses, white lilies, and baby's breath filled the middle space. Wendy's name was printed on a sash across the front.

I heard a rustle behind me, and Kimmie joined me in the pew. She wore a tight black business suit with her skirt a good two inches shorter than what was appropriate. Atop her head, a wide-brimmed black hat looked big enough to serve dinner on. A veil hung down to cover the upper portion of her face. People were bound to talk about her outfit, which was probably her intention.

"Oh, good, you didn't forget," she whispered out of the side of her mouth, causing the netting on her hat to billow outward.

"I think it's about to start." I saw that Kurt still hadn't shown up, but Detective Palmer had arrived. He gave me a slight nod of greeting. I smiled back and turned around as fast as seemed natural before he noticed the flush I felt creeping up my neck. I'd guessed he might be here, but still found myself swallowing convulsively. How was I going to talk to people with him lurking around? And how could I tell him everything I'd learned without admitting I was snooping against his direct orders?

Jason appeared at the end of the row, and I smiled at him.

"I wanted to say hi before the service starts," he said.

I gestured to the space next to me. "Did you want to sit here?"

"Wish I could, but I'm on the clock."

I watched as he walked back a couple of rows and sat down next to Detective Palmer, probably trying to squeeze extra info out of him for an article.

Someone near the front cleared his throat. While I'd been watching Jason, a pastor in a dark gray suit had appeared at the pulpit. I automatically straightened up and placed my hands in my lap. Next to me, Kimmie flipped her veil up onto her hat, took out a compact, and touched up her lipstick.

"Dear friends," the pastor said, "thank you for gathering here today to remember a life gone too soon." He continued speaking at length, talking about Wendy's childhood and her success as a businesswoman. When he finished, Preston went up and spoke a bit about his wonderful marriage, which seemed the polite thing to do, even if he had been considering a divorce. On the other hand, his speech was a tad hypocritical if he'd been the one who killed Wendy.

He sat down, and Kimmie tapped my knee. "I'm up," she said, as though auditioning for *American Idol*, not speaking at a memorial service. She pushed her skirt down, thank goodness, and sashayed to the front.

"Everyone here must already know I'm the owner of Le Poêlon, the best restaurant in town, but what you may not know is that I was also one of Wendy's closest friends." She pulled a handkerchief from her shirt cuff and dabbed at her dry eyes. "We met back in fourth grade when she was a lonely outcast and I broke away from my own circle of besties to befriend her. That's the type of person I am."

At this point, I tuned her out. Instead, I worked

on a mental list of features I wanted an apartment complex to have before I moved in. Low rent was at the top of my list. Even with Ashlee and me both working full-time, we couldn't afford much. A safe neighborhood was a must, maybe at a complex with some sort of neighborhood watch program or security gate. I was still debating whether the place needed a pool, when I noticed Kimmie had stopped talking. She stood behind the pulpit as if waiting for applause. When none came, she flipped the veil down and returned to her seat.

The pastor stepped back up and said a few final words. When he finished, a taped recording of organ music filled the air. Everyone stood and filed out, stopping on the front steps to chitchat. Several people must have snuck in after the service started, and I was glad to see the crowd amounted to a respectable turnout. I was surprised that Lily wasn't among the group, since she was such a devoted Invisible Prints customer, but maybe she hadn't heard about the service.

Helen approached Preston and shook his hand, while I sidled closer. "I'm so sorry for your loss."

Preston bowed his head. "Thank you. I still can't believe she's gone."

"I told her the festival might not be a good idea. We need large companies as customers, not individuals, but she insisted on participating." Helen sighed. "To think that decision ultimately got her killed."

"You know how Wendy loved dealing with the public. She wanted to build that company one person at a time."

"Still, I saw a man selling dog poop there," Helen said. "It's not exactly the type of festival we need to be associated with."

I bristled at her comment but kept silent. Now was not the time to make a scene.

"Anyway," Helen said, "I hate to rush off after such a touching service, but I have to meet a repairman to replace the windows at Invisible Prints, then hurry to an appointment."

"What's wrong with the windows?" Preston asked.

"Someone broke all the ones facing the highway."

I stifled a gasp. Who could have been so destructive?

Preston shook his head. "How horrible. My poor Wendy just died."

Helen pointed to Detective Palmer, who stood near the entrance. "I spoke with the police about it, and he chalked it up to vandals. No connection to Wendy's death."

That answer sounded too pat. Had someone broken into the company? They could have smashed all the windows to give the appearance of vandalism and divert attention from a possible burglary.

As Helen moved away, Kimmie took her place,

clutching one of Preston's hands with both of hers. "Thank you so much for letting me speak at Wendy's service." She raised her gaze toward the overcast sky. "I know she was up there watching."

"I'm sure you're right," Preston murmured.

"Call me if you need anything. I'm always willing to help whoever needs it." She dropped his hand. "Now, excuse me, I must be going." She headed to her car, veil flapping in the breeze.

Jason stepped next to me. Now that I could get a good look at him, I couldn't help but admire his slim physique in his black suit and gray-and-black-striped tie. He looked pretty darn hot.

"Did you hear what Helen said a minute ago?" I asked, trying not to drool openly while I spoke. "Someone busted all the windows at Invisible Prints. What do you think it means?"

"Some parents aren't watching their kids close enough."

I pulled him closer to the door and farther away from the others, noting how warm his body felt. "You don't think it's connected to Wendy's death? Maybe someone was trying to break in and steal something related to her murder."

Jason pulled on his tie, looking relieved as the knot loosened. "Helen didn't notice anything missing. There's no evidence it was anything other than kids being destructive."

"If you say so," I said.

"He does," Detective Palmer said behind me.

Man, that guy is sneakier than the neighbor's cat when it's trying to catch the birds around Mom's feeder.

I turned slowly, giving myself a pep talk about how the detective was sure to appreciate my help. "Detective Palmer, so nice to see you again. Do you have any leads on Wendy's murder?"

He gave me a half smile. "Plenty, but none that I can share with you."

"I didn't want to know anyway," I lied. "I was simply looking for some assurance that Wendy's killer would be arrested."

"The police department thanks you for your concern," he said without a trace of sarcasm. He must practice that.

Jason retrieved his notebook and pen from an inside jacket pocket. "Anything you want to share with Blossom Valley's citizens?"

The detective didn't blink. "The residents have nothing to fear. This was a targeted crime, not a random killing."

Not exactly the breakthrough of the week. "Of course it wasn't random." I held up two fingers for emphasis. "I already know of at least two people who might want her dead."

I probably should have kept my voice down, because more than one head swiveled in my direction, including Preston's. He broke away from the group he'd been talking to and made his way over to our little trio.

"Who would want Wendy dead?" he asked, his

eyes tearing up. He grabbed my arm in a firm grip, his tone pleading. "You have to tell me."

My gaze darted all around as I tried to think. One of my suspects was Preston. What was I supposed to say?

18

I waited for one of those California earthquakes to rattle the ground and distract Preston from our conversation, but those tremblers never happened when you wanted.

Preston still held my arm. The pressure increased slightly as more tears leaked out.

I patted his hand, but his grip didn't ease. "Well, I shouldn't mention names." I jerked a thumb at Detective Palmer. "I mean, the police might need to keep the list of suspects quiet so they don't tip anyone off."

"That's correct," Detective Palmer said.

Do I detect a smirk?

Preston released his hold on my arm, but then he took my hand, only increasing how flustered I felt. "If you know anything that can help the police, you've got to tell them."

I snuck a peek at Jason to see if he would step in, but he was busy writing in his notebook and didn't seem to be paying any attention. I nodded at Preston. "Absolutely. In fact, I was about to speak with the detective, but first I want to tell you again how sorry I am about Wendy's passing." An awkward silence settled between us.

Preston looked past me and let go of my hand. "Please excuse me. I need to speak with the other guests."

As he moved away, I smacked Jason on the arm.

"What?" he asked.

"Why didn't you help me there? You could have said something."

Jason spread his hands. "What did you want me to say? The poor guy clearly wants to know who murdered his wife."

"And so do I." I tapped Jason's notebook. "Which reminds me, who is it that we can talk to?"

"How about you leave the talking to me?" Detective Palmer said.

Oops, I'd forgotten he was standing there. "Right, I meant who can *you* talk to?" Trying to act casual, I glanced around and saw that Drew was the only one left anyway. Even now, she was moving toward her car. I felt Detective Palmer's gaze on me and said, "I wasn't kidding when I told Preston I'd pass information on to you. I mean, I'm not investigating or anything, but I've heard a few things that I want to tell you."

Detective Palmer crossed his arms. "Let's start with those motives you were talking about a few minutes ago."

Beside me, Jason raised his notebook, at the ready.

"Well, her brother, who missed today's memorial service, I might add, is upset that Wendy inherited their mom's money." Considering Jason had told me the information, I wasn't surprised when he didn't write anything down. Detective Palmer looked similarly unimpressed. I quickly went on. "Her brother seems to think Wendy was scamming people with her company. That fits in with the man I saw yelling at Wendy at the festival, the one I already told you about. He invested two million dollars in Invisible Prints and now believes the money wasn't used for any green-living projects."

"No kidding," Jason said as he started writing. I couldn't help but feel a little smug that I'd found out information before him.

"You're sure it was the same man?" Detective Palmer asked.

"Yep, saw him at the festival, then a couple of days later at Invisible Prints. His name is Marvin Stevens." I hoped he was making a note of how helpful I was being.

The corners of Detective Palmer's mouth almost moved upward. So close to a smile, yet not quite there. "This is confirmation he was at the festival around the time of the murder."

A woman standing nearby began coughing rather forcefully. After listening to her hack for a few seconds, I rooted around in my purse, shoving aside my lip gloss and phone. Detective Palmer and Jason started chatting while I searched for the elusive cough drop I knew was in the bottom somewhere. Just as I was about to give up, my fingers brushed the wrapper and I held it up as though it were the magic ring everyone longed for in *The Lord of the Rings*.

I handed it to the woman, who nodded her thanks, and tuned back in as Detective Palmer told Jason, "Marvin's suspicions might be correct that Wendy embezzled the money."

My breath caught. Even though Marvin was absolutely convinced Wendy had stolen the two million, I hadn't really believed it. Well, really, I didn't want to believe it. The Wendy I had known was honest and good, other than that little class president scandal. Still, there was a huge difference between tampering with a school election and stealing an enormous sum of money from your own company.

I noticed a silence and looked up. Detective Palmer was studying me.

"Forget you heard that."

"But Marvin had both opportunity and motive. He was at the festival at the time of the murder, and Wendy really did steal the money. Does this mean you'll arrest him now?"

"We need a little thing called evidence first." I must have looked a little too excited because Detective Palmer practically growled, "Don't get any ideas. I'm in charge of *that part*."

I batted my eyelashes, a technique I'd picked up

from Ashlee. "I wouldn't dream of interfering." I could swear that Detective Palmer and Jason snorted at the same time.

"I need to get back to work," Detective Palmer said. "Don't forget what I said about keeping out of my investigation."

I gave him a two-fingered salute. "Aye, aye, Captain."

He shook his head and walked away, leaving me alone with Jason.

"Have time for a cup of coffee?" Jason asked.

The service hadn't lasted long, but I had one more stop—a stop I didn't want Jason to know about. "Not this time, I'm afraid. I need to get back to work." I watched Preston climb into his Lexus and pull out of the lot. "What do you think Preston's going to do now?"

Jason watched the car merge onto the highway. "What do you mean?"

"I wonder if he'll take over as president of Invisible Prints, or if he even has any interest in it."

"Hard to say. I'm not sure how the company is set up. But if he stands to inherit, he could probably sell it and make a tidy profit, although this possible embezzlement could mess up everything. Even so, he doesn't need to worry about money right now."

His tone made the little hairs on my arms stand up. "Why's that? I thought he was out of work."

"Palmer let it slip that Preston is the beneficiary of a hefty life insurance policy."

"How much?" I held my breath, visions of dollar signs floating through my mind.

"Eight hundred thousand."

Eek! That was definitely enough for Preston to kill for, especially if he was already considering leaving the marriage. But if that was really true, where did the adoption fit in?

I gave Jason a quick kiss. "I'd better get back to the farm."

I climbed into my car, feeling a tad guilty that I'd misled him about my plans, but I didn't want another lecture about how I shouldn't be poking around in Wendy's murder. I wasn't sure why he hadn't said anything when I'd told the detective everything I'd found out, but I didn't want to press my luck. Besides, it was a teensy-weensy lie, so small I shouldn't even worry about it. I squashed my remaining guilt down into a ball and rolled it into the corner of my mind for later.

I drove the few miles down the highway and turned in the driveway for Invisible Prints. Even from a distance, I could see the jagged edges of the broken windows. A man in coveralls stood near a truck loaded with glass panes in slots, talking on his cell phone. Drew and Helen were nowhere in sight, and only one car was parked in the small lot.

Since I knew the window guy would be here awhile, I parked behind his truck and got out. I pulled my black blazer closed as a gust of wind blew in off the coast, sending my blond hair swirling around my head. I tried to brush it down as I made my way to the front door.

Inside, the temperature didn't increase much, thanks to the gaping holes in the windows. Drew stood behind the counter, typing on a keyboard. She'd placed coffee mugs and packages of multi-purpose paper on top of any loose sheets of paper, but the edges still fluttered in the constant breeze.

She glanced at me and hit a few keys on the keyboard. "Did you have an appointment with Helen? I don't remember making one."

"No appointment. I was on my way home, but I had to stop and see the damage for myself. I can't believe someone would break all these beautiful windows."

Drew threw up her hands. "Tell me about it. I was sweeping up glass all morning. I don't know what's wrong with kids these days."

"You don't think someone was trying to rob the place?"

"Why not break the window by the front door and leave the rest alone?"

I looked around the room, but nothing had changed since my last visit. "To cover up the fact that it was a robbery. What's more distracting than breaking half-a-dozen plate-glass windows? Did you at least look to see if anything was missing?"

Drew sneered. "There's nothing worth stealing. Have you seen how cheap our office equipment is?

This computer is at least five years old. Wendy bought it refurbished."

"What about the computers in those cubes? They must be worth a few bucks."

"There are no computers."

I squinted at the cubes, although I knew my eyes were working fine. "I can see the tops of the monitors from here."

Drew spoke so low, I had to wonder if Helen was upstairs after all, even though I hadn't seen her car. "Sure, we put monitors in there, used ones we picked up on the cheap, but they're not attached to anything."

"Then why are they there?" I whispered back.

"Like I told you last time, we want to give possible investors the idea that we're a thriving company that will earn them money."

Maybe this company was a complete and total con job after all. "So you deceived potential investors with phony employees."

Drew held up a finger. "Not me. Wendy."

I didn't belabor the point that Drew was basically an accomplice. That accusation wouldn't get me anywhere. "What can you tell me about the day Wendy was killed?"

Drew took a step back. "Nothing. What do you mean? I had nothing to do with her death." She started twitching. For a second, I worried that she was having some sort of seizure.

I moved back too so she wouldn't think I was crowding her. "I'm not accusing you of anything. I remember you and Helen were at Wendy's booth in the early morning, and I was wondering if you saw anything strange."

Drew smoothed down her hair several times, as if calming herself, but the tips just sprang back up. "Oh, right. I was there that morning for a little while. I had to get back here to handle the phones, and Helen had to see a customer."

I wondered if anyone could verify she'd returned to the office when she claimed. Who's to say she didn't stay in Blossom Valley and hide until she went back to the festival to kill Wendy? Had she gotten some inkling that Wendy had embezzled all the investor money? But why would she kill her over that? It might put her out of a job, but not much else.

The man in the coveralls stepped inside. "I'll need some insurance information before I get started," he said.

"Sure," Drew said. She looked at me. "Is there anything else?"

"No, I guess not." As I walked out the door, I took another look at the gaping holes. Maybe the broken windows were a random act of vandalism after all. But so close to Wendy's murder?

I got back into my car and drove over the hill, taking the turns too fast as I rushed to get back to work. As I rounded a blind curve, I came up behind a slow-moving truck and slammed on my brakes. My purse slid off the passenger seat and hit the floor. I could hear the contents fall out and roll around.

Shaking at the close encounter, I kept a more reasonable speed as I entered the valley and reached the edge of town. The truck lumbered down the freeway, but I took the first exit and eased to a stop at a stoplight. While I waited for the light to change, I reached down to grab my purse and placed it on the passenger seat. Then I retrieved everything that had fallen out and crammed it all back in. I picked up the program from Wendy's memorial service last, and my thoughts turned to the attendees. Had Preston even notified Kurt about the service?

When the light turned green, I pushed down on the gas pedal, one hand still on the program. I hadn't known how long the memorial service would run, so I hadn't told anyone at the farm when to expect me. I was all caught up at work, and Zennia could easily handle the current guest load for lunch service.

Mind made up, I headed across town and reached Kurt's place in minutes. I pulled in front of the main house and got out, holding the memorial service program to my chest as though it were a talisman.

As I approached the garage at the end of the long driveway, I noticed the main door was lifted up a few inches. Loud voices reached me, and I slowed my steps to listen to what they were saying. Maybe the argument was related to Wendy's murder.

Clutching the program tighter, I crept toward the garage door.

19

The closer I got to the gap in Kurt's roll-up garage door and the angry voices, the more I doubted my "find." If I wasn't mistaken, Kurt had his television turned up too loud. I heard the distinctive accent of Robert De Niro blasting through the open door. Here I was prepared to hear incriminating words about Kurt's involvement in Wendy's death. Instead, I was faced with *Taxi Driver.*

Still, I listened a few more seconds and heard, "You talkin' to me?" Yep, definitely De Niro.

As I took a step toward the side of the garage, Kurt flew around the corner, dressed in a wife-beater shirt and torn jeans. "What the hell do you think you're doing?"

I felt the urge to duck behind the nearby trash can to put distance between us, but I stood my ground. "I came to see you."

His face got redder and the veins in his forehead bulged. "You were spying on me."

I crossed my arms. "I was not. How dare you make such an accusation." Even if it was true.

Kurt pointed at the gap in the garage door. "I could see your feet."

Oops . . . this was embarrassing. I thrust the memorial service program at him. "I wanted to bring you this, but I thought I heard you arguing with someone and didn't want to interrupt."

Kurt grabbed the program, glanced at the cover, and shoved it into his back pocket. "Looks like a ten-year-old made that. Good to see that husband of hers pulled out all the stops."

"Well, uh, I think he planned everything on rather short notice. I saw you weren't at the service this morning and thought you might want a copy."

Kurt rubbed his balding head. "Sure, I could use a souvenir of my sister's death." I cringed at his comment, and Kurt chuckled. "Sorry, I'll try to pretend I care when you're around. Not that I expect to see you here again."

I sighed, not hiding my dismay. "I remember when you and Wendy used to play together all the time as kids. We'd follow you around when you were hanging out with your friends. I know a lot's happened since then, but maybe one day you can remember the fun times with her."

"After what she did? Don't bet on it."

I was no therapist, but Kurt really needed to let go of his bitterness. It wasn't helping him any.

"Maybe your mom gave Wendy all her money to say thank you. I heard Wendy really did a great job taking care of her at the end."

"Oh, she took care of her, all right. Ran Mom's life like she was running a board meeting. Told her when to eat, when to sleep, who it was that she could talk to. I tried to visit a couple of times, but Wendy made sure Mom was always conveniently napping. I got shut out of Mom's life, and then Wendy probably told her that I'd abandoned her." The words poured out of him as though he'd wanted to tell someone for a long time about all the injustices he'd suffered. I found myself feeling sorry for him.

"That's terrible," I said, sensing my words were completely inadequate.

Kurt cleared his throat and spit off to the side. "Whatever."

"Maybe Wendy left you some of the money in her own will," I said.

"Fat chance. If she even has a will, she probably left everything to her little hubby. Besides, I needed the money back when Mom died, not now."

The hurt in his voice was so clear that I almost reached out to touch his arm, but I thought better of it. "What would you have used the money for?"

He let out a sigh so filled with exhaustion that it made *me* tired. "Not that it's any of your business, but I wanted to save my house. And my marriage, as it turns out." He gripped his jaw and moved it back and forth as though trying to loosen it up.

Must be sore from all that tension. "Our mortgage was upside down, and when our adjustable rate reset, I couldn't swing the payments. The bank was threatening to foreclose, and I was counting on Mom's money to pull me out. Then Wendy went and stole it. I even asked her for a loan, but she said she needed all the money for that phony company of hers. What a witch."

I flinched. "Look, I didn't know any of this. I'm really sorry."

"It's not your fault. It's Wendy's. And that wife of mine. When I lost the house, she moved out. She said she didn't want to live with a loser anymore. You think you know somebody. . . ." His words trailed off.

"Now I understand why you weren't at the memorial service today." This time, I did lay a hand on his arm. "Maybe, after enough time passes, you'll forgive Wendy."

"And maybe a money tree will grow out of my ass."

"Won't the branches hurt?" I asked, trying to lighten the mood.

Kurt gave me a disgusted look. Guess he wasn't ready for jokes. He jerked his arm away and disappeared inside the garage, shutting the door without another word.

I walked back down the driveway, thinking about how Kurt had suffered one blow after another, all stemming from Wendy inheriting their mom's money. Kimmie had described Kurt as too weak-willed to actually commit murder, but maybe she didn't know how far Wendy had pushed him.

As I reached the curb, I heard someone behind me say, "Hey, you there."

I turned, half expecting Kurt to be trotting down the driveway after me.

Instead, the old man I'd seen on my earlier visit stood on the porch of the main house, a three-pronged cane in one hand. I climbed the porch steps and joined him, noticing as I got closer that he had to be close to ninety. His skin was papery thin. His hair was wispy and sparse. With these heavy winds we'd been having lately, he'd do better to stay indoors before a solid gust blew him away.

"I've seen you here before," the man said, giving me the once-over. The middle of one eye was obscured by the start of a cataract.

"Right, I was visiting Kurt."

"No, I mean I saw you looking in my windows. Were you casing the joint?"

Geez, first Detective Palmer found me peering in the windows, and now it turns out this guy had, too. Not to mention Kurt had spotted my feet while I'd been eavesdropping. The Peeping Tom profession required a lot more skill than I'd realized.

"No, of course not. When I was here before, I thought Kurt lived in the house, and I didn't want to bother him if he was too upset about—"

"What happened to his sister." The old man leaned on his cane. "Terrible stuff. I lost my own sister a few years back. She wasn't murdered, mind you, but I still miss her like the dickens."

Somehow, I suspected this guy missed his sister a whole lot more than Kurt missed Wendy.

"I'm close to my sister, too. I can't imagine what I'd do if anything happened to her. I'm Dana, by the way."

"Buck." He held out his hand and we shook. "Kurt mentioned he and his sister had a falling-out, something to do with their mom, but still, it's a sad thing. Made me ashamed when I yelled at him about his car."

For the life of me, I couldn't see the connection between Kurt's car and his sister's murder. "His car?"

"I have a rule with my tenants. They're welcome to park in front of the house, but not in the driveway. I save that space for my guests."

I tried to hide my impatience at the sudden shift in conversation. "And Kurt parked in the driveway?" I guessed.

"All day. He'd never done it before, so I almost let it go, but I got fed up by suppertime and went over to tell him about it. That's when he told me his sister had been murdered that very morning. Made my whining about his parking job seem downright petty."

"Murder does have a way of putting things in perspective," I said, the first answer that came to mind as I tried to hide my excitement. I doubted the old guy realized it, but he might have just provided Kurt with an alibi for the time of Wendy's murder. If his car had been parked in the driveway, then he must have been here, and not off killing Wendy. What else could Buck tell me? "How well do you know Kurt?"

He poked at a beetle with his cane, guiding it toward the edge of the porch and away from his front door. "I don't. I respect my tenant's privacy. He pays his rent on time, and that's all I care about."

"Does he have a lot of visitors?" Maybe I could find some of Kurt's friends to talk to.

"I don't keep track. I have my own life."

A mailman walked up the path and handed a bundle of envelopes to Buck, while I debated whether I should ask anything more. Buck didn't seem the type to gossip, and I didn't think I'd learn much more about Kurt.

After the mailman departed, I stepped off the porch. "Sorry about looking in your windows."

"That's okay." He patted his stomach. "With this hot body, I can understand." He laughed and shambled into the house.

I walked to my car and noted the time. Ugh, it was already after one. Definitely later than I was planning to get back to work. Good thing we didn't have set schedules at the farm.

With a glance in my side mirror, I started the car and pulled away from the curb. I zipped home, changed from my funeral attire to my work uniform, and got back into the car. Once on the highway, I drove the short distance to the farm and parked in my usual spot in the corner. I made my way past the vegetable garden, pool area, and herb garden, and entered the kitchen. Zennia was placing a mound of something pale into a bowl.

I went to the sink and squirted soap on my hands. "Sorry I wasn't here to help with lunch service, Zennia."

"That's fine. Not many people showed up to try my chicken salad with cod-liver oil dressing. Must have gone over to the coast or eaten in town."

Or else they'd gotten wind of the cod-liver oil and hidden in their rooms.

Zennia held the bowl aloft. "I've got plenty of leftovers, if you're hungry. It makes the most wonderful sandwich with my chia seed bread."

I rinsed my hands and grabbed the hand towel on the counter, wondering if I should rinse out my ears. "Did you say 'chia seed'?"

"The seeds are full of omega-three fatty acids."

I bit back a smile. "If I eat chia seeds, will grass sprout out of my head? Will guests think I'm a Chia Pet?"

Zennia wagged a finger at me. "You can't hide behind your white bread and commercial-bought mayonnaise forever. You'll come around sooner or later."

I raised my hand. "I vote for later."

I left the kitchen before Zennia could convince me to try the cod-liver oil dressing and went into the office. After I replied to a handful of new blog comments, I pulled up the document I'd drafted about the spa facial for a final read-through. As I made a small change in the last paragraph, Esther appeared in the doorway.

"Dana, honey bear, the UPS man delivered a bunch of boxes for the spa. Would you mind taking them back and unpacking? Gretchen has a full schedule today, and I want to make sure she has everything she needs. They're on the porch."

"I'll take care of it." I saved my document and stood. "The spa certainly seems to be attracting a lot of customers lately."

Esther beamed. "Mercy me, yes. Even people who live in town are showing up for this new spa stuff. I never dreamed when I turned this itty-bitty farm into a bed-and-breakfast last year that it would be such a success, knock on wood." She reached over and rapped her knuckles on the desk. "Especially after all those troubles a few months back."

"People love this place with all the animals and nature trails. I'm not surprised in the least that it's becoming more popular." That was a bit of a stretch. More than once, the farm had been on the verge of collapse, and none of us knew if we could stay open. I could only hope this latest stretch of guests was the start of stability.

"Since things have steadied out, I'm going to help my friend with her organic chocolate business. She'll give me a big discount if I'll put a bar in every room. It'll help get her name out there."

"I'm sure the guests will love that. Sounds like a win-win for both of you." I moved past Esther. "I'll get those boxes now."

I went out to the front porch, where the stack waited. I picked up the first box and wondered if Gretchen was teaching classes in weight lifting on the side. Either that, or she'd ordered a box of rocks for some sort of hot-stone massage. I staggered off the porch and down the path, while the ducks watched from the pond. One even quacked in encouragement.

Once I reached the spa tent, I dropped the box inside the door with a thud. I could hear Gretchen talking to someone, so I went to retrieve the other boxes, rather than disturb them with my unpacking. Three trips later, I was out of breath and out of upper-body strength. I sat down in one of the rattan chairs in the waiting area, but I popped right back up when Gretchen appeared. I glimpsed brown hair over her shoulder as her client followed behind her.

Gretchen stepped to the stand, which held the appointment book, and I saw that the client was Lily, Invisible Prints' loyal, earth-loving customer. My eyes lit up at this unexpected opportunity.

She smiled shyly. "The spa looked so gorgeous in the brochures you were handing out at the festival that I had to stop in and try a massage for myself."

Wow, someone had actually come here because of my brochure. I stood a little taller right then. "And how was it?"

"Spectacular. Gretchen has magic hands."

Gretchen waved away her compliment. "Oh, stop. I see here we have an opening a week from today. Will that work?"

"Perfect. How much do I owe you?"

Gretchen gave her the total, and Lily handed over a credit card. While Gretchen ran it through the machine, Lily turned back to me. "I had to get these knots out of my neck. After everything that's happened this week, I was too tense to concentrate at work."

I rubbed my neck, as though the mere mention of tension had caused my own muscles to tighten. "Wendy's death was definitely a shock."

She accepted the slip from Gretchen, along with a pen. "Not even her death. The lies that Wendy told. The evil, evil lies. She wasn't doing a thing with all that money I gave her." She pressed so hard when she signed her name that she tore through the paper. "Here I thought I was helping the world." She jerked the paper toward Gretchen.

This was definitely a new side to Lily. Maybe she wasn't the meek, little environmentalist I'd pegged her as. Ever the professional, Gretchen pretended she hadn't noticed Lily's agitated state as she accepted the signed copy. She stowed it in the cash register and moved toward the back of the tent, raising her eyebrows at me before going around the corner.

I shifted in the doorway so Lily couldn't get past me and leave. "Did you pay Wendy a lot?"

"At least thirty thousand dollars."

My eyes widened. Yep, that was a lot. "You must have been pretty mad when you found out the truth."

Lily swiped at a strand of hair in her face. I noticed that her nails were bitten down and ragged. Her beautiful French manicure was destroyed. "I felt more betrayed than anything. You put your trust in somebody you look up to, and then they turn out to be a phony? It hurts."

I thought back to how upset Lily had gotten when I'd asked her what she'd heard the day of the festival. She'd obviously overheard Marvin accuse Wendy of stealing all the investment money. Maybe she'd been so mad at Wendy that she'd killed her without planning to do so.

"So what are you going to do now?" I asked.

Lily chewed on an already-bedraggled nail. "What can I do? If Invisible Prints stays in business, I can try for a refund, but Wendy probably already spent my money. I guess I'll have to file it away under a life lesson."

I wasn't letting her off the hook that easy. I crossed my arms and stared at her until she made eye contact. "That's an expensive lesson. You must have been furious."

"You have no idea. I just—I just . . . I had to do something." Lily burst into tears and brushed past me. She ran from the tent, and her last words rang in my ears.

What exactly had Lily done?

20

Gretchen came out from the back in time to see Lily run down the path. "Is she all right?" she asked.

Explaining the situation seemed too complicated, so I thought up a quick excuse. "She remembered an appointment she was late for."

"Getting all stressed again is going to ruin the effects of her massage."

"At least she'll be a repeat customer," I said.

A pregnant woman, who looked to be five or six months along, entered the tent, and Gretchen and I ceased our conversation. Gretchen greeted the woman and led her to the back, while I found a pair of scissors and cut open the first box. Instead of rocks, I found bottles of creams and oils. I moved among the partitioned sections, avoiding the one with the customer, while I unpacked the shipment.

After I'd placed the last bottle on a shelf, I gathered up the empty cardboard boxes and left the tent. I followed the path past the chicken coop, where several chickens pecked at the ground or clucked at each other. I wondered what they were talking about. Farther down the path, Wilbur and his friends lay around the pen, and I stopped near the fence. Wilbur rose and lumbered over to where I stood, sticking his snout through the wood railings.

I set down the empty boxes and patted his nose. "Hey, buddy. You guys having a good day?"

Wilbur snorted.

"Mine's been okay," I told him. "Right now, I'm trying to picture this woman, Lily, as a killer. She seems much too nice. People who buy organic produce and save the whales usually don't slit someone's throat at a festival."

Another snort. I could always count on Wilbur to agree with me.

"I know, right? And she got really upset when talking about all that money she paid Invisible Prints. Could she have killed Wendy over it?"

Wilbur remained silent.

"Yeah, probably not. I need to keep digging." I grabbed the boxes and carried them to the recycling bin, where I broke them down and tossed them in. I entered the kitchen, my stomach rumbling. The fridge contained packages of tofu, the bowl of chicken salad with cod-liver oil dressing, and vegetables, lots of vegetables. In the back, hidden behind the Brussels sprouts, a package of sliced turkey breast waited.

I snatched the pack up as though it might turn into tofurkey if I didn't act fast enough. Success! Now what to do with it? The only bread in the kitchen was Zennia's chia rolls. The only mayonnaise was Zennia's homemade tofu mayo. But plain turkey was too . . . well, plain. Maybe if I piled on the meat, I wouldn't taste the other ingredients as much.

I pulled out a chia roll, added a thin layer of tofu mayo, and stacked up the turkey slices. With one final look at the tiny seeds that populated the bread, I took a bite. Not bad. The seeds added an unusual crunch and the mayo was soft and creamy. I'd even be willing in a pinch to eat another one sometime. I was popping the last bit into my mouth when Gordon walked in.

He set his clipboard on the table and noticed the half-empty turkey package on the counter. "Isn't that my turkey?"

"Yours? I figured Zennia bought that for any guests who refused to try her other offerings."

Gordon glowered at me. "When has Zennia *ever* purchased processed deli meats? I keep a pack here so I can guarantee an edible lunch in this place."

"Sorry. I'll buy you a replacement pack."

He twisted his pinkie ring around and around before letting his hands drop to his sides. "Don't worry about it. There's still some left."

I all but gaped at Gordon and his new personality. If I'd eaten his turkey three months ago, he'd have driven me to the store himself to make sure I bought more. I'd noticed with the farm's recent steady reservations that he was becoming a much more agreeable person, but extra guests couldn't completely explain his new attitude. I'd have to watch him, make sure he didn't suddenly explode in a rage and blow up the whole farm.

Gordon picked up his clipboard and stepped over to the stove. He opened a cupboard to one side and began counting the salad plates, jotting down the number. That done, he moved on to the dinner plates. Guess he hadn't given up all his obsessive-compulsive habits. Did he think Zennia was stealing dishes to add to her personal collection, or that guests threw away their food, plates and all, when they didn't like something?

I rinsed my plate in the sink, wondering if Gordon had included it in his tally, and went to the office. After a couple of hours working on a magazine ad and a newsletter, I found my mind turning to everything I'd learned so far about Wendy's murder.

Lily had lost thirty thousand dollars to Wendy's bogus company while she tried to offset all her cross-country flights to see that online boyfriend of hers. Not nearly as much as the two million Marvin might have lost when he provided the venture capital funds to Wendy, but still a considerable chunk, especially on a nurse's salary. Lily probably overheard the argument in the festival booth, but would she immediately assume it was true or give Wendy the benefit of the doubt? Were those flowers she'd brought to the booth the next day a sign of mourning or of guilt?

Marvin had the better motive. Did he have any way to recover that money? He'd left the festival in an awful hurry after Wendy's body was found. But if he was the killer, why hadn't he left even earlier, as soon as he killed Wendy?

Maybe Helen had found out about the embezzlement and killed Wendy, outraged that Wendy had ruined the company Helen had helped build. But with Wendy gone, Helen might not be able to save Invisible Prints. All that work would have been for naught.

What about Kurt? He had plenty of reasons to kill his own sister. His landlord said Kurt's car was in the driveway the entire day, which would imply Kurt was home, but Buck hadn't seen him until that evening. Buck had also mentioned that Kurt had never parked in the driveway before. The festival wasn't too far from where he lived. Had he parked in the driveway so Buck could provide his alibi, and then walked to the festival to kill Wendy?

And then there was Preston. Kimmie felt positive that Preston had wanted to end the marriage, and Ashlee had heard much the same. Was it true he'd get nothing in a divorce? With that large life insurance settlement Jason had mentioned, maybe Preston had decided that murder was the more profitable option.

I put my thoughts about Wendy's murder away. Time to get home. I updated my time card, shut down the computer, and left through the lobby. As I crossed the parking lot, I tried to dig my keys out of my purse, marveling at how they always managed to hide at the bottom. Once I'd extracted them, I glanced up and froze. The keys slipped from my hand and clanged against the pavement.

Someone had keyed my car. No, that wasn't quite right. Someone had scratched an entire message on it.

BACK OF was etched in huge block letters on my hood, the ugliness of the marred paint screaming at me. Whoever did this must have gotten spooked because he or she had only started the vertical line of the last *F,* but I didn't need the missing letter to understand the message. Someone was threatening me.

21

My hands shook as I stooped down and felt along the ground until my fingers closed on my dropped keys. I couldn't take my eyes off the hood. Who could have done something so vicious?

My mind instantly flew to Kurt. He'd been plenty upset when I'd dropped off the memorial service program earlier. Maybe he hadn't believed me when I'd said I wasn't spying on him. Or else he didn't like the questions I'd been asking. This could be his way of scaring me off.

Well, he could forget that idea. One little scratched-up hood wasn't going to stop me from finding out what had happened to Wendy. In fact, it made me want to ask even more questions. But maybe I'd bring Jason along next time. Just in case.

Still shaking, I went back to the office and put a call through to the police. I had no proof that Kurt was responsible, but I at least wanted the incident documented. Plus, my insurance company would most likely require a police report.

The nice thing about living in a small town was that the crime rate was low. An officer arrived within minutes of my call, eager to take a look. My scratched hood was probably the biggest case he'd seen all day. He inspected the car, took some notes, and gave me a case number for the insurance forms. I asked about fingerprints, but he politely informed me that the police didn't usually dust for fingerprints in vandalism cases.

A short while later, I'd provided the insurance company with all the necessary information, and they'd promised to have a claims adjuster meet me at the body shop in the morning. I got into my car, thankful that I couldn't see the letters on my hood from the driver's seat.

As I drove, I found myself checking the rearview mirror more often than usual, but no one appeared to be following me. When I reached home, I found Ashlee's Camaro in the driveway and felt momentary panic that she'd see my hood and demand an explanation. I had absolutely no idea what I would tell her. With any luck, she'd want to talk about apartments as soon as I walked in.

Sure enough, I'd barely crossed the threshold before she popped out of the living room. "Finally! I thought you'd never get home."

"Wow, such a grand welcome. You must have really missed me today."

"Not really, but I've got photos of those two

apartment complexes up on my laptop. Let's go look at them." She walked back toward the living room, and I followed after her, glad to have a distraction from the attack on my car. She sank onto the couch and leaned toward her laptop, where it sat open on the coffee table. I set my purse on the floor near the couch corner and sat down beside her, angling the laptop until I could see the screen without any glare.

Ashlee tapped the keyboard. "Both places have okay rent and a pool," Ashlee said.

I glanced at the pictures as she clicked through, but the two looked almost identical. "What about utilities and garbage service? Are those included in the rent? What type of security deposit do they require?"

"I didn't bother to find out about that stuff, but look." She pointed at the screen. "This one has a gym. That means lots of hot guys getting all sweaty."

Or it might mean two weight machines stuck behind the boiler in some utility closet.

"I'll need more information than that," I said. "We need to visit these places."

Ashlee slapped her laptop closed and stood. "Perfect, let's go."

"What about dinner?" Mom usually made us dinner. It felt rude to run off when she'd gone to all the trouble.

"I asked Mom, and dinner's not till seven tonight. That gives us time to run over there."

Might as well go now. Otherwise, Ashlee would pester me all night. I retrieved my purse from the floor. "One complex. We don't have time for both." I walked to the front door, with Ashlee practically stepping on my heels. Before I could twist the knob, Mom came in from the kitchen.

"Oh, good, you're both here. I have big news."

Big news? For a split second, I thought she might tell me she was marrying Lane. How would I feel about that? What if she asked me to be a bridesmaid? My hand tightened on the knob.

"I got a job," Mom said.

Relief ran through me, swiftly replaced by confusion. I released the knob and moved toward Mom. "A job? Where?"

"Don't sound so surprised," she said. "It's not time to put this old cow out to pasture yet."

Mom and Esther should get together some time and compare farm phrases. "That's not what I meant. It's just that I didn't realize you were even considering a job."

"I've been bored lately. You can only play so much bunco. Janine, who owns that Going Back for Seconds clothing store, is an occasional alternate for our group and mentioned she was looking for a new salesclerk. I convinced her to hire me."

I gave Mom a hug. "That's wonderful. I bet you'll love it."

"Yeah, Mom," Ashlee said. "Congratulations. Do they have a family-and-friends discount?"

"I'll find out," Mom said. She seemed to notice

for the first time that we were standing by the front door. "What are you two up to? Are you on your way out?"

"We're gonna check out an apartment complex," Ashlee said. "See how many single guys live there."

At the mention of apartments, I realized that with Mom getting a job, money wouldn't be so tight. Dad's survivor pension didn't provide much, and I'd been contributing to Mom's bills, though she always protested. In the back of my mind, I'd been saving the excuse that Mom needed my paycheck as a last-minute way to bail out of this apartment hunting. With Mom's new job, that excuse vanished. I wasn't sure if I was delighted or terrified.

"Do you need me to hold up dinner?" Mom asked. "We're having baked fish, with steamed broccoli."

Wait . . . if I move out, I can eat whatever I want for dinner. No more brown rice and plain chicken. No more whole wheat pasta and low-fat salad dressings. Then again, no more Mom making my dinner for me. I'll have to cook my own.

"Dana, let's go," Ashlee said. While I'd been wondering how many days in a row I could eat Top Ramen, she'd pulled her phone and car keys out of her pocket.

"Right. We'll be back for dinner, Mom." I hurried after Ashlee as she headed to her car. I climbed into the passenger seat and clicked my seat belt, yanking on it to make sure it was securely fastened. You never knew what Ashlee's driving would be like.

She buckled up behind the wheel, started the engine, threw the car in reverse, and hurtled backward out of the driveway. Behind us, a horn blared. I whipped my head around as a car drove into the other lane to avoid getting broadsided by Ashlee.

"Where did that guy come from?" Ashlee muttered.

The good thing about backing up so fast was that Ashlee had completely missed seeing my scratched hood. "I think that's why car manufacturers put rearview mirrors in cars. So you can look behind you before you back up."

At the mention of the mirror, Ashlee glanced in it, but only to fix her hair. "Ha-ha. You're such a comedian."

She barreled down the street, slowed down at the stop sign, and roared ahead. In less than ten minutes, we'd arrived at the Walnut Hills Apartments. From the outside, the place looked decent enough. Flower beds bordered the parking lot. Rows of purple and white blooms bobbed in the breeze. The buildings appeared to have been painted recently in a dark brown color. Flags flew in front of a single-story building, which I took to be the rental office.

Ashlee parked in a guest spot, and we walked to the office. Except for a single car driving by, the complex was quiet, a good sign. In the office, a young woman in a business suit sat behind a desk. When Ashlee explained we were interested in renting a place, she grabbed a set of keys out of a desk drawer and walked us across the lot, pointing out the gym and pool along the way, as well as the laundry facilities.

Ugh, I'll have no more free access to a washer and dryer. Another thing I hadn't considered. It was amazing how much I'd forgotten about living on my own in San Jose.

The two-bedroom apartment reminded me of any other, with plain white walls, neutral carpeting, and older appliances in the kitchen. The woman rattled off all the amenities as she walked us back out, locking the door behind us.

"Feel free to walk around the grounds," she said. "Most people here work all day, so the area is quiet. We have the occasional Saturday-night party, but the office staff is sensitive to noise control."

Guess Ashlee wouldn't be having any of those keggers she'd been hinting at.

"Thanks for the tour," I said.

"I should mention that we have only two 2-bedroom apartments left, so you might want to grab one before it's gone." She headed back to the office.

She could try the pressure sale all she wanted, but I needed time to think about the place. "Ready to get home?" I asked Ashlee. "Mom will be waiting with dinner."

"In a minute," Ashlee said, "I want to see if any guys are working out in the gym."

Knowing Ashlee, this was probably the biggest factor for deciding where we would live. Maybe she could bed down on a weight machine at the local gym and save herself some rent money.

As I turned to follow Ashlee, I noticed a familiar dark blue Lexus pull into the guest spot next to Ashlee's Camaro. Sure enough, Preston, dressed in jeans and a plain gray sweatshirt, stepped out of the driver's side.

Forget hot guys lifting weights. What was he doing here? Suppose I was wrong about Kurt scratching my hood. Maybe it had been Preston. I swallowed hard.

Did he follow me here to make sure I'd gotten his message?

22

Oh, God. What if Preston really did follow me? I needed to get the hell out of here before he saw me. Before I could make a dash for the gym, I heard Preston call, "Dana!"

Shoot. He's already spotted me.

I pretended not to hear him and started walking away, but Ashlee stopped and said, "I think that guy called your name."

"No, I'm sure you're mistaken," I told her, taking her hand and trying to pull her along.

"Dana!" Preston called again. This time, I looked back and saw he was heading our way.

Ashlee pried her hand out of my grip. "Why are you acting so weird, Dana? I'll go peek in the gym, while you talk to whoever that is."

I felt my panic level rise. "Wait, you need to stay here with me."

"Don't be silly. I'll be right back." Before I could

stop her, she'd entered the gym door. I started to
go after her, but I felt a hand on my arm.

I faced Preston, moving my arm away so he'd
have to let go of it. My muscles tensed. Surely, he
wouldn't attack me in the middle of the parking
lot. Would he?

"Dana, I'm glad I ran into you. Have you heard
anything else from the police about Wendy?"

*He certainly sounds sincere. Have I misread the situation? But if he wasn't following me, why else would he
be here?* "Nothing yet, I'm afraid. What brings you
all the way to Blossom Valley?"

An annoyed look crossed his face, and the
muscles in my body tightened even more. "I'm
looking for an apartment."

As simple as that. Preston hadn't followed me at
all. He was apartment hunting. "Hey, me too. My
sister and I might share a place." We faced each
other. Preston's closed expression was a clear indication he wouldn't be helping the conversation
along, now that we weren't talking about Wendy.
Then a thought struck me. "Why do you need an
apartment when you have that beautiful home in
Mendocino?"

Preston exhaled noisily and crossed his arms.
This might be a short conversation. "That beautiful home has a rather ugly mortgage to go with it."

"Sorry to hear that. Guess you can't afford the
payments, huh?" I mentally shook my head at
myself. If they ever held a contest for the world's

most obvious question, I'd have a good shot at taking home the trophy.

He pinched the bridge of his nose. "I don't work, so that'd be hard."

"What about the life insurance?" *Oh, shoot, Jason told me about the insurance in confidence.*

Preston's jaw visibly tightened, and he pursed his lips. "What life insurance? How do you know about that?" Behind us, a car pulled into the complex but went by, probably a resident coming home from work.

I shifted my feet, sensing sweat along my hairline even though it couldn't be more than seventy degrees outside. "Someone mentioned Wendy had a sizable policy and you were the beneficiary."

"Who's this someone?"

Would he suspect Jason? Would he complain to the newspaper that one of their reporters was blabbing secrets? "I don't remember. I heard it around somewhere."

"Did Kimmie tell you?"

Oh, I hadn't considered he would blame Kimmie. I shrugged slightly to imply he might be right. If he wanted to think Kimmie had a big mouth, then that was totally fine by me.

"You can tell her that there is no life insurance. When I called the number on the policy, the lady on the other end informed me that Wendy had stopped paying the premium a few months back. The policy is now defunct."

Ouch. That must have burned.

"Invisible Prints must be worth something." Even as I said this, I realized it wasn't, not with the allegations of mismanaged funds. Preston confirmed my thoughts.

"The money for Invisible Prints might be tied up in court for years. I'll be lucky if I don't owe money on that stupid company." He rubbed a hand up and down his face. "I can't believe the years I wasted with that woman."

I probably should have offered more condolences and walked away, found out what was taking Ashlee so long at the gym, but I found myself saying, "Surely, you loved her." I'd almost swear the setting sun dipped even farther behind the mountain, because the sky definitely darkened.

"I used to," Preston said. "We had plans when we first married. Start a family, build a life. Maybe Wendy believed in those plans once, but in the end, her job always came first." He shoved his hands into his sweatshirt pockets so hard that I listened for the sound of stitches tearing. "I quit my job and gave up my career so I could be a stay-at-home dad, but then Wendy admitted she might never be ready to have children. It'd mess up her professional plans. She wanted a house husband to clean the floors and balance the checkbook, someone to meet her at the door every night with dinner and a kiss." He clutched the zipper on his sweatshirt and ran it up and down.

I tilted my head and tried to appear guileless. "You always could have adopted," I said, knowing full well that was his plan. "Then she wouldn't have had to worry about pregnancy interfering with her career."

Preston gave me a sharp look. "You must be a mind reader."

Or someone who knew more than she was supposed to know.

"I was looking into adoption before Wendy was killed," he said. "She had refused to have a natural child with me, but if I showed up one day with an adopted baby, she couldn't exactly stick it on the curb, although she might have tried."

I pictured a baby seated on a curb with a sign around its neck that said, FREE. Not a good image. "Are you going forward with your plan, now that Wendy's gone?" I didn't know what the odds were for a single guy to adopt, but other men must have done it.

Preston let go of the zipper and rubbed his hands together. "You bet. Even without the insurance money, I think I found a way to get the money I need. I have to look into a few things first."

Well, that was curious. Had Preston stumbled upon the missing business funds, or was he referring to something else? Before I could ask any more, I heard Ashlee behind me.

"Dana, you ready?"

Not exactly, but Preston probably wouldn't say any more with Ashlee here. I was surprised he'd said as much as he had.

"Sure, I'm ready," I said as she joined us. I gestured toward Preston. "By the way, this is Preston Hartford, Wendy's husband. This is my sister, Ashlee."

Ashlee held out a hand and they shook.

"Sorry about Wendy," she said. "Are you thinking about moving here?"

Preston looked at the buildings, indecision etched on his face. "I might. It depends how this other thing pans out."

Ashlee tucked a lock of hair behind her ear. "Well, if you do, feel free to stop by our apartment anytime to borrow a cup of sugar or hang out."

My head swiveled from Ashlee to Preston and back. Was she hitting on him? His wife hadn't been dead a week.

I swatted Ashlee's shoulder. "Let's go."

She beamed at Preston, using the smile she always reserved for new guys. "It was *so* nice meeting you," she said. She flipped her hair back and practically pranced to her Camaro.

I gave Preston a much smaller smile and followed after her. By the time I reached the car, she was already gunning the engine, a warning that I'd better move it. I hurried into my seat and was struggling with the seat belt as she backed out of the space at warp speed and zipped toward the street.

"Slow down," I said.

"You gotta make a big exit with guys. Make an impression so they won't forget you."

I snapped my belt into place. "Show some respect. Preston's wife just died."

"Right. That means he'll need someone to comfort him on these cool fall nights."

Had my sister really sunk so low as to hit on recently widowed men? I'd rather not know. "Did you mean it when you told Preston you wanted to move here, or were you just flirting with him? I think this place could work," I said.

Ashlee blew through a yellow light. "Up until five minutes ago, I would have said not a chance. Exactly one guy was working out in the gym, and he was at least forty."

"What happened five minutes ago?"

"Didn't you see those two cars waiting to turn into the complex when we pulled out?"

"You drove by too fast. At the speed you were going, I would have missed a jumbo jet parked in the street."

Ashlee pushed down on the gas, as if to show me what the car could really do. "You think a Greyhound bus is too fast."

I pulled on my seat belt to make sure it was secure. "Have you seen the way some of those guys drive?"

"Man, you kill me sometimes, Dana. Anyway, I saw the drivers of those cars. They were guys, and they were hot. Maybe all the ones our age are still getting off work. We should come back on a Saturday and see who's in the gym."

"Or we could take our chances that plenty of men live here. This place has everything we're looking for, and it's in a good part of town. I think maybe we should sign a lease." Not having to look at any more apartments with Ashlee while she hunted for men would be an added bonus.

"I'll think about it." She pulled into the driveway at home, tires screeching as she made the turn. She shut off the car. "Next up, furniture shopping."

Aw, man, I hadn't even considered the furniture situation. Ashlee didn't own any and I'd sold all mine on Craigslist before moving back home, even giving away the Papasan chair and futon for free at the end so someone would haul them away for me.

I unbuckled my seat belt. "We haven't even signed the lease yet."

"We could still figure out what we're going to buy for when we do."

Knowing Ashlee, she really wanted an excuse to go shopping, but I liked the idea of getting all of my ducks in a row. "We could at least look," I conceded. "We do need a few things." Such as beds. And a table. And chairs. And everything else. I pushed open my car door and stepped out, grateful to be alive after Mr. Toad's Wild Ride.

Ashlee got out on her side. "Great, when can we go shopping?"

"Does that mean you want to move into this place?" I walked up the path to the house, glad it was now dark enough that Ashlee wouldn't notice my hood.

"Unless I find a better one. Are we going for a theme when we decorate? All pink maybe?"

I shoved the front door open so hard, it banged against the wall. All pink? Were we moving into Barbie's Dreamhouse? Not to mention, all those hot guys Ashlee was so interested in would run screaming when they entered her pink palace. "Absolutely not. We're getting basic black or brown furniture that won't collapse when we sit on it." Too bad the nearest Ikea was over a hundred miles away.

"You'll change your mind. Pink's awesome." Ashlee moved past me and headed for the kitchen. "So how does tomorrow look?"

"It's normally my day off, but now that we need to buy furniture, I might work a few extra hours. How about your lunch break?"

"Great. We'll start at Have a Seat. I saw the cutest sofa there a while back, and it was only fifteen hundred dollars."

I stifled a groan. Forget about a few extra hours at work. Between buying furniture, laying down a security deposit, and paying the first month's rent, I might need a second job.

23

The next morning, I arrived at the body shop and found the claims adjuster waiting. He assessed the damage on my car and approved the request for repairs. The guy at the shop inspected the scratches and promised to start the work immediately. Feeling somewhat better and thankful that neither one had asked who was mad enough to do such damage, I climbed into the loaner car and headed to work.

Once at the farm, I checked in with Zennia, who requested a handful of parsley from the herb garden. On my way out of the kitchen, I grabbed the bag of leftover bread crumbs Zennia had been collecting from various meal preparations and went out front to the duck pond. In the last few months, the ducklings had gone from fuzzy yellow feather balls to full-sized birds. Now, they eyed me with little interest as they tried to warm themselves in the rays of the feeble morning sun.

Until I raised the bag of bread crumbs.

As one, the ducks hopped to their feet and advanced toward me, quacking menacingly. I jammed my hand into the bag for a fistful of crumbs and flung them toward the duck army. That stopped the first rank, but the rest kept marching, getting closer with each step. Their bills opened and closed, ready to eat anything in their path. I threw another handful and jumped back.

Two ducks had ignored the crumbs but stopped at the edge of the sidewalk as if held back by an invisible force field. Still, I wasn't taking any chances. I hurried around the house to the herb garden, glancing back to see if I was being followed, and, at the same time, feeling foolish that I was running from a bunch of ducks. But those ducks could get mean when they were hungry.

With no ducks in pursuit, I squatted before the parsley plant and broke off several stems. The fresh, grassy scent of the herb filled my nostrils as I snapped off a few more sprigs. That finished, I carried my bundle and the remaining bread crumbs into the kitchen.

Zennia stood at the counter, slicing a peach. Juice glistened on the cutting board, and the sleeves of her loose-fitting blouse looked ready to unroll into the moisture at any minute. My mouth watered as I inhaled the fruit's sweet scent.

I waved the herbs in the air. "Parsley for the chef."

"Thanks, Dana." Zennia pointed her knife at

the refrigerator. "Could you do me one more favor and see if the gooey duck has finished thawing?"

I set the parsley on the counter. "If not, maybe we can cover it with a blanket, help warm it up." I swung the fridge door open, wondering why the duck was gooey. Was she making a special sauce? Marinating it in a thick liquid?

I scanned the shelves, noting the packages of tofu, soy milk, and a bowl full of what appeared to be rubber hoses attached to rocks. I wasn't sure that belonged in the fridge, but the kitchen was Zennia's domain. I moved the milk to the side, but only a head of lettuce and a cucumber waited. "Doesn't packaged duck look the same as the chicken I buy at the supermarket?" I called over my shoulder.

Zennia broke into peals of laughter, and I turned to stare at her as a piece of peach slid onto the floor. She hurriedly picked it up and tossed the slice into the sink, laughing all the while. "Sorry," she said when she could speak again, "but gooey duck isn't an actual duck. It's a clam."

"What? Then why is it called a duck?"

Zennia wiped her hands on the kitchen towel and joined me at the open fridge. "No one knows, although they think it was a translation error." She reached past me and pulled out the bowl full of rocks and hoses.

I stared at what I now realized were pale and rubbery clams. The things were even uglier up close.. What was with that giant hose? "You're going to make people eat that for lunch?"

She poked at one. "Maybe dinner now, since they're not done thawing."

I grimaced. "But why? What's wrong with regular clams?"

"These taste much better than the ones you'd normally find at the store, and I can guarantee most guests won't have tried them before. I want to offer unique cuisine to make the spa stand out from our competitors."

"Oh, your cuisine is unique all right."

Zennia put the clams back in the fridge and shut the door. "I wish some of these items weren't so expensive. Heaven help me if Gordon starts tracking how I spend my budget."

"As long as the guests are happy." Of course they probably wouldn't be happy if they saw those clams in their natural form. I sure hoped Zennia was planning to chop them up.

"Speaking of Gordon, he had to run into town to talk to a supplier and asked me to cover the front desk, but I need to start my sauce," she said as she resumed slicing. "Would you mind watching the desk for fifteen minutes? I believe one person is checking in today, but I don't know what time they're arriving."

I was already halfway out the door when I said, "I'm on it." Anything to get away from the giant clams. They might suck my face off.

In the lobby, I stood behind the counter and

took in the silence of the room. Most guests were probably walking on the nature trails or sleeping in. Out the window, I watched the ducks waddle around the grass, occasionally slipping into the water for a swim. They'd calmed back down now that they'd gobbled up all the bread crumbs.

I checked the clock on the wall. Two minutes had passed. No wonder Gordon was always working on his clipboard or futzing on the computer. Manning the front desk was boring.

But, wait . . . a maroon BMW glided down the road and into the parking lot, pulling into a vacant space near the lobby. Was this the new guest Zennia had mentioned?

The driver's-side door opened, and out stepped Marvin in a black business suit and orange dress shirt. What was he doing here? I leaned on the counter and watched as he popped the car's trunk and removed a black briefcase and a suitcase, setting the suitcase's wheels on the pavement and pulling up the handle. I moved to the computer and brought up the reservation system. Sure enough, Marvin Stevens was our expected guest for the next two nights.

I bounced on my toes while I awaited his approach. He wheeled the case across the parking lot and up onto the curb, with what I considered infinitesimal slowness. Eventually he maneuvered the suitcase around a duck on the sidewalk and entered the lobby.

I stood behind the counter, hands folded on the surface, the picture of professionalism. "Good morning, sir. Checking in?"

He parked the carry-on and gave a curt nod. "Reservation for Marvin Stevens."

I pretended to type on the keyboard, even though his information was already in front of me. Couldn't let him know I'd been spying on his reservation. "Oh, yes, here you are. And what brings you to the O'Connell Organic Farm and Spa today?"

"Every bed-and-breakfast in Mendocino is booked solid. Is it normally like that?"

"People usually take one last vacation before the cold weather settles in." I hit a button on the computer. "I'll need to swipe a credit card and then I'll get your key."

Marvin pulled his wallet out of his pocket and extracted a card. "Still, it's inconvenient for me."

"Mendocino's loss is our gain. We appreciate your business." I ran his card through the machine.

"I refuse to stay in chain hotels. The walls are paper-thin in those places. I can't have people overhearing my business dealings."

I handed back his card. "You sound busy."

He pulled out his smartphone and thumbed the screen. "I've got several meetings later today to handle a deal that went sour. I need to find out where my money situation stands."

Aha, now we're cooking. "You mean with Invisible Prints?" I asked.

Marvin's eyes narrowed as he looked up from his phone. "How do you know about that?"

"I was there at the company when you, um—" I'd been about to say "yelled," but that seemed antagonistic—"*asked* where your investment money went."

"You were there?"

"Standing next to Drew."

Marvin glanced at his phone again. "Guess I didn't see you. I was too mad to focus."

"Any word on what happened to your money?"

"Not yet. The accountant is looking at the books. With Wendy dead, we may never know."

I laid Marvin's room key on the counter. "Couldn't you sue for the money? Invisible Prints must have some assets."

"If there's no money to recoup, there's no money. This wouldn't be the first company my firm has invested in that went bankrupt."

That was odd. I hadn't realized a firm had invested the money. I'd assumed it was from Marvin's private bank account. "How'd you discover the embezzlement, anyway?"

Marvin studied me. "What's your interest in this?"

I held up my hands. "I went to school with Wendy. I'm having trouble believing she would do this."

"Well, she did. And she got caught, thanks to an

anonymous tip." He snatched up the key. "Now excuse me. I have to get ready for my appointment."

"Of course. Can I show you to your room?"

"I can find it." Marvin's tone was clipped, and I wondered if he was upset by my questions or the loss of the money. Probably both.

"Follow the sidewalk to the vegetable garden, hang a left, and the path will take you right to the cabins. You're in number nine."

He nodded his thanks. I watched as he wheeled his suitcase out the door and down the sidewalk. Who had been the source of the anonymous tip? With such a small company, only a handful of people could have discovered the embezzlement. Helen was the likely choice, as vice president, but why would she tip off Marvin and effectively ruin the company? Drew hadn't worked there long, but maybe she had access to the company's files. Still, wouldn't she go to the police if she discovered money was missing?

That left Preston. But again, why squeal to Marvin? Wouldn't he have asked his own wife about the money first? And Wendy's income was their only income. Preston would be risking their entire lifestyle if he turned in his wife.

I'd managed to rule out everyone, but I couldn't think of anyone else who might have found out about the embezzlement.

Who am I missing?

24

While I mulled over the source of the anonymous tip, my cell phone rang. I pulled it from my pocket and smiled when I saw Jason's name on the screen.

"Hello!"

"Dana, hi. Are you busy?"

"Never too busy for you." I didn't mention that I was standing around waiting for imaginary guests. He might not be as impressed with my answer.

"Great. Are you free for dinner tonight? My parents are leaving town tomorrow and wanted to see you again before they go."

My stomach plummeted to my toes. "Dinner? Did you say 'dinner'?"

"Yeah, that meal that follows lunch."

"With your parents?"

"Right."

Really, I had no legitimate reason not to agree, except I was a bigger chicken than Berta.

"Dana?" Jason asked.

I told myself to get a grip. It was dinner with two very nice people, not a couple of serial killers. "I would be delighted."

"Glad to hear it. Let's meet at Table for Two at six. I'll need to come straight from work, or else I'd pick you up."

"That's fine. I'll see you then," I said, and hung up. At least I had the afternoon off. If I survived furniture shopping with Ashlee, I could use the extra time to figure out what to wear. My work clothes weren't going to cut it.

Zennia appeared from the direction of the kitchen, fresh spots on her apron from the ripe peaches. "All finished. Now that my prep work is done, I am once more feeling centered. Thanks for watching the desk."

Maybe I could use some of Zennia's techniques to center myself before tonight. I tapped the keyboard. "Our guest arrived. I put him in cabin nine."

"Great. Gordon should be back soon. I can take over until then in case we get any drop-ins." She pulled her apron over her head and wadded it up to place on a shelf below the counter.

"I'll be in the office." I walked down the hall to post the day's blog, not happy that it was a few hours later than normal. I wondered if anyone would appreciate that the topic was all about avoiding tardiness.

I spent the rest of the morning doing odd jobs

around the farm: skimming the muck from the pool, skimming the muck from the hot springs, and cleaning the muck from the pigsty. Life didn't get much more glamorous. I stowed the equipment in the toolshed, washed my hands at the outside faucet, and said my good-byes to Zennia and Gordon, who had returned from his errands.

Once in the loaner car, I used the drive to give myself a pep talk about shopping with Ashlee. I decided to squash any thoughts of my dinner with Jason's parents, for fear I might drive off the road in a panic.

At home, I took a quick shower, then threw together a chicken sandwich. I was finishing the last bite when Ashlee waltzed through the door. Even though she wore a standard vet smock to work, she still managed to look fashionable with her tousled hair, which probably took an hour to style, and her carefully applied makeup.

"Did you want to eat lunch before we get started?" I asked.

"I'll grab something on my way back to work." She clutched my hand and pulled me to my feet. "Let's get shopping."

After having already suffered through the car ride to the apartment complex, I immediately walked to my rental car. "I'm taking the wheel."

Ashlee pouted. "I only have an hour for lunch. We don't have time for your turtle driving."

"Pipe down and get in," I said, yanking open my door.

Ashlee paused near one headlight. "Whose car is this?"

I still hadn't planned what to tell people, but an abbreviated version of the truth seemed easiest. "I got a bunch of scratches on my hood and decided to get it painted."

"Those must have been some major scratches. When did it happen?"

I put one foot on the floorboard, eager to end the conversation. "Yesterday. At least that's when I noticed them." I got in.

"Huh." She walked over to the passenger side and climbed inside.

As Ashlee buckled herself in, I got in my side and gunned it out of the driveway, just to show her I was a better driver than she gave me credit for, never mind that I bounced off the curb on my way. She did that herself all the time.

I motored through town and pulled up to Have a Seat. It was essentially the one furniture store in Blossom Valley, which is why the guy jacked up the prices a good ten percent. I was already grumbling under my breath about how unfair that was before I'd even stepped into the store. As I swung the door open, the smell of leather and furniture polish greeted us. The store consisted of one giant room, with bedroom furniture on the left, dining-room tables in the middle, living-room fixings on the right.

Ashlee darted to the right before the door had even closed behind us, and I trailed after her, running my hand along a suede couch until I hit the armrest, where a bright-colored tag announced this beauty could be mine for a mere two thousand dollars. I yanked my hand back. On to the good old-fashioned stiff-and-scratchy couches.

While I'd been admiring the suede couch, Ashlee had plopped herself on a plush-looking sofa, where one end served as a recliner. As I approached, she pulled the handle to lift the footstool and settled into the cushion.

"We should get this one."

I flipped the tag over to read the price. "Way out of the budget. We need something for less than a grand."

Ashlee closed the footstool. "Dana, nothing in here is that cheap. We need to find something comfortable but sexy."

"Stop worrying about 'sexy' and start worrying about what we can afford."

Ashlee waved her hand. "We can charge it."

I planted my hands on my hips, feeling more like a mother than a sister. "I'm not spending the next five years paying off some couch for your little love nest. Besides, these prices are outrageous. Maybe we should stop by a Goodwill store."

Ashlee stared at me, horrified. "But all their stuff has cooties," she whispered.

"It does not. Now, look, we stick to a budget or the deal's off."

Ashlee stuck her tongue out at me. "Fine, you win. We'll keep looking." It wasn't often that Ashlee conceded defeat. I almost did a victory dance right there in the sofa aisle.

We spent the next half hour wandering through the store. Ashlee pointed out every overpriced piece of furniture in the place, while I shook my head and reminded her again and again about our budget. We eventually settled on some mid-priced items to keep in mind for when we signed a lease on a place. By the time we left the store, I was more exhausted than if I'd cleaned out Wilbur's pigpen ten times in a row. How did my sister wear me out so fast?

In the parking lot, I pulled out my keys, glancing around as I neared my car. Across the lot, Drew stood by a Ford Focus, the rear passenger-side tire flatter than the cushion on one of the discount couches in the clearance section. Why was she here instead of working at Invisible Prints right now?

I turned to Ashlee. "Hang on a second. I know that girl. Let me see if she needs any help."

"Make it snappy. My lunch hour's almost up." Ashlee whipped out her iPhone. "I'll pin photos of the furniture on Pinterest. See what my friends say."

I hoped her friends didn't say the furniture looked cheap and that she needed to get the sectional sofa with the double recliner and side panel that housed a refrigerator. We'd both have to sleep on the thing, since we wouldn't be able to afford beds.

As I walked over to Drew and her car, a cool wind blew across the pavement and made me shiver. Drew must be freezing in her T-shirt and pajama pants. I could see the bottom of the panther tattoo peeking out below her cap sleeve.

Up close, I started to doubt that this was Drew after all, even with the tattoo. Did she have an older sister? She'd aged a good five years since my last visit to Invisible Prints. Her spiky hair drooped and her puffy eyes were sunken in her pale face.

"Drew?" I asked, just to make sure.

She'd clearly been wrapped up in her own thoughts as she stood by her car, but now she blinked twice and focused on me. "Oh, hi. Sorry, I forgot your name."

"Dana Lewis." I pointed to her flat tire. "Need me to call anyone?"

She showed me her automobile membership card. "I'm waiting for a tow truck, thanks." She glanced at the tire, and tears appeared in her eyes. "One more thing that's gone wrong."

I never knew what to do when people who were practically strangers started crying. Heck, I didn't know what to do when longtime friends started crying. "Well, I'm sure George over at Spinning Your Wheels can fix your tire. You'll be on your way soon enough."

"On my way where?" She let out a sob, and I put a hand to my temple. Guess I'd picked the wrong thing to say. "Helen told me not to come to work until this whole mess with Wendy gets cleared up. She thinks the place will be shut down. Without a job, I can't afford rent. Now I have to pay for a new tire on top of everything else." She kicked the flat tire for good measure, not that it could get any flatter.

"Maybe Wendy didn't embezzle any money," I said. "Maybe she put it in a special bank account that no one's found yet."

Drew sniffled. "That would be a neat trick. But the money's gone. Like Wendy." Tears trickled down her cheeks. I'd been hoping she was all done crying, but apparently not.

"It's a terrible shock, all of it," I said.

"This wasn't supposed to happen. I keep thinking about how different it should have turned out."

"What do you mean?" I wasn't sure if she was talking about Wendy's death or the state of the company.

Drew swiped at the tears. "It's just that . . ." The rumble of a tow truck interrupted her sentence. Her words trailed away as she watched its slow approach across the pavement.

"It's just what?" I asked, trying to bring her back to the conversation.

She continued to look at the truck. "I'd better go talk to the driver. Show him my card."

I watched her walk away. My insides were a bundle of loops and knots. Drew definitely knew something, but with her car and job troubles, she wouldn't be sharing the info with me. At least not today.

I walked back to where I'd parked the car. Ashlee leaned against the hood, thumbs flying as she texted. I slid into the driver's seat. When Ashlee didn't move, I hit the horn. She jumped off the hood, glared at me, and got into the passenger side.

"God, Dana, you're so rude."

"Sorry, I thought you heard me get in the car."

"I was too busy asking Brittany what she thought of that sofa. She agrees we should go with something more pink."

"No pink."

"But the brown's so boring."

She says it's "boring"; I say it's "easy to coordinate."

"You can add pink pillows. How's that?"

She sighed. "Fine. But we still need to decide what we want to hang on the walls, and where we're going to get dishes."

I didn't remember living on my own being this expensive. Then again, my salary had been about three times higher. "We'll figure it out later."

Right now, I needed to decide what to wear tonight. I had a date with my boyfriend's parents.

At three minutes to six, I pulled into the Table for Two parking lot, feeling slightly uncomfortable in my knee-length skirt and tights, topped off with a sweater. I scanned the rest of the lot and spotted Jason's parents by the entrance. Where was Jason? Parking the car? Reserving a table with the hostess? Maybe I'd sit right here for a minute until I saw him.

Stop it, Dana. You're a grown woman. You can make small talk with two people for a few seconds. You did it all the time down in San Jose. Think of them as a couple of Silicon Valley clients.

Exhaling slowly, I opened the car door. I reached back for my purse, checked my reflection one last time in the rearview mirror, and then shut and locked the door. I'd moved as slowly as possible, and yet, still no sign of Jason. Great.

I stiffened my spine, figuratively and literally, and marched across the parking lot. Jason's dad saw me coming and nodded in my direction. His mom turned to watch my approach, and that made me stand up even straighter.

Mrs. Forrester held out a hand. "Dana, I'm so glad you could make it. I was worried you might cancel, once you found out Jason wouldn't be here."

My smile froze along with the rest of my body. "Jason's not coming?" I squeezed out as my brain told my hand to rise up and shake Mrs. Forrester's.

"Didn't he call you? Oh, dear, he was in an awful hurry. Called away on a big news story, though he couldn't give us any specifics."

Jason wasn't coming. At all. For the entire meal.

With his parents. I took a deep breath to steady my nerves and reminded myself that if I was mature enough to move into my own place—even if Ashlee would be there, too—then I was mature enough to eat dinner with my boyfriend's parents all by my little lonesome. "Well, we'll have to order him something to-go when we're finished," I said.

"Splendid," Mr. Forrester said, the first word he'd uttered. He opened the door, and Mrs. Forrester and I entered the restaurant, my appetite shrinking by the second. At this rate, I'd be ordering a cup of soup. Or nibbling on the contents of the bread basket.

The hostess seated us at the same table where Jason and I had eaten earlier in the week, but there was nothing romantic about this situation. Mrs. Forrester pulled her napkin from under her silverware and placed it in her lap, and I followed suit. She sipped her ice water. I sipped my ice water.

We couldn't play Simon Says all night, so I cleared my throat. "How are you enjoying your visit?"

"It's been lovely," Mrs. Forrester said. "Of course, Jason's been so busy with this murder that we haven't seen as much of him as I'd prefer, but I know his work is important to him."

"He's extremely dedicated," I agreed. "Being lead reporter is a huge responsibility."

Mr. Forrester reached over and squeezed his wife's hand. "That's why we're so proud of him."

I'd have to pass this on to Jason, let him know his parents approved of his profession after all.

"You'd have to be awful committed to pass up dinner with a girl as lovely as yourself," he added.

I felt my face grow warm. Must be sitting too close to the fireplace.

"I have to confess," Mrs. Forrester said, "I was hoping Jason would become a doctor like his brother, but sometimes parents have to readjust their vision of their children's lives."

Mom had probably made the same adjustment when I'd moved back home.

"And seeing how happy he is," she said. "I believe he made the right decision."

The waiter arrived to take our orders. Though my full appetite hadn't yet returned, I found myself requesting the fish special. As soon as Jason's parents ordered and the waiter departed, Mrs. Forrester said, "Tell me more about your job at the spa."

"Between collecting chicken eggs, helping with the meals, and covering the marketing side of the business, Esther, the owner, keeps me pretty busy."

"Sounds fun," Mr. Forrester said neutrally.

What did he mean by "fun"? Did my job sound frivolous? "I'm looking to establish a more serious marketing career," I said.

"Oh, don't get me wrong," he said. "Nothing wrong with having a job you enjoy. Our daughter-in-law is a top-notch lawyer—"

The waiter brought our drinks, interrupting Mr. Forrester.

A lawyer? And not just a run-of-the-mill lawyer, but a really good one. How can I compete against that?

"Her parents must be quite proud," I said.

"Sure, but she hates it."

"Really?" I asked. Who could hate the stature and money that came with being a successful lawyer?

"She works constantly, including weekends," Mr. Forrester said. "Travels all the time. Barely gets to see her husband. That's Jason's brother. But she owes a fortune in student loans and has built such a solid reputation in the industry that she feels she can't quit now."

Mrs. Forrester dabbed at her lips with her napkin. "Poor dear is worn-out all the time. I don't know how she does it."

Maybe working at the farm wasn't so bad after all. At least I had time to enjoy the rest of my life.

The conversation moved on to new topics, and our entrees arrived a short time later. As dinner progressed, I found myself more at ease with Jason's parents, even managing to eat the entire platter of grilled trout and mashed potatoes. They really were wonderful people, and I wondered why Jason didn't visit them more. By the time we said our good-nights, I felt like I'd known them for years. I drove home with my heart as warm and fuzzy as a baby duckling.

As soon as I got inside the house, I slipped into

my room to call Jason and tell him about the evening. His phone rang three, then four times, and I started to suspect he'd turned off the ringer to focus on whatever story had kept him from joining us for dinner.

I was about to hang up, when he came on the line. "Dana, what's up?" His tone was curt and business-like. Definitely still working on the story.

"Your mom mentioned you were working, but I wanted to let you know that dinner went great. I really enjoyed talking with your parents."

His voice warmed considerably. "I knew you guys would hit it off. I'd love to hear about it, but not right now."

Curiosity got the better of me. "Can you give me a little hint as to what big story you're working on?"

"Of course. It won't be a secret much longer anyway." He paused. "It's Preston. Someone killed him."

25

I pulled the phone away from my ear to check the reception, though I knew I'd heard Jason correctly. "Preston's dead? Why didn't you tell me?"

"I've been working nonstop since I found out. I haven't even had dinner yet."

The way the food in my stomach was flip-flopping right now, I kind of wish I'd missed my fish and potatoes. "What happened?"

"Someone killed him at his home, slit his throat, the same MO as Wendy."

I shuddered as I sank down onto my bed. My breath didn't come as easy all of a sudden. "I can't believe it. I talked to Preston yesterday."

"When?" Jason asked, his voice tight. "About what?"

My mind replayed the conversation from the previous evening. "I ran into him at the Walnut Hills complex when Ashlee and I went to look at an apartment. He was thinking about renting as well."

"Why would he do that? He had all that insurance money coming his way."

"He said Wendy let the policy lapse. Plus, I guess, the house had quite a mortgage on it. Preston couldn't afford to stay."

"No kidding."

I heard talking in the background.

"Are you at the office or the crime scene?" I asked, picturing the cops with flashlights, searching for clues in the dark.

"The office," Jason said. "And I'm afraid I have to go. I'll pass what you said on to Detective Palmer. He may want to speak to you."

"Fine, keep me in the loop."

As I hung up, I remembered what Preston had said about finding a way to get some money. I thought about calling Jason back, but he was obviously busy and I didn't have any real details.

Instead, I tossed my phone on top of the covers and tried to grapple with this unexpected death. Was his murder somehow related to the money he'd mentioned? Had he told someone he'd found Invisible Prints' missing funds, and they'd killed him for it? If Detective Palmer didn't contact me tomorrow, I'd reach out to him. He needed to know this, even if I didn't have more specific information.

I leaned back on my bed, planning to rest for a moment. When I opened my eyes again, it was half past ten. Shoot. I'd taken a nap right up until my regular bedtime. I could forget about a good night's sleep. I put on my pajamas, wandered into the living room, and clicked on the TV. The house was quiet, and I could only assume that Ashlee and Mom were already asleep. I kept the volume low as I flipped through the channels. After I'd rotated through the lineup twice, I clicked off the set, went to my room, and grabbed a farming magazine Esther had lent me, but my mind couldn't concentrate on the words. All I could picture was Preston when I'd last seen him, talking about adoption and how much he wanted a family. After a few more minutes, I closed the book, flipped off the light, and lay in the dark, staring at the ceiling. That's the last thing I remembered.

The next morning, I awoke to a room full of sunlight. That's what happens when I forget to set the alarm. I stumbled out of bed, took a quick shower, donned my usual work clothes, and staggered out to the kitchen a mere fifteen minutes after I'd gotten up, a new personal best.

Mom was already seated at the table, wearing a pair of black slacks, a cream silk blouse, and a red blazer, with gold hoops hanging from her ears.

"Wow, you're dressed up this morning."

Mom blushed under her rouge. "It's my first day at Going Back for Seconds. I hope I do a good job. I haven't worked in almost thirty years, not since I had you girls."

I gave her a quick hug. "You'll be fantastic, and I know you'll sell a ton of clothes."

"Thank you." She glanced at the clock. "Aren't you normally at work by now?"

"Slept in, but I'm on my way right now." I picked out a banana from the fruit bowl on the counter, retrieved my purse, and opened the front door.

Detective Palmer stood on the porch, dressed in a brown suit and matching tie. His Ford Taurus was parked across the street. I lowered my banana. Guess I wouldn't be heading to work just yet.

"Morning, Detective."

"May I come in?" he asked.

Mom poked her head out from the kitchen. "Who are you talking to, Dana?" She caught sight of the detective. "Oh, dear, is anything wrong?" I noticed Mom had paled considerably. She'd first met Detective Palmer when Ashlee was involved in a murder, and I'm sure his presence brought back a lot of bad memories.

"Not really," I told her. "I didn't want to say anything, but Wendy's husband was murdered last night." I heard Mom inhale sharply as I turned back to the detective. "I assume that's why you're here?"

"That's correct."

I pushed open the screen door and held it while he stepped into the house. "Let's talk in the living room," I said, creating the illusion of privacy. If Mom listened closely, she could hear every word from the kitchen. And I was pretty sure she'd be listening closely.

"I'll get you some coffee, Detective Palmer," Mom said.

"Thank you, Mrs. Lewis."

I led Detective Palmer into the living room, my palms clammy. I had nothing to do with Preston's death, yet I suddenly felt like a suspect, just like when I'd talked to the detective after finding Wendy. I gestured toward the sofa and took the recliner for myself. I didn't need the detective to get poked in the butt by a loose spring in the worn-out cushion.

He pulled out a notebook and clicked his pen. "It has come to my attention that you spoke with Preston Hartford two days ago. Is that correct?"

"Yes. Did Jason tell you that? He mentioned he'd pass that along to you."

Detective Palmer ignored my question. "What did you and Mr. Hartford talk about?"

"Don't let me interrupt," Mom trilled as she bustled into the room with a tray. She set the tray on the table and placed a cup of coffee in front of Detective Palmer, along with a sugar bowl and creamer.

He nodded his thanks, and Mom rushed back out with the tray, no doubt in a hurry to get back to the heater vent, her official eavesdropping station. Detective Palmer took a sip of coffee as I figured out the clearest way to answer him.

"Well," I said, "we were both considering renting

apartments at the Walnut Hills complex. I asked why he was interested, and he said he couldn't afford to keep his house."

Detective Palmer jotted in his notebook. "What, then?"

I drummed my fingers on the armrest while I thought. "He said something strange about having an idea where to get some money, so he might not be renting after all." I waited for Detective Palmer to leap up from the couch and hug me after this big revelation.

Instead, he glanced at his notes, then up at me. "And?"

I leaned forward, back straight. "What do you mean 'and'? This is huge. Don't you think he figured out where Wendy put the missing money? That must be connected to why he was killed."

"You're making a leap. He could have been borrowing the money from his parents, or getting a loan from a friend. Maybe he was planning to sell some of Wendy's possessions."

Oh, I hadn't thought of any of those ideas. I sagged back in the recliner.

"What else did you talk about?"

"That was it."

He didn't say anything. Clearly, I hadn't provided the information he was hoping for.

"So when was Preston killed?" I asked. I pressed my lips together, curious to see if he'd answer me.

Detective Palmer tucked his notebook into his inside jacket pocket. "Guess you haven't read the paper this morning. He was killed around lunch-time."

I thought back to yesterday. I'd been munching on a chicken sandwich when poor Preston had been murdered. "Did someone really slit his throat?"

"Appears that way." He stood. "If you think of anything else, you know how to reach me." He handed me a business card, though I already had a couple in my room from previous encounters.

"Sorry that I wasn't more help," I said as we walked to the front door. "I really thought I had something there."

"You never know what's important. That's why we follow up on all leads." I couldn't tell if he was being sincere or if he was saying that to make me feel better.

I watched him head down the front walk. As soon as I closed the door, Mom popped out of the kitchen.

"Why didn't you tell me Preston was mur-dered?"

"You were already in bed when I found out last night. I'm surprised Sue Ellen didn't call you at the crack of dawn to tell you."

As if by magic, the phone rang. Mom pursed her lips. "I'm sure it's someone else."

She picked up the receiver, with me watching the entire time. She turned away from me, but I heard her say in almost a whisper, "Oh, hi, Sue Ellen."

I knew she'd be on the phone for a while, so I grabbed my purse, ready to drive to work.

As I was digging out my keys, Ashlee emerged from her room. Her blond hair was sticking out in all directions.

She yawned. "What are you still doing here?"

"On my way right now," I said. "Wendy's husband was murdered last night. Detective Palmer stopped by to ask what we'd talked about the other night."

Ashlee stopped in mid-yawn. That had woken her up a little. "Bummer for Preston. Guess we won't be neighbors after all."

"Guess not." I unsnagged my keys from my wallet and yanked them out of my purse. "See you later."

I hopped into the loaner, noted that the detective's car was no longer parked across the street, and sped to work. Clouds sat atop the mountains. An icy wind ruffled my hair as I walked past the vegetable garden. I found Zennia in the kitchen, rinsing bits of scrambled eggs off a plate. Berta and the other chickens had come through for her again.

"Big turnout for breakfast?" I asked as I picked up a dish towel and dried a plate.

Zennia shook the next plate to get the last drips of water off and propped it in the dish rack, feeling her long-sleeved tie-dyed shirt to make sure it hadn't gotten wet. "Almost every guest showed up.

If I have this many for lunch, I might need your help."

"Absolutely." I set the dried plate down and grabbed the next one. "Say, how did the guests like your slushy-duck thing?"

"The gooey duck? They loved it. That new guest raved that the meal was better than many of the fine-dining restaurants in San Francisco that he frequents." Zennia placed a hand on my arm. "I always knew people would embrace my cuisine."

"You're a great cook," I said. "I just don't always know what you're cooking."

Zennia chuckled. I placed the dishes in the cabinet and started to walk out of the kitchen. As I reached the doorway, I realized that the new guest Zennia was referring to must be Marvin. She might be able to tell me if Marvin had been at lunch yesterday as well, which would be right around the same time that Preston was supposedly killed.

I cleared my throat. "So what did the new guest think of your lunch offerings?" I asked in my oh-so-casual voice.

Zennia tilted her head. "I don't remember him being there, but then I only served my tuna salad with tofu mayonnaise, which isn't too exciting."

The tuna might not be exciting, but the fact that Marvin wasn't in the dining room was. He'd mentioned a business meeting, one that involved finding out about a money situation. Any chance that meeting was with Preston? Was he convinced that Preston knew where the money was? Had he killed him when he wouldn't reveal the location? Or was my mind off on a wild-gooey-duck chase?

"What are you thinking about, Dana? You almost look like you're meditating."

My thoughts about Preston vanished. "Sorry, I got distracted. Guess I'll go write today's blog." I went to the office and stared at the blank computer monitor for a good five minutes, trying to think up a topic. I brought up my list of backup blog subjects and decided to describe how to use lemons for cleaning.

As I was typing the last line, Esther came in the room, dressed in a checkered shirt and denim overalls, looking every bit the farmer.

"Dana, dear. Can you help me clean the rooms this morning?"

An idea formed, and I all but jumped from the chair. "I'd be delighted."

Esther took a step back and slapped a hand to her chest. "My goodness, I've never seen you so excited to vacuum a cabin before."

"Guess I'm in a cleaning mood today." Really, I was in a snooping mood. If I could make sure I cleaned cabin nine, the cabin where Marvin was staying, I might uncover something useful, maybe even a clue to Preston's or Wendy's murder.

I brushed past Esther and around the corner into the laundry room, dragging the maid's cart into the hall before Esther had even reached the doorway. She followed me as I pushed the cart through the dining room, across the patio and pool area, and over to the row of cabins.

"How about you start with the first one, I'll start with the last, and we'll meet in the middle?" I said.

"We'll be done in no time." She gestured toward a stack of organic chocolate bars. "Don't forget to leave a candy bar in every room."

"You got it." I made short work of the first cabin as I swapped out the towels, wiped down the bathroom, and ran the vacuum over the carpet. I stripped the linens in record time and remade the bed. Then I remade it again when I noticed that the comforter was all bunched up and the sheet was upside down. Maybe I should slow down. When the room looked clean, I added a chocolate bar to the nightstand and carried the cleaning supplies to the cart, shutting the door behind me.

I pushed the cart next door and stood before Marvin's cabin. Thank goodness the DO NOT DISTURB sign wasn't hanging from the knob. I clutched the key in my hand, noticing I was trembling, and knocked on the door. When no one answered, I inserted the key into the lock.

It turned easily, and I pushed open the door.

"Dana," someone said right behind me.

"Gah!" I jerked back. The keys flew from my hand and skittered across the pavement. I gave Gordon a sheepish grin as I retrieved the keys. "I mean, yes?"

He ignored my theatrics, thank goodness. "I wanted to congratulate you on your spa giveaway.

It's attracted a lot of interest to our Web site, which is translating into a higher reservation rate."

"Great, glad to hear my efforts are working." I mentally willed Gordon away so I could get back to snooping, but he reached over and picked up a chocolate bar from the pile on the cleaning cart. "Was there anything else?" I asked.

He studied the red-and-gold wrapper. "These look pretty fancy. How much do they cost?"

"You'd need to ask Esther. I think she's friends with the company owner. Now she wants to leave one for each guest in his cabin." I picked up a bottle of cleaner and a rag, hoping he'd take the hint.

"We can't afford to splurge on overpriced chocolates. We need to keep costs down."

His stern tone made me wonder if the old Gordon was returning. I flipped over a bar and read the label, but the price wasn't printed on it. "Esther's frugal. I'm sure they're affordable."

He set the chocolate bar back down on the cart, and I felt hope bubble up that I'd get into Marvin's cabin now. Before he could walk away, Esther emerged from the cabin at the other end. Drat.

Gordon immediately raised his arm and motioned Esther over, picking up the bar once more. I thought about darting inside while they talked, but they'd probably follow me into the room, cutting off all chance of my looking around.

"Esther, how much do these bars cost?" he asked.

She took the bar and smiled at the wrapper. "My friend has started a chocolate artisan business. She offered me a huge discount if I'd pass them out to the guests. That's great advertising for her and a yummy treat for the guests."

"As long as it's a decent discount. I don't want to waste all our profits on candy."

Gordon moved toward the path that led back to the house, and I released a breath I didn't realize I'd been holding. But then Esther stepped into my line of vision.

"Need help with this cabin?" she asked.

"What? No. I mean, no, thank you." *Maybe all these interruptions are a sign I shouldn't snoop in guest rooms?* I'd have to mull that theory over while I was poking through Marvin's things.

"Call me if you need anything," Esther said.

"You too." As soon as Esther reached the end of the row, I hurried into Marvin's cabin, shut the door, and leaned against it. Finally! I did a visual inspection of the room and felt my excitement wane. The room was almost bare, with a suitcase in the corner, a paperback book on the nightstand, and a small binder on the coffee table. I moved over to the partly opened closet and saw two dress shirts—one orange, one white—and a pair of dark slacks. The dresser top was bare.

I gripped a drawer pull, but I didn't open the drawer. Even though I couldn't wait to get inside the room, searching through drawers was a huge invasion of privacy. I didn't mind looking at things in plain view. I mean, Marvin knew whoever cleaned the room would see anything he left out, but drawers were private sanctuaries. I took my hand off the knob and focused on the small binder.

Upon closer viewing, the binder appeared to be a day planner. With the advent of smartphones and tablets, I didn't realize anyone still carried an actual paper planner around. I undid the clasp on the side, but then I froze again. Was opening his day planner any different than opening the dresser drawer?

I heard a noise outside the cabin and whipped around toward the door. My cleaning bottle smacked into the planner and sent it hurtling off the table and onto the floor. It bounced open, loose scraps of paper spilling onto the brown carpet. Oops!

I dropped to my knees and scooped the papers into a pile, glancing at a couple of sheets as I cleaned up. One was a gas station receipt, another was from an office supply store. I straightened everything into a tidy pile and placed them back inside the day planner. When I scooted back, I noticed a stray scrap of paper near the coffee table's leg. It had obviously been torn from a larger page and contained a number and a street name. Why did that address seem so familiar?

Oh yeah, it was Preston's address.

Why did Marvin have it?

26

I stared at the scrap of paper, wondering if I had the proverbial smoking gun in my hand. Then I dropped it onto the stack, slammed the day planner shut, and placed it back on the table.

Of course Marvin had Preston's address. It was also Wendy's address, up until a few days ago. Preston himself had remarked that Marvin came by the morning of Wendy's death, looking for Wendy. The address meant nothing.

Grabbing the cleaning bottle with more force than was necessary, I abandoned any further search. Esther would be wondering what was taking me so long. I hurriedly wiped all surfaces in the bathroom, and then ran the dust rag over the coffee table, nightstand, and dresser. That done, I changed the linens and vacuumed.

When the room was finished, I loaded the supplies into the cart and moved next door. By the time Esther and I cleaned the last cabins, it was approaching lunchtime. I stowed the cart in the laundry room and entered the kitchen, washing my hands at the sink.

At the counter, Zennia was scooping her Asian-style tofu and vegetables onto bright green lettuce leaves resting on white plates. The scent of teriyaki sauce wafted toward me. For a second, I was tempted to try a nibble. Then I looked at all those vegetables I didn't recognize and decided to skip it.

"Need any last-minute-prep help?" I asked.

"I'm putting the finishing touches on now. I'll need you to serve these lettuce cups to the guests while I get started on dessert."

I moved the finished plates to the kitchen table and wiped a few errant drops of sauce off the white ceramic. As soon as the big wing and little wing of the rooster clock pointed to twelve, I poked my head in the dining room to see if any guests were waiting.

Marvin sat alone at a table near the French doors, staring at the pool and patio area through the glass. His smartphone rested on the table near his silverware. The rest of the room was empty. Either guests had opted to eat out—which is what I would do, given Zennia's odd food choices—or else more people would be showing up at any minute.

I retrieved a plate from the kitchen and hurried

to Marvin, hoping to speak to him before anyone else arrived. He looked up at me as I approached the table. Then he let his gaze drop to the cream tablecloth.

"Is anything wrong?" I asked as I set the plate down.

Marvin propped his elbows on the table and placed his head in his hands. "Preston's dead."

"I heard. What a terrible thing."

He groaned and his head sank lower. "Especially since I was the last one to see him alive. Wendy, too, at that damn festival. I've been talking to the police all morning."

So that's why he hadn't eaten Zennia's lunch yesterday. He really had been meeting with Preston. I dropped into the seat across from him. "What did they say?"

Marvin eyed me. "I probably shouldn't tell you."

I laid my hands on the table, palms down. "We're in the same boat. A detective came to my house first thing this morning. I'm wondering if he asked you the same questions that he asked me."

"I wouldn't think so." Marvin's phone buzzed, but he barely glanced at it. "Unless you saw Preston right before he died, too."

"What did you talk to Preston about?"

Marvin closed his eyes and didn't respond.

"Marvin," I said, but I stopped talking as two people drifted into the dining room, chatting quietly. I recognized them as a married couple spending part of the week here to celebrate their anniversary.

Once they sat down, I rose. "Back in a jiffy," I told them.

I went to the kitchen for two more plates and set them before the couple, then checked on Marvin. He was looking out the French doors again and cracking his knuckles.

I sat back down across from him. Considering his plate of food was untouched, it wasn't as if I was interrupting his meal or anything. "You know, I was telling that police officer who visited that Preston might have come across some money. Did he admit anything to you? That must have been what you went to see him about." I figured if I was willing to share with him, he might return the favor.

He tore his gaze from the pool and looked at me. "Preston said he didn't have the money and Wendy never took it. Then again, I didn't expect him to tell me any different."

"Maybe Preston was right and Wendy didn't take the money," I said.

"She must have."

"Is that why you went to see her at the festival?"

"Yes, but she wouldn't tell me anything. Now that they're both dead, it'll take a miracle to find that money." Marvin squeezed his eyes shut and pinched the bridge of his nose. "What a mess. This could ruin me."

Marvin sounded downright desperate, and I

had to wonder how far that desperation could have fueled his actions. "I'm sure it'll all get sorted out," I said.

"If it's not too late already. This isn't the first bad investment I've made in recent months. I've heard rumblings that upper management isn't happy." He rubbed his eyes and let his hands drop back to the table. "Never mind, I'll take care of it. I'm not going down without a fight after everything I've done for that company." He picked up his fork and poked at his food.

I took that as my signal that he wanted to be alone and returned to the kitchen as another guest entered and found a table. I continued serving lunch as people straggled into the dining room. At one point, I noticed Marvin's chair was empty, and most of his food was still sitting on his plate, the lettuce cup intact. Losing two million dollars would ruin my appetite, too, especially if I was also a potential murder suspect.

When all the diners had eaten, I cleared the remaining dishes, stripped the tables, and threw the tablecloths into the industrial-sized washer. After that, I helped Zennia tidy up the kitchen before drifting into the office to work on a promotional brochure. I hammered out the details, saved the file, and then raised my arms over my head to stretch out the kinks in my back. Time to count the ducks and tend to the pigs.

I nodded to Gordon on my way through the lobby. He raised his head from whatever he was jotting on his clipboard and gave me a half wave. Out front, low-lying clouds cast a gloomy gray atmosphere over the parking lot and duck pond. The ducks huddled in a cluster on the lawn above the waterline, their beaks tucked under their wings. I did a head count. When the ducks had been younger, they'd constantly wandered off. Now that they'd grown, few strayed.

With no ducks missing today, I cut through the gap in the hedge and walked across the patio area, watching the breeze ripple the surface of the pool. Past the redwood tree, I stepped onto the Chicken Run Trail and stopped at the pigsty. Wilbur and his friends snorted a greeting, and I thought about running back to the kitchen for a spare apple or two. These pigs sure had me trained.

My cell phone rang, and I pulled it from my pocket. When the pigs saw I wasn't getting out a treat, they grunted and turned their backs. Well, they could forget about the apples with that kind of attitude.

I hit the green button on my phone. "Hello?"

"Dana? Jason. I wanted to make up for missing dinner last night by taking you to the movies tonight. Are you free?"

"As a matter of fact, I am. What time will you pick me up?"

"Movie starts at seven-thirty. How about seven?"

I had no idea what movie he was referring to, but our tastes for action and comedy flicks matched, so I knew he'd pick one we would both enjoy. "See you then," I said, and clicked off.

Wilbur was still giving me the cold shoulder, so I walked past the hen house, offering a wave to Berta, and followed the path around to the front of the cabins. Helen Goldstein, VP of Invisible Prints, came around the corner from the other direction, and I stopped up short.

"Helen?"

She'd been texting on her BlackBerry and looked up in surprise. "Oh, you're that friend of Wendy's, right?"

"Right." I ran my hands over my shirt to try to smooth out the wrinkles, feeling underdressed compared to Helen's navy blue business suit and sensible heels. "What brings you all the way to the farm? Are you here for a massage?"

She looked at her BlackBerry again. "I'm here to meet with Marvin about this fraud investigation. Business has come to a standstill, now that the company assets are frozen."

"I'm sure you can understand how he'd want his money back," I said.

"If he'd given me a little more time, I might have found the money on my own. Now I have to figure out how to save the business. I already had to lay off Drew. I can't pay her if I don't have access to the bank accounts."

I thought about Drew crying in the parking lot of Have a Seat. "Drew seemed to think that her time-off was temporary." Helen raised her eyebrows and I felt compelled to explain. "I ran into her yesterday. She filled me in."

Helen scratched her neck. "Well, to be honest, her time-off might be permanent. I'm starting a new position at a solar panel company in San Francisco."

"But what about Invisible Prints?" I demanded.

"With the missing money and Wendy's death, the future of that company could be in limbo for years. I can't afford to wait. I need a paycheck as much as anybody."

Helen glanced at her watch, and I felt her attention drifting away.

"So, you have no idea where the money went?" I blurted out.

Helen's mouth screwed up in a look of annoyance. "I already told the police, I have no clue. Wendy insisted on taking care of the books. I had no idea the money was gone until Marvin showed up and started shouting accusations." She stepped toward Marvin's cabin. "Which reminds me, I'd better get to this meeting." She raised her hand to knock.

"What about Preston's murder?" I asked, and her hand froze.

Helen turned to me, with her eyes wide. "Preston's dead? How? When?"

"Someone killed him yesterday afternoon at his house." I watched for her reaction, but she only shook her head.

"My God, who would do such a thing?"

Exactly what I am wondering. "The police are looking into it."

She laid her fingers on her lips. "I suppose it could be whoever benefited from both his and Wendy's death. I have to assume Wendy left everything to Preston, so maybe whoever is next in line didn't want to wait his turn. That's the most logical answer."

Before I could ask who might inherit from Preston, Marvin opened the door. I had to wonder if he'd been listening on the other side. He certainly didn't seem surprised to see me again as he ushered Helen inside and shut the door.

As I walked back to the office, I pondered Helen's last remark. Who stood to gain with both Wendy and Preston gone? Kurt was the obvious choice, except I knew that Wendy had essentially left Preston nothing. That meant Kurt, in turn, would also get nothing. But maybe Kurt didn't know that. If Wendy and Preston didn't have wills, would Kurt be the automatic heir? Was he the closest surviving relative? I didn't know a lot about estate laws, but it gave me something to think about. Along with all the other bits that made no sense.

Like who would kill Wendy in the first place? Were the broken windows at Invisible Prints an act of vandalism or a break-in? Who had provided the anonymous tip to Marvin, and what did it have to do with Wendy's death?

I had too many questions and too few answers. I

cut through the dining room and entered the office. I spent the rest of the workday at the computer. When quitting time arrived, I shut everything down, updated my time card, and walked to my car, shivering in the cool air.

Traffic was moderate on the drive home. When I pulled in front of the house a few minutes later, I found Ashlee's car already hogging the driveway. I gathered my purse, locked my car, and headed up the front walk. Before my foot touched the bottom porch step, the front door flew open and Ashlee popped out.

"Dana, let's go sign the lease for that apartment. I talked to Brittany, and she used to date a guy who lived in the complex. She said everyone there is supernice and no one ever steals your parking space."

"How about I put my purse down first, and then we'll talk?"

Ashlee stepped onto the porch, crowding me, and closed the door behind her. "What's to talk about? We both liked the place."

"Didn't you find another one online that you wanted to visit?"

Ashlee shrugged. "I don't think we need to now, especially since the rent on this one is so good."

"Speaking of rent, how is that going to work? Not to mention the utilities and security deposit."

"We'll split everything fifty-fifty. I might need

you to spot me my half of the security deposit, but I'll pay you back."

That's exactly what I was afraid of. We hadn't even moved in, and she was already missing a payment. "Maybe I don't have enough money saved for the entire deposit." In reality, I'd been setting aside a small amount each month and had built up a nice little nest egg, knowing I'd be moving out of Mom's house someday, but I didn't care for the way she was railroading me here.

"Then I'll borrow the money from Mom."

I put my hand on the doorknob. "Speaking of Mom, isn't she expecting us for dinner?"

"She's out with Lane."

Again? How serious were these two getting? "Then I'm at least eating a sandwich before we go. Jason's picking me up later for a movie, and I might not have another chance."

"They sell snacks at the theater," Ashlee said.

"At ridiculous prices. If I bought a large popcorn, I wouldn't be able to afford my half of the deposit." I shoved past her and went inside. "It'll only take a minute."

I dropped my purse on the table and opened the fridge door, studying my options. Pretty soon, this was how all my dinner preparations would go, except the house would be full of Pop-Tarts, frozen waffles, and Top Ramen, not low-fat dressing, fat-free milk, and vegetables. Not seeing much else, I threw together a sandwich of natural peanut butter and sugar-free jelly.

I settled down at the table to eat. Ashlee sat across from me, staring at me as I took each bite. I chewed slower and slower and watched her press her lips together to keep from saying anything. I may have smirked a little, because she slapped her hand on the table.

"Knock it off, Dana. We need to hurry or that apartment could be gone."

"Funny, when I suggested we might want to sign the lease, you couldn't be bothered until you'd done a single-male head count."

"Well, now I'm ready."

"Fine, I'm almost done." I resumed chewing at regular speed and finished the sandwich. I put my plate in the dishwasher, washed my hands, and picked up my purse.

Ashlee grabbed her keys and darted for the door. "I'll drive."

I couldn't have argued if I wanted. By the time I reached the driveway, she was buckled in. I got into the passenger side and watched the houses whiz by as Ashlee raced across town.

We told the woman in the rental office why we were there, and she escorted us to the apartment for a walk-through. We noted minor things that needed to be fixed, and then the rental agent walked us back to the office for the paperwork. According to the hours etched on the door, the rental office was open until seven, and the woman behind the desk seemed determined to keep us there until closing. She hummed to herself as she sorted through papers in a file folder, eventually pulling out a pair of forms. She chatted with us while we filled in the blanks, making it nearly impossible to concentrate. When we handed back the finished forms, she double-checked our information in case we'd missed anything.

As she chattered on about the potlucks and singles mixers they occasionally held, I kept an eye on the wall clock, watching as each tick brought me a second closer to half past six. Jason was picking me up at seven, and I was still in my scuzzy work clothes. Not good.

Another three minutes zipped by while the woman nattered on about the new gym equipment and landscaping improvements, as though we were still considering moving in, rather than filling out the paperwork to reserve a place.

"Yes, the place is lovely," I interjected as she got ready to launch into a description of every machine in the gym. "What do we need to do, now that we've completed the paperwork?"

The woman shuffled the papers into a stack. "I'll need the security deposit, and, of course, I'll have to do a credit check, though you two seem like nice, honest girls."

I knew a lot of nice, honest girls with poor credit, but I didn't comment. Instead, I pulled out my checkbook and wrote out the specified amount. "You can pay me your half when we get home," I told Ashlee.

"You bet, sis," she answered, which was her way

of saying I'd be chasing her all week for her share. I didn't have time to argue with Ashlee right now. I needed to get home.

I tore the check out and handed it over. The woman paper-clipped it to our forms and shoved it in an already-brimming drawer. I had to wonder if the paperwork would actually get processed.

"How long until we can move in?" I asked.

"As soon as I get the results of your background check and our maintenance crew cleans the place," the woman said. "I'll give you a call when that's done."

I stood, and Ashlee matched my movements. "Thanks so much for your help," I told the woman. I hustled through the exit and waited with one hand on the car door handle while Ashlee clicked the lock button on her remote. The good thing about Ashlee's driving was that we made it home in record time, giving me precious extra minutes to shower and change. I was zipping up my dark blue jeans, which accompanied my V-necked blouse, when I heard the doorbell ring. I didn't need to check the clock to know it was seven. Jason was never late.

When I entered the room, Jason smiled in a way that let me know he liked my outfit. He held out his arm, elbow bent, and I linked my arm through his. Ashlee was grinning all the while.

"Don't wait up," I told her.

She snickered. "Oh, please, you'll be home by nine-thirty."

Jason leaned toward me. "Just for that, I say we stop for coffee after the movie."

"An excellent idea, sir." I picked up my jacket, and we walked to his silver Volvo.

As we passed my rental car, Jason nodded at it. "Whose car is that?"

"Mine, temporarily. I'm getting some work done on my Honda." No way was I telling Jason about the threatening scratches on my hood. He'd only get upset.

Jason held the door while I climbed inside and we drove to the theater. He parked in the half-full lot, and we walked to the ticket window, which was lit well in the dark. As we got into line, I noticed a couple near the front. They kept offering each other quick kisses. The guy's hand appeared to feel some sort of magnetic pull toward the girl's butt, but she kept brushing his hand away. *Man, am I glad Jason isn't into public displays of affection.*

The couple moved forward and closer to the light from the ticket window, giving me a clear view. The man was Wendy's brother, Kurt. The girl he kept groping was Drew.

27

At the sight of Kurt, my stomach sank. Had
he gotten his anger out of his system when he
scratched up my car, or would he freak out when
he saw me?

Once the attendant handed over the tickets,
Kurt didn't so much as glance over his shoulder as
they entered the theater, but I still edged behind
Jason just in case. I nudged him. "Did you see
that?"

Jason craned his neck to see around the guy in
front of him. "See what?"

"Wendy's brother and Wendy's admin were
making out up there."

Jason stepped to the side for a better look. "Are
you sure? She's the one with the spiky hair, right?"

I eased past him. "I'm going to see which movie
they're here for." I ran to the entrance and peered
through the large window, knowing Kurt couldn't
see me outside in the dark. The lights inside illu-

minated the lobby like a stadium at a night game. Kurt and Drew were easy to spot in line at the snack bar. I returned to Jason.

"They're getting food," I told him.

"Did you want me to write about that in my next article?"

I poked his side, and he let out a grunt. "No, silly, I want to see what they're up to. Besides watching a movie, obviously."

Jason exhaled loudly. "I knew you were investigating. I knew you'd ignore my request that you stay out of this."

Oh yeah, I'd forgotten about his lecture at dinner the other night. Good thing I hadn't told him about my car. "Look, Wendy was my friend. We have to make sure the killer is caught. Especially now that the same person most likely killed Preston, too."

"*We?* How about the police? Seriously, Dana, what if that person comes after you?"

I spread my hands. "All I'm doing is talking to people. And you can help. Let's go find out where Drew and Kurt went."

Jason tried again to change my mind. "What if they're seeing that foreign romantic movie with the subtitles? I don't want to sit through that."

"They don't strike me as fans of subtitles any more than we are." The line moved forward. Now only one couple stood between us and our ticket purchase. "Don't you want to know what they're doing?"

"If they were making out, I'd guess they're on a date."

I tugged his sleeve. "But were they dating before Wendy was killed, or did they hook up after?"

Without answering, he pulled out his wallet, stepped up, and requested two tickets for the action movie. So much for buying tickets to whatever movie Kurt and Drew had selected. While he waited for his change, he said, "I'm not sure it makes a difference."

"What if they were in cahoots? Maybe after they started dating, Kurt found out Drew worked for his sister and convinced her to help kill Wendy."

Jason looked at his tickets. "Maybe we should go with a nice romantic comedy instead. These action movies are messing with your brain."

I stamped my foot, feeling like a little girl. "There's nothing wrong with my brain. It can't be a coincidence that those two are dating. We need to follow them."

"Watching them watch a movie won't tell us anything. You need to talk to them, which you can't do during a movie, unless you want to get thrown out."

Besides the fact that I wasn't sure I was ready to talk to Kurt yet—despite everything I'd told Jason about asking questions—Kurt scared the bejeezus out of me now. "We can sit behind them and eavesdrop. Maybe they're the annoying types who talk through movies." I grabbed his arm and pulled him toward the usher at the door. He allowed me to drag him along, probably figuring it was easier than arguing all night.

Inside the lobby, a handful of people milled about the displays and snack area, but Drew and Kurt weren't among them. "They must have gone inside already," I said.

"We need to get to our auditorium, too. The movie's about to start."

I paused, torn between tracking down Kurt and enjoying my evening. "Fine. We probably wouldn't have found out anything anyway."

I checked my ticket stub and found the right entrance. Inside, the lights were still up as ads played on the enormous screen. "Let's sit near the middle," I said to Jason. I climbed the first three steps and brushed the leg of the person sitting in the aisle seat. "Excuse me," I said automatically as I looked over.

Kurt looked back, and I saw his jaw clench. Next to him, Drew glanced at him nervously. I'd swear she looked guilty of something, but maybe it was the lighting.

"What are you doing here?" Kurt asked.

"We came to see a movie." I felt Jason step up beside me, and his presence gave me a surge of courage. "I didn't know you two knew each other," I said, nodding toward Drew.

Kurt straightened in his chair, and Drew rearranged her shirt and wiped at her lips. They'd clearly been pawing each other before I interrupted.

"We do," Kurt said. Short and to the point, much like the message on my hood.

"Have you known each other long?" I asked, locking eyes with Drew.

She licked her lips. "Sure. We've been seeing each other for months."

Interesting. "That was before you started working for Wendy, right?"

Drew started to answer, but Kurt placed a hand on her knee, and she closed her mouth.

"Did Wendy know you two were dating?" Jason asked. I was glad to know he had my back.

The lights in the theater dimmed as the ads on the screen faded to black.

Kurt shifted in his seat and faced forward. "Movie's starting."

The first preview appeared as music blasted from the speakers. Jason placed a hand on my back and guided me to the row behind Kurt and Drew. I plopped down in the seat and stared at the outline of Kurt's head. He leaned over and whispered something in Drew's ear. They both looked back at me. I lifted one hand in acknowledgment, but they didn't wave back. Instead, they rose, stepped into the main aisle, and headed for the exit.

Either the preview for the latest horror movie had offended them, or else my presence had made them nervous.

* * *

When the movie let out, Jason and I walked back to his car. The night air was much cooler than when we'd gone in. Jason placed an arm around my shoulders, and I snuggled up against him while we crossed the lot. He popped the locks and held the car door while I climbed inside.

He went around to his side and slid behind the wheel. "How about that coffee?"

"Sounds perfect. Might help thaw me."

Jason gave me a devilish grin. "I could help you with that."

That remark alone shot my internal temperature up a good five degrees. "Let's start with coffee and see where it goes."

He drove a few blocks and pulled into the Daily Grind parking lot. Once inside, we placed our orders at the counter and found a corner table.

I removed my jacket and hung it on the back of the chair. "I don't think I told you that Ashlee and I placed a deposit on an apartment right before you picked me up. We'll be moving in pretty quick." I felt a slight tug at my heart when I said that. I hoped Mom wouldn't be lonely.

Jason must have seen the indecision on my face. "Is your mom okay with the move?"

"She's probably more ready than I am. With her new job and Lane, she's clearly open to change." I marveled at how I'd originally been reluctant to move back home, and now I wasn't sure I wanted to leave. "By the way, Ashlee gave us permission to make out all the time in the new place."

"She's going to regret that offer." He gave me a salacious wink. "I'll be all over you."

Our banter was interrupted by the barista calling Jason's name. He hopped up to retrieve our drinks. After I'd sipped my white-chocolate mocha, I said, "I can't get Kurt and Drew out of my mind. Drew must have been hired at Invisible Prints after she started dating Kurt. She mentioned a while back that she'd only worked there a couple of months."

"You think Wendy hired Kurt's girlfriend as a favor?" Jason asked. "They didn't strike me as having the best sibling relationship."

"I haven't figured it out yet, but there must be a reason Drew chose Invisible Prints. Maybe she and Kurt had hatched a plan to kill Wendy, and the festival was their first opportunity."

"Would Drew agree to such a thing? She has no reason to kill Wendy."

"I know it's pretty far-fetched, but why else would she work there? Even if she really needed a job, I can't imagine she'd work for a woman who screwed over Kurt like that." I swirled the coffee around in my cup. "I wonder if the police know about their relationship."

Jason pulled his notebook out of his jacket pocket and jotted something down. "Detective Palmer hasn't mentioned it."

"Speaking of the good detective, has he told you anything new about Preston's murder?"

"All I know is he was killed in his living room. Someone probably attacked him from behind."

A chill ran up my back, and I clutched my coffee cup for warmth. Should have kept that jacket on. "So either someone snuck up behind him, or the killer was someone he knew well enough that he'd turn his back on them." The coffee in my stomach churned. "Any suspects?"

"No new ones. Preston didn't have much of a life outside of Wendy."

"Did the neighbors see anything?"

"One neighbor saw a man enter Preston's house not long before the murder. Police identified him as Marvin."

I pushed my coffee away. "He mentioned he had an appointment with Preston and that the police think he was the last one to see him alive. Maybe Marvin murdered him on his way out the door."

"That's definitely something the police are considering."

"But why would Marvin kill him? Preston was the last link to the missing money."

Jason used a napkin to wipe up a few drops of coffee, which had leaked from his cup. "Agreed. If he'd killed him in a fury, I'd expect him to stab him repeatedly, not slit his throat."

I realized that the folks two tables over were staring at us openmouthed. Our conversation must have been easy to overhear in the nearly deserted coffeehouse. I smiled in what I hoped was a reassuring manner. "Our movie let out a bit ago. We're trying to figure out the plot."

They both busied themselves with stirring their coffee, obviously not convinced.

I faced Jason. "What are the cops planning to do next?"

"I asked, but they didn't share their plan with this reporter."

Whatever course of action the police had outlined, I still needed a plan of my own. Before the killer struck again.

28

The next morning, the sky remained overcast as the sun tried to muscle its way through the mass of clouds. I dressed in my long-sleeved work shirt and khakis and grabbed a sweatshirt for good measure. Mom and Ashlee were still asleep when I got behind the wheel of the loaner car and drove to the body shop. I hadn't realized how much I'd missed my Honda until I spotted it waiting in the side lot. I studied the freshly painted hood from every angle. The guy had done a fantastic job.

I paid him and drove to work, parking in my usual corner spot. As I passed the dining room on the way to the office, the sounds of early-morning chatter and the clink of silverware reached me. Once inside the office, I shut the door to block out the noise and booted the computer. I was brainstorming potential new ad campaigns when the door opened, and Esther walked in.

Today she wore a denim shirt with embroidered

pigs along the bottom and little pink pig buttons down the front. I knew she loved finding embroidered shirts at craft fairs and street festivals, and she had a closet full to prove it.

"Morning, Dana. Are you busy today?"

"I'm working on new ideas to promote the farm, now that the festival is over. Is there something you needed me to do?"

Esther fiddled with a pig button. "Would you mind checking on Gretchen? She mentioned she has a hen house full of spa customers this morning, and she might need an extra hand."

"I'd be happy to. Let me wrap this up."

"Thanks, Dana. You're a dear." She walked out the door.

I finished the paragraph I'd been struggling with, saved the file, and stood. With breakfast now over, I cut through the dining room, where Zennia had already removed the tablecloths for laundering, and crossed the patio area. The path in front of the cabins was empty, and I wondered if Marvin had been at breakfast this morning or if he was hiding in his cabin. It certainly looked bad that he was the last person to see Preston alive. The police must be focusing closely on him.

I slipped through the tent opening to the spa and found Gretchen studying her appointment book. The creases in her forehead disappeared when she saw me.

"Dana, thank goodness. I've got back-to-back

appointments starting in five minutes and no time to mix ingredients for the facials. Could you do it?"

"If you'll give me instructions."

Gretchen led me to the area where I'd had my facial a few days ago and handed me an apron. I surveyed the table of jars and bottles full of mysterious items. She pointed to a jar of dark goo. "Don't worry about the black moor mud. That's ready to go." She laid a hand atop two other jars. "For the mix, you'll start with the clay and lavender flowers." She tapped a bottle with a stopper. "Add two drops of this essential oil." She listed a few more components and then ran back to the desk to greet her first client.

I repeated Gretchen's instructions in my head as I carefully measured out the ingredients and stirred them in the correct order, hoping I got the mixture right. When I finished, I set the bowl to the side and washed my hands at the nearby sink. I could hear Gretchen talking to someone in hushed tones in another section of the tent. I straightened the jars and bottles I'd moved around, used a nearby towel to wipe the sink area, and tidied up the rest of the stack.

As I headed outside, I met Lily on her way in. Her brown hair was swept up in a bun, wisps falling out the sides. With her long floral dress and old-style boots, she reminded me of an extra from an old *Little House on the Prairie* episode.

When she saw me, she flinched and clutched her head with one hand.

"Lily, are you okay?"

She rubbed her temple. "I can't get rid of this headache. I'm sure it's from the stress of Wendy's death. I'm hoping one of Gretchen's massages will help."

I moved aside as a woman exited the tent. Her relaxed countenance was the exact opposite of Lily's. "Wendy's death has hit us all hard," I said. "And now Preston's dead, too."

Lily dropped her hand. "Who's Preston?"

First, Helen didn't know, and now it was Lily. How had I become the official spokesperson for announcing Preston's demise? "Preston was Wendy's husband. He was also murdered."

Lily gasped. "My God, someone killed Wendy's husband? But why?"

Either Lily was taking acting lessons, or she truly had no idea who Preston was. If she didn't know Preston, then she had no reason to kill him. "The police are trying to answer that very question."

Her hand crept to her temple again. "Oh, I can't believe it. Now I feel even worse."

My curiosity meter swung to "High."

"What do you mean?"

"I . . . I've done some terrible things," she said, not meeting my eyes. "With everyone dealing with so much already, I can't believe I acted like that. I've got to fix this." She hurried toward the parking lot.

"But what about your massage?" I called after

her as she practically ran down the path. *And what about telling me what you feel so guilty about?*

"I'll reschedule," she yelled back.

I watched her disappear around the corner of the cabins. What exactly had she done? She didn't seem to be confessing to murder, but what else could it be?

"Was that my next client?" Gretchen asked behind me.

I turned toward her. "She had to leave."

"That was sudden." She gave a last look toward the path and shrugged. "Guess that frees up my time, and I owe you for helping me earlier. I could give you that cactus massage I mentioned a few days ago. You said you wanted to write about more spa services on our Web site. Now's your chance."

Here I'd helped the woman mix her mask ingredients, and to show her gratitude, she wanted to poke me with cactus needles! Some thanks. "Sorry, but I have a project to work on in the house." If I couldn't find anything, I'd make up something.

Gretchen raised her eyebrows. Her eyebrow ring moved along with them. "Can't it wait?"

Could my imaginary project wait? For a moment, my mind went blank, but then I remembered the file I'd been editing earlier. I crossed my arms. "I'm working on an important marketing document."

She peered at me. "You do know that the cactus paddles don't still have needles on them, right?"

They didn't? Well, that was a relief. "Sure, of course I knew that," I said. Gretchen grinned at me, clearly not fooled by my denial. "All right, so I didn't know."

"Does that mean you want to try the massage?"

I wavered for a moment. "Now that I know I won't be suffering some twisted acupuncture torture, I'm definitely interested, just not right now. I really do want to finish my project."

"Suit yourself." Gretchen went back inside the tent, humming.

I followed the back path behind the cabins to where Berta and her chicken cohorts pecked at the dirt, hoping to snag an extra seed they'd missed during an earlier feeding.

"I think you got it all," I told her.

Berta's head snapped up, a mean gleam in her eye. With a flutter of wings, she ran at the fence, trying to peck me through the wire.

"Hey, I was only trying to save you some time," I said. I moved on before Berta flew the coop and pecked my eyes out. At the pigsty next door, Wilbur wallowed in the mud, not bothering to stand when he saw my hands were empty of treats. What was with these animals today?

I cut past the redwood tree and was walking by the pool, when I saw Detective Palmer exit the dining room through the French doors. I did a double take. What was he doing here?

As he started across the patio, I intercepted him. "Looking for me?"

Detective Palmer gave me the once-over. "No. I was told the guest cabins are back here."

I clasped my hands together in anticipation. "Is this about Preston's murder?"

The detective pulled a stick of gum from his pocket, unwrapped it, and folded it into his mouth, placing the wrapper back in his pocket. "What makes you ask?"

"I know Marvin is staying here." I stepped closer. "Are you about to arrest him?"

"I'm here for follow-up questions. Nothing more."

"Oh." I felt disappointment bloom. Not only did I want the police to catch Wendy's killer, but I would have loved to see the big arrest before I read about it in one of Jason's articles. The detective started to walk away, and I spoke before he got too far. "Hey, I was at the movies last night."

"Congratulations," Detective Palmer said with nary a hint of sarcasm as he turned back.

I stopped myself from rolling my eyes. "There's more."

"I was hoping."

"I saw Wendy's brother, Kurt, there, with her assistant, Drew."

"Sometimes other people go to the movies, too."

Geez, this guy should do stand-up. "But they were together. And Drew said they've been in a relationship for a while."

He chewed his gum. "Yes, she told us the same thing."

This time, I did roll my eyes. "You mean you already knew?"

Detective Palmer's gum chomping sped up. "Believe it or not, we are professionals. We don't sit around all day waiting for clues from private citizens who fancy themselves modern-day Nancy Drews."

I felt my cheeks heat up. "I'm trying to help."

"Then stop involving yourself in this case."

Where was the fun in that? "Look, I want to make sure Wendy isn't forgotten. She was a good person, no matter what anyone says."

"Which is why we're logging so many man-hours. To make sure she gets justice, as well as Preston. That's our job, not yours."

I looked at my shoes. "Duly noted." Of course, if I found a clue or two myself, the police could wrap up the case that much faster.

Detective Palmer shook his head and moved toward the cabins. I watched his retreating back, troubled by the thought running through my mind: *Is he any closer to solving the case, or is he as stumped as I am?*

29

I went back into the office and worked steadily
on the marketing campaign until lunchtime.
Zennia waved off my offer to help serve, and I
decided to take an actual lunch break for a
change. I grabbed my keys and purse, jumped
into my car, and revved down the road, swinging
through the McDonald's drive-thru for a Big Mac
and an apple pie.

Taking my delicious treasures home, I settled in
at the kitchen table and unwrapped my burger. As
I was sinking my teeth into the first bite, Mom
came out of her bedroom. She eyed the take-out
bag and the sauce on my chin, but she didn't comment as she adjusted the collar on her navy blue
blouse, then felt along her pearl necklace to make
sure the clasp wasn't showing.

I chewed and swallowed. "You look fabulous."

"Thank you. I'm off to work."

Oops, what kind of a bad kid am I? I hadn't even

remembered to ask about the first day at her new job. Must be because of all the people dying around here. "How do you like your job?"

"I think I've found my element. The customers are so friendly and seem to appreciate my advice on colors and accessories."

"You're a natural. I've always thought you were one of the best-dressed ladies in town."

Mom tittered. "Oh, stop. You're just buttering me up so I won't mention that lunch of yours. Is that an apple pie peeking out of your bag?"

I folded down the top of the bag. "Thanks for not mentioning it." I winked at her.

Mom sat down and adjusted one earring. "What have you been up to lately? I haven't seen much of you."

I wiped my mouth. "The usual. Work and a date with Jason." I left out all my activities related to Wendy's and Preston's murders, knowing my involvement would ruin her good mood.

"Didn't you have dinner with his parents the other night? How did that go?"

"Great. They were very friendly."

Mom stopped fiddling with her earring and folded her hands on the table. "What does this mean for your relationship with Jason? Are you two getting serious?"

I pulled at the lettuce on my burger, considering. "I think we're both happy with where our relationship stands right now. I freaked out a bit when he first said he wanted me to meet his parents, but then I decided he was just taking advantage of their visit. They don't come to Blossom Valley very often. I don't think he meant anything more by it." If he did, he hadn't shared it with me.

"If you say so. Jason's a nice boy." Mom stood and kissed the top of my head. "I'd better run. I'd hate to be late on my second day."

I took another bite of burger as Mom gathered her jacket and purse and went to the garage. I listened to the garage door rumble up, the car engine start, and the door rumble down. While I ate my food in silence, I thought about Lily and what terrible thing she could have possibly done. Had she forgotten to bring her reusable bags to the store? Left the water running while she brushed her teeth? Obviously, the issue was more serious than that, but what was it?

Too bad I didn't have some way to get in touch with her. She was obviously hiding something. Maybe I could ask Gretchen later if she had her number. In the meantime, I'd just have to focus on someone else. Like Drew and Kurt. I needed to learn more about how Drew got her job at Invisible Prints. Struck with an idea, I pulled out my cell phone. *Why don't I just track down Drew and ask her?*

I looked up the number for Invisible Prints and dialed. I wasn't sure if Helen would be at the office, now that the place was basically shut down, but she seemed to be the type who wouldn't quit working until the police chained the door shut.

Sure enough, on the third ring, Helen picked up. "Invisible Prints."

"Hi, Helen. This is Dana Lewis. I spoke with you at the spa yesterday when you stopped by to see Marvin."

"Yes?" She sounded perplexed.

I gripped the phone tighter. I'd rehearsed in my head what I was going to say, but now I worried my story would sound as fake as the processed cheese on my burger had tasted. "I was trying to reach Drew and was hoping you'd have her home number. I feel so bad that she's out of work right now, and as luck would have it, Esther might have an opening for her." I leaned my forehead on the table. All this lying was exhausting.

"How nice, Dana. I'm sure Drew would love to hear from you."

I wouldn't bet on it, not after our brief conversation at the movie theater last night, but I didn't argue.

"Let me see if I can find her number."

I heard pages rustling. "If it's not too much trouble, could I have her address, too?"

"Her address?" Definite reservation in her tone this time.

I scrambled to put her at ease. "Yes, last time I saw her, she mentioned how much she loved snickerdoodle cookies, and I baked a fresh batch this morning." This last part was definitely over the top. I felt like my insides were being squished in a vise.

"I guess that would be fine." She listed the address and phone number, and I entered the information into my cell phone. Then I thanked her and quickly hung up before she thought too hard about my preposterous story.

Mission accomplished, I took a few minutes to savor the apple pie, the filling still plenty hot. I was chewing the last bite when I heard the front door open. Ashlee bounced into the kitchen, her arms up in victory.

"Dana! The apartment manager called! We passed the credit check, and they've already cleaned the place. What do you think about moving in this weekend?"

I almost gagged on my pie. "This weekend? It's a little soon, isn't it?"

Sure, I'd signed the lease. Sure, the apartment was empty and ready. But deep down, I still didn't quite believe that we were moving out of our childhood home and into an apartment together.

Ashlee dropped her Coach knockoff purse on the table and plopped onto a chair. "What are you waiting for?"

"I need to pack."

"Pack what? Your five shirts and your old Cabbage Patch doll?"

I wanted to smack her, but she had a point. Packing would only take me a couple of hours—if I folded my clothes really slowly. I pulled a napkin from the take-out bag and wiped my hands. "We haven't even ordered the furniture we picked out yet. Where will we sleep?"

"We can buy the furniture tomorrow and set up delivery. If they have to ship it, we can drag out our sleeping bags for a few days. It'll be like a camp-out."

The image of draining my nice little nest egg even further filled my head. The pie in my belly bubbled up. "I guess we could buy a couple of really necessary items," I managed to choke out. "Maybe Mom'll let us take that old TV in the garage she doesn't use anymore."

"God, Dana, do you know how old that thing is? It's got that huge bulb in the back. I can't even lift the thing."

I flexed a bicep. "We'll lift it together. New TVs cost money."

Ashlee groaned. "I can suffer for a while with that thing, but then we're getting a brand-new plasma TV, no arguments."

I had plenty of arguments, but I'd save those for when we went TV shopping.

Ashlee went into the kitchen and started rummaging through the refrigerator. I crumpled up my napkin, tossed it in the paper bag with the rest of my lunch wrappings, and stuffed everything into the trash can under the sink. Talking with Ashlee had momentarily distracted me from my plan to visit Drew. One look at the clock showed I'd have to wait until after work. I didn't have time now.

With a resigned sigh, I got back into my car and returned to the farm, already thinking about questions to ask Drew, such as whether Kurt had anything to do with her being hired at Invisible Prints. And what, if anything, she knew about Wendy's death. Every time I saw Drew, she looked more tired and stressed. Considering her boss had been murdered, two million dollars was missing, and she'd been laid off, I didn't blame her for seeming so concerned. But was there more bothering her, just in case that wasn't enough?

The afternoon crawled by. No matter how many times I looked at the clock, it didn't move any faster. When I'd about given up hope of ever ending the day, I hit my eight-hour mark. With renewed vigor, I yanked the bottom desk drawer open, removed my purse, and updated my time card. By now, my expectations for my talk with Drew were so high that I knew she'd have to confess to Wendy's and Preston's murders for me to feel satisfied. In truth, she'd probably reveal nothing.

But you never knew how these things might go. And that's what I was counting on.

30

Drew lived in one half of a duplex on the south side of town. The paint was faded and the venetian blinds in the windows on her side were bent in places, but the yard was tidy and the flowers in the beds were fresh.

I rang the doorbell. After a moment, footsteps sounded from within and the door swung open. Drew blinked at me, momentary confusion written on her face.

"Oh, it's you," she said, her words slightly slurred.

Had I awoken her from a nap, or had she been drinking?

"Hi, Drew. I was in the neighborhood and thought I'd stop by. Mind if I come in?" I stepped forward before she could give my request too much thought. She automatically moved back.

Three short steps brought me into a modestly furnished living room. The slightly stained brown carpet looked freshly vacuumed. The battered coffee table was recently polished. I settled onto the sofa and sank into the cushions. I noticed the slipcover felt crisp and new under my hands.

Drew stood near the couch, swaying slightly. I got a whiff of fruit mingled with the stronger odor of alcohol. Yep, she'd definitely been drinking. Any second, she might topple over like a mighty redwood at the hands of a saw blade.

I hurried across the room, removed a straight-backed chair from the corner, and then placed it behind her, easing the seat into the backs of her knees. She collapsed and stayed there. I reclaimed my spot on the sofa.

"You okay, Drew?" I asked, praying she didn't slide off the chair and onto the floor. I wasn't sure I could lift her, and I'd hate to leave her there.

Tears ran down Drew's cheeks. "Nothing's okay. This wasn't supposed to happen."

"What exactly are you talking about?"

Drew gave me an incredulous look as though I was the drunk one. "Wendy. She's dead. And Preston."

"Do you know something about that?" I scooted to the edge of the cushion. "If so, you need to tell the police. It might help them figure out who's behind these deaths."

Drew started to jab a finger in my direction, but then she let it fall back in her lap. "Don't you think I want to? Kurt would kill me."

I pressed my hands together. *Is she telling me that Kurt was responsible?* "Did Kurt murder his sister?"

I whispered. My voice sounded deafening in the silent room.

More tears slid down her cheeks as she shook her head. "No. I got Wendy killed."

My heart beat faster. "Are you saying that you did it?" I was still whispering, afraid Drew might clam up if I spoke too loud.

"No, but I blabbed to Marvin that all the money had disappeared at Invisible Prints. I know that's why Wendy was killed."

I nearly fell off the couch. Drew was the source of the anonymous tip? "The police don't know for sure why Wendy was murdered," I said. Though odds were good, the missing money was involved.

"The day after I told Marvin, Wendy got her throat slit. For all I know, he's the one who did it." She slumped down on her chair, sliding a bit.

I wondered if I should prop her back up, but I decided not to disrupt the conversation. "How did you know about the missing money, anyway?"

Drew hiccupped. "I'm thirsty." She staggered to her feet, momentarily clutched the chair for balance, then lunged across the room in what, I could only assume, was the direction of the kitchen. I heard a refrigerator door open, bottles were clanking, and then the fridge door slammed shut. A *clink* here, *bang* there, and Drew reappeared, gripping a wine cooler in both hands as though it might slip out of her grip and run away.

I stared at the bottle, transfixed. She was drunk

on wine coolers? I'd never been positive those things even contained alcohol.

Drew tried to sit back on the chair, missed, and fell to the floor, landing on her butt. "Good enough," she mumbled. She licked where the wine cooler had sloshed out of the open bottle and spilled on her hand.

I thought about helping her up, but she looked pretty comfortable on the floor. "So how did you discover the money was missing?" I asked again.

She waved the bottle at me. "You think you're so smart, don't you?"

I put a hand to my chest. "Not at all. That's why I need your help figuring everything out." Time for a new tack. "How'd you meet Kurt?"

"At the bowling alley. My friend threw a singles party and we ended up on the same team. We can't bowl at all, but we hit it off all right."

"Were you working for Wendy then?"

Drew held up the bottle and studied the label. "Naw, I was in between jobs."

I took the bottle from her hands and set it on the coffee table. "Did Kurt get you hired at Invisible Prints?"

She snorted. "Guess you're not that smart after all."

I worked to keep the exasperation out of my voice. "Why don't you help me out here?"

"Kurt told me all about his sister. How she took everything he ever wanted his whole life. How she always kissed up to their mom and dad so they'd love her best. She even got their mom to leave all the money to her so poor Kurt was left flat broke."

I'd heard all this before, but I nodded along to keep her talking. "What else did he tell you?"

"He knew she was a crook. Always had been. So he came up with this great idea to get back at her."

"Tell me about it," I said.

Drew hiccupped again. "Kurt saw an ad in the paper for a receptionist at Invisible Prints. He helped me dummy up a résumé, make some fake references. Then I lowballed my salary requirements. Kurt knew Wendy would want to hire cheap." She let out a laugh and used the back of her hand to wipe the spit from her lip. "She even called one of my friends I'd listed as a reference, and my friend pretended she was some muckety-muck at a big company. And Wendy was dumb enough to believe her."

I stiffened at this attack on my friend. "Wendy never struck me as dumb."

Drew sniffled. "No, and now she's dead." She reached for the half-empty wine cooler on the coffee table and stared into its depths.

"What happened when you started working for Wendy?"

"Kurt was sure she was running a scam. Once I got hired there, he wanted me to spy on her. If I could find something that would prove she was a big phony, Kurt would expose her and ruin her reputation. I followed her to appointments and dug through company e-mails, but I never could find anything. Not until I went old-school."

I waited, but Drew's gaze focused on a stain on the carpet and stayed there.

"What did you do?" I asked.

Drew's head snapped up. "What?" She took a swig from the bottle. "Oh, right, I went through the shredder clippings. Wendy bought these cheap-ass shredders for everyone. She thought 'cause it was crosscut that you couldn't read anything once you shredded it, but you can. It's just in shorter strips. The strips clump together sometimes, so it's easy to figure out which strips go together."

I made a mental note to replace the shredder at the farm. "And you found proof that Wendy was stealing?"

"I wasn't sure what I'd found, but I told Marvin about it. I would have found it sooner, only it was the wrong shredder."

Before I could ask what that meant, someone knocked on the door. I'd been so intent on what Drew was saying that I literally jumped, all my nerves springing to life. I stayed silent, willing Drew to do the same. Maybe a magazine salesman was at the door, one who would give up and go away, so we could get back to who had killed Wendy.

The knock came again, and Drew used the seat of the chair to rise, almost pulling the chair down on top of her instead.

"Wonder who that could be," she said as she reeled to the door.

She turned the knob. Whoever was on the other side shoved it open, whacking into Drew and sending her back to the carpet on her rump.

"Jesus, Drew," Kurt said as he appeared in the doorway. He grabbed her arm and yanked her to her feet. "Why aren't you answering your cell? I got worried."

I felt sweat break out all over my body. If Kurt had scratched up my car over me asking a few simple questions, what would he do when he found out his girlfriend had been blabbing to me?

31

Kurt hadn't noticed me yet. I rose from my spot on the sofa, readying myself in case he reacted badly to my presence. "Drew and I were talking," I said, sounding a lot braver than I felt.

He jerked his head around and glared. "What are you doing here?" He gripped Drew's shoulders and gave her a little shake. "Have you been drinking?"

"Drinking away my pain," she said.

Oh, boy.

"Drew told me she's the one who blew the whistle on Wendy's embezzlement," I blurted out. "After you convinced her to spy on your sister, that is."

Kurt let go of Drew and moved toward me. I wondered if I'd overstepped my bounds. With a drunken girlfriend as the only witness in this tiny place, who knew what he might do to me?

"I was sure Wendy was conning people," he

growled at me. "She always had something going. I wanted to ruin her, like she ruined me. She took away my whole life."

"Do you blame her for your wife leaving?" I asked, mentally cursing my inability to keep quiet.

Kurt squeezed his hands into fists. "My wife always had expensive tastes, and that requires money. If I'd gotten my fair share of the inheritance, I'd still be married." Drew let out a little whimper, and Kurt patted her arm. "Hey, I'm glad we met, honey. Don't get upset." He faced me again. "Once Drew told Marvin what she'd found, I could watch Wendy's life fall apart. No way could she talk her way out of this one."

"So, you're saying you didn't need to kill her, since you were going to mess up her life instead?"

"You got it. I planned to sit back and enjoy the show. That's it. I'm not a violent guy."

I put my hands on my hips, completely forgetting to keep my defenses up. "Then how do you explain my car hood?"

Confusion crossed Kurt's face, and I felt an inkling of doubt. "I don't know anything about your hood."

"Are you saying that you didn't scratch 'back off' in the paint?"

Drew leaned against Kurt, and he used one hand to prop her up. "If I wanted you to back off, I'd tell you to your face. In fact, I have, more than once, but you don't seem to be getting the message."

If Kurt hadn't done it, who else would have scratched my car? I looked at Drew. "Was it you?"

"Nope." She waggled a finger at me. "Somebody doesn't like you." She slapped a hand to her mouth and gagged a couple of times. Then she threw up all over the carpet.

That was my signal to leave. I moved to the door as the first acidic smells of the mess on the floor assaulted my nose. Kurt made a disgusted noise and disappeared into the kitchen, returning almost immediately with a roll of paper towels. Drew stared at her shoes, mesmerized by the goo that ran down the sides.

"I can show myself out." I slipped out the door, keys already in hand, the faint stink of vomit still clinging to my nostrils. As I headed to my car, I almost bumped into Helen as she came up the walk.

She raised her eyebrows. "Dropping off your snickerdoodles?" she asked.

For a second, I had no idea what she was talking about. Then I remembered my ridiculous excuse for needing Drew's address. "All taken care of," I said vaguely. "What brings you here?"

Helen held up an envelope. "Drew's two-week severance. With me leaving, and the company in limbo, I have no idea when, or even if, she could return to work. I don't want to string her along. I had business in town today, so I thought I'd deliver the check in person."

I studied Helen with her business suit and professional haircut. "You sure got hired at that new place fast. Any chance you were already looking?"

She narrowed her eyes. "I'm a well-respected member of the green community. I'm often approached with job offers from other companies."

I wasn't buying it. "But Wendy just died. Either the place where you're going has a very streamlined hiring process, or else you accepted the offer before Wendy's death."

Helen clutched the envelope tighter, leaving creases in the paper. "Perhaps."

"But Invisible Prints was your life. I can't imagine that you'd accept another job, unless you felt Wendy's company was failing." Then I had another thought. "Did you know about the missing money before Wendy was killed?"

Helen tossed her head. "Wouldn't I have said something if I'd known?"

Not exactly a denial. "I don't know, would you?"

Helen checked her watch. "Oh, for heaven's sake, I don't have time for this."

I crossed my arms. "Tell me the truth, and I'll stop pestering you."

"Do you have any idea how hard it would be to stay in this industry if word got out that Wendy stole all that money? No way would people believe that I wasn't involved."

"What about all that respect you were just talking about?"

Helen shook her head. "That's no good against the rumormongers. They would have dragged me down, right along with Wendy. As soon as I realized what she'd done, I started looking for another job. Once I landed something, then I would have gone to the police, but Wendy was killed before that happened." She moved forward and I stepped aside. "Happy now?" she asked.

"Very. Thanks."

She huffed past me, and I turned toward my car, thinking about the information I'd just gathered. I'd confirmed why Drew was working at Invisible Prints and who had told Marvin about the missing money. And Helen had admitted she knew about the money before Wendy was killed, but she had decided to pursue a new job before reporting it. But what, if anything, did all of that have to do with Wendy's murder?

The next morning, I parked my Honda in a vacant spot at the farm and walked along the path past the vegetable garden. As I neared the corner of the cabins, I saw Lily over by the spa entrance.

"Lily!" I called.

She looked back, a frown on her face. "Why are you here?" she demanded as I caught up to her.

Yikes, how offended should I be? "Well, I do work here."

"Sorry, that sounded terrible."

She put a hand to her temple, as she had during our previous conversation, and I had to wonder if I was the cause of her headaches.

"If I'm ever going to soothe my spirit, I need to surround myself with positive things."

Am I negative? I'd always thought of myself as rather upbeat. "Something still bothering you? I didn't expect to see you back so soon after you rushed off yesterday."

"Gretchen was able to squeeze me in for an early-morning appointment. I've cleared my mental tensions, and now I must rid myself of the physical constraints."

"Good luck with that."

Lily reached into her purse and pulled out an envelope. "It must be divine intervention that I ran into you. I was planning to give this to Gretchen, but if I'm going to atone for my deeds, I need to face them head-on." She shoved the envelope into my hand. "Now, excuse me. Gretchen's waiting."

Wondering exactly what wrong she was righting, I opened the envelope. Inside was a stack of twenties, several hundred dollars' worth, judging by the thickness.

Why on earth is Lily giving me this? What is she paying for? Realization dawned.

"Hey," I called before she could disappear into

the tent, "you're the one who scratched my hood. Why?"

She stopped in midstride and faced me. She looked like she was ready to protest her innocence, but then her shoulders sagged. "I'm so embarrassed. I've been working on my anger issues with my therapist, but sometimes I can't control myself."

I didn't hide my irritation. "You scared the crap out of me."

"I'm sorry. I don't know what came over me. But you were asking all those questions like I was a suspect. Me! I'm a nurse. I help people, and you went and accused me of something as horrible as killing a person." She was starting to talk faster, her words flying. "All you were doing was stirring up trouble, and I wanted you to stop."

"That was a reason to vandalize my car?" A flash of inspiration struck. "Did you break all the windows at Invisible Prints, too?"

She flushed. "I didn't mean to. I went there that night to talk to someone and see where all that money went, but no one was there." She looked off toward the hills, but I was pretty sure she was really looking toward her memories of that night. "I stood outside, staring at the building that represented all these lies, and I was filled with such rage." She searched my face.

I couldn't condone her actions, but I could

definitely understand her fury at being duped. "You lost a lot of money," I said.

"It's not so much about losing the money, but that it wasn't used to do anything good. No one planted trees. No one supported the wind farms. While I was busy flying all over the country, my money did nothing." The flush reached the tips of her ears. "I only meant to break one window. I picked up a rock and threw it at the closest one. The sound of the breaking glass, the sense of power, it was so cathartic. I couldn't stop myself. I scooped up anything I could find and broke them all." Her face was colored a full-fledged fire engine red now. "I've been ashamed ever since, which is why I gave you that envelope a moment ago and sent Invisible Prints money to cover the damages." Lily laughed. "Funny, isn't it? As much money as I've already given them, I shouldn't have felt obligated, but I still did. And I got my first night's sleep last night."

"Now that I know who marked up my car, maybe I can sleep, too."

She had the good grace to drop her gaze. "I should really get that massage," she mumbled. With a sweep of her long brown hair, she turned and disappeared inside the tent.

I carefully tucked the envelope into my pocket and resumed my course toward the house, with my thoughts on Lily. She might have moved on, now that she'd paid for her actions, but I hadn't. If she was so angry that she couldn't stop herself from breaking those giant windows and scratching my car, then surely that same anger could have propelled her to kill Wendy. It only took a second to slit someone's throat. Lily could have acted before she even knew what she was doing.

Of course that didn't explain Preston's murder. Maybe he knew something, and Lily had killed him to protect herself, even if she'd claimed she'd never heard of him. What could he have known? And how could I find out?

32

I sidestepped a line of ducks headed for the pond out front, wondering about the motive for Preston's murder. Maybe the killer, either Lily or someone else, only *assumed* Preston knew something he shouldn't. That would make identifying the culprit almost impossible, but I felt confident that whoever killed Wendy was responsible for Preston's death as well.

Shoving these thoughts from my mind, I stopped at the office to stick the envelope full of money into my purse, type up the morning's blog, and post an update on Facebook. I then placed a call to Detective Palmer to let him know about Lily's anger management issues. He didn't answer, so I left a detailed message. He might need that information for the murder investigation. After I ended the call, I went to the lobby to see if Gordon had gotten feedback on the festival yet.

He was typing on the computer, referring to his

clipboard from time to time. His dark suit and striped tie added a touch of formality to the casual lobby. He held up one finger to indicate he'd be done in a moment. I straightened the brochures on the coffee table, plucked dead leaves off the ficus, and watched out the window as the ducks slid into the pond.

When Gordon cleared his throat, I swung around to face him and asked, "Have any vendors returned their comment cards for the festival?"

He reached under the counter and pulled out a stack of papers. "Most have, and the majority was positive. They liked the selection of vendors, the advertising, and the location."

"What about the negative comments?"

He shuffled through the stack. "They had the opposite opinion. Complained there wasn't enough advertising, the location was limited, and some of the vendors shouldn't have been included. One guy said he was disgusted to see a man peddling dog poop."

I laughed. "Yeah, Helen, a woman from Invisible Prints, said the same thing. We might need to deny that guy access next year."

"Speaking of next year, let's plan to hold the festival again. If we make the event big enough, even more people from out of town will visit, and they'll need a place to stay."

"Great. I'll work with the committee to come up with some new ideas for expansion."

Gordon straightened his tie. "I'm sure you will."

I stared. That was at least two votes of confidence this week. I could really get used to this new Gordon.

He resumed his work, and I saw him frowning at whatever he was reading on his clipboard. "'Gooey duck,'" he muttered under his breath. "What on earth is 'gooey duck'?"

"It's a clam," I volunteered. "Zennia made a clam dish for the guests a few days ago."

He jabbed the page with his index finger. "It cost how much?" he bellowed.

Uh-oh. "Zennia mentioned the gooey duck is expensive, but she really wants to draw more foodies to the spa, so she's offering unusual dishes."

Gordon violently twisted the ring on his pinkie. "I can't take it anymore."

Time for some damage control. "Have I mentioned how nice it's been to work with you lately? You've been so open-minded and pleasant."

He threw the clipboard on the floor, and I took a step back.

"Look where it's gotten me," he snapped. "Zennia's buying overpriced seafood. Esther's passing out free chocolate bars to every Tom, Dick, and Harry who shows up, and you . . ." He pointed his finger at me, and I gulped. "You ate my turkey!"

I pointed right back at him. "Not all of it. And I offered to buy you a new package."

Gordon threw a pen on the floor. It landed near the clipboard. He paced behind the counter. "I knew that instructor at the management seminar was full of it. He said I should be more trusting of my employees. He said that if I'd back off, you guys would excel at your positions. But have you? *No!*"

I started to defend myself, but he wasn't done. "You didn't even ask me about those stupid oinking pens you handed out at the festival. I'm surprised we're not bankrupt the way everyone around here spends money."

Gordon paused for breath, but I knew his ranting could last all day. Suppressing a smile at his antics, I hurried down the hall before he threw the computer monitor.

Esther and Zennia sat at the kitchen table, hunched over an open cookbook. They looked up as I entered.

"The jig's up," I said. "Gordon's back to his old management style. You know, the one where he yells at everyone."

"Oh, dear," Esther said.

"And here I was starting to like the new Gordon," Zennia said. "His aura was such a healthy color."

"Well, his aura is a solid black now. Just so you know, that gooey duck helped send him over the edge."

Zennia closed the cookbook and slid it on the shelf with the others. "Better make myself scarce for a while. Think I'll run into town for supplies." She grabbed her sweater and disappeared out the back door.

Esther rose and tugged down her denim shirt. "I suppose I should talk to Gordon. See if I can soothe his ruffled feathers." She walked toward the lobby.

Alone in the kitchen, I listened to the ticking of the rooster clock. My stomach growled. Driving home for lunch was a waste of gas, and stopping for fast food was a waste of money, especially since I needed to pay rent now. Instead, I rummaged around the pantry until I came up with a can of line-caught tuna and a box of whole wheat crackers. I added green onions and a small dab of Zennia's homemade tofu mayonnaise to the tuna before smearing it on a cracker. Not the most delicious lunch, but it'd get me through the day.

After I'd eaten, I cleaned up the kitchen and headed out back to see if Gretchen needed any help. The temperature had dropped in the last hour. Dark clouds hovered on the horizon. A blue jay squawked in the redwood tree.

I heard shoes crunch on the gravel and looked over to see Jason approaching. I felt a rush of pleasure at the sight of him, quickly replaced by concern. He rarely visited me at work.

When he reached me, I took his hand, noticing how warm his long fingers were. "Jason, is everything okay?"

"Can't a guy surprise his girl at work?" He planted a kiss on my lips and it sent a sizzle down to my toes.

When we broke our lip lock, I gave him a goofy grin. "You can surprise me like that anytime you want. Every day, in fact."

Jason chuckled. "I just might."

We settled at one of the picnic tables, and I rested my elbows on the wood surface. "Have your parents gone home?" I asked. "You mentioned they'd be leaving."

"Left this morning. By the way, my mom adores you. Says you're so polite and well-grounded."

I practically glowed at the compliment. "She couldn't have been nicer to me. I wish I hadn't let my own insecurities get the better of me. I would have enjoyed their visit more."

"Don't worry. Every time I see them, I feel like I'm twelve years old again."

"Funny how moms have that effect on their kids." I traced a groove in the surface of the redwood table and picked at a sliver that stuck out. "Any news on the murders?"

Jason gave me a crooked smile. "Here I thought we were having a pleasant conversation about mothers."

"We were. Now I'm ready to talk about murder. A total coincidence, by the way." It was Ashlee, not my mom, who usually led me to thoughts of murder.

"I do have some news," he said. "Detective Palmer said they're closing in on the killer."

I straightened up in anticipation. Was this madness about to end?

Then why didn't Jason look happy?

33

Jason's serious expression curbed my elation as questions flew out of my mouth. "The police have identified the killer? Do you know who it is?"

He shook his head. "No. Detective Palmer won't release the name until they have enough evidence. The DA would refuse to press charges with what the cops have right now."

"Did Detective Palmer give you any indication about who it might be, or at least if it was a man or a woman?"

"Not a clue. You know how tight-lipped he can be. But he's confident they have the right person in their sights."

I broke off the wood sliver I'd been fiddling with and dropped it on the patio. "How infuriating. I can't imagine being a cop and watching someone I knew was a killer walk around, free as anybody."

"They'll get him."

"The sooner, the better."

We chatted for a few more minutes before Jason kissed me again and walked to his car. I watched over the hedge as he climbed into his Volvo. My warm feelings for him intermingled with my frustration over the police being unable to make an arrest. At last, I rose and stretched. Time to get back to work.

The rest of the day passed quickly as I hammered out more details for my marketing project. As I was approaching the end of the day, my cell phone rang. I pulled it from my pocket and checked the caller ID. Kimmie. What did she want?

"Hello," I said.

"Dana, it's Kimmie. I still haven't received those status reports from you. I feel completely in the dark on this whole Wendy thing."

Considering I was the only one of us working on Wendy's murder, I wasn't surprised. "I'm making progress," I said. "How about you?"

"I haven't had time, but I thought we could meet at Le Poêlon tonight. You could give me the details in person, instead of typing everything up."

I glanced out the window and watched where the afternoon clouds had continued to move in. The air held the threat of rain. Did I want to risk driving to Mendocino during a storm? "Would this meeting include a meal?"

Kimmie sighed. "I suppose feeding you is the

least I can do. Even though you're not sending me updates, I know you've spent a lot of time talking to Wendy's associates."

Kimmie was finally acknowledging my efforts. And I'd get to try her food, too. That was definitely worth getting stuck in a deluge for. "How does seven work?"

"Make it eight. See you then." She clicked off.

As usual, Kimmie had the last word.

I finished up the day's work and drove home. I found a note on the kitchen table from Mom, letting me know she was out with Lane. I had no idea where Ashlee was, though odds were good she was on a date as well.

I watched television for a while, then went to my room and dressed for dinner in dark jeans, a drape-front white blouse, and boots. With my purse and keys in hand, I locked the front door on my way out. The first raindrops began to fall as I reached the driveway. Great.

Once at my car, I got inside and slammed the door before I got any wetter. Then I started up the engine and flicked on the wipers and headlights. The wipers made a squeaking sound as I drove through town, but at least traffic was light. People were probably settling onto their couches for the evening, not driving through a rainstorm on a twisting road for a free meal. But talking to Kimmie might shake a few ideas loose in my head.

I merged onto the highway and sped down the road, slowing as I reached the first curves. The dark pavement blended into the night. The white fog line was barely visible. At least the towering redwoods provided some cover from the rain.

As I eased around a curve, headlights from an oncoming car blinded me. For a moment, I couldn't tell if the car was in his lane or mine, and all I could do was send up a quick prayer. The car whizzed past, and I slowed down even further, wondering again what the heck I was doing.

By the time I came out of the trees, my hands were cramped from gripping the steering wheel, and my face hurt from clenching my jaw. I reached the intersection with Highway 1 and loosened my hold on the wheel, glad to be on a straight stretch of road. The parking lot to Le Poêlon was jammed with cars, but I managed to squeeze my Honda between an oversized SUV and a four-door sedan. I held my purse over my head as I ran for the entrance.

Inside the restaurant, I stopped at the hostess stand. A stylish young woman with platinum-blond hair cut short, and an impossibly thin body, looked down her nose at me. "Do you have a reservation?" Her cool tone implied she already knew I didn't.

Before I could answer, Kimmie swept in from the opposite direction. "She's with me."

The hostess immediately switched from condescending to acquiescent. "Of course, Mrs. Wheeler."

Kimmie grabbed my hand and led me through the dining room, winding past a series of small tables pushed close together. At last, we reached a

table for two next to the swinging door, back
where servers brought food from the kitchen. I
smirked. Not the best table in the place, but at
least she wasn't making me eat *in* the kitchen.

As I sat down, a waiter appeared so fast, I was
almost convinced he materialized right there at
our table. He started to offer me a menu, but
Kimmie waved it away.

"We're famous for our seared scallops," she
told me.

"Sounds delicious," I said.

Kimmie tilted her head. "I suppose you'll want
something to drink, too. A glass of chardonnay,
perhaps?"

"Just iced tea, thanks." No way was I ordering alcohol when I had to drive home in this weather.

The waiter disappeared as fast as he'd appeared,
and Kimmie leaned forward. "I've got ten minutes.
Is that enough time to fill me in?"

I unrolled my silverware and placed my napkin
in my lap. "I'll try. Earlier today, I found out that
Lily was the one who broke the windows at Invisible Prints. She also scratched up my car. Did I tell
you about that?"

Kimmie drew her head back. "No, but she
sounds crazy."

"She definitely has problems with her temper,
which makes me wonder if she flipped when she
found out about the missing money and killed
Wendy on the spot. I don't know why she would
have killed Preston, though."

"If she's nuts, maybe she didn't have a reason."
I looked down at my hands. How sad if Preston had been murdered for no reason. Kimmie was watching me, so I continued. "I also discovered that Drew and Kurt are dating. Kurt convinced Drew to get a job at Invisible Prints and spy on his sister. Once Drew found out Wendy had stolen the money, she reported it to Marvin. I can't imagine Kurt would kill Wendy before he witnessed the fallout. And Drew barely knew Wendy. It's possible that Wendy discovered Drew had blown the whistle on the embezzlement and confronted her about it that morning at the festival. Drew could have waited until Wendy was alone and killed her, but that scenario doesn't make much sense. As for Helen, it turns out that she had already discovered the missing money, but she was keeping quiet until she could line up another job. Maybe Wendy was feeling guilty about stealing the money and was going to confess, and Helen killed her to keep her quiet, hoping the missing money wouldn't be noticed right away. But thanks to Drew, Marvin found out about it anyway."

"Wow, you've really learned a lot." Kimmie used one long nail to scratch at a speck on the tablecloth. "I can't believe the police haven't solved this case. Why do I even pay my taxes if I can't expect better service?"

I almost told Kimmie about the police identifying a solid suspect, but I decided against it. Jason had told me that in confidence, and I'd already slipped up once before when speaking with Preston. Instead, I said, "It's only a matter of time."

She checked her watch. "Speaking of time, I keep meaning to stop by Invisible Prints, but I've been too busy. Wendy and I had tickets to a very exclusive fund-raiser tomorrow night. Everyone who's anyone will be there. The tickets are in her office, but that place is creepy, and I don't want to pick them up alone. Can you go with me?"

"You want to go now? No one will be there this late. How would we get in?"

"Wendy gave me a spare key, remember?"

My two earlier visits to Invisible Prints had both been brief, and I'd learned little. Surely, Wendy's office held some information. "Count me in."

A sizzle announced the arrival of my scallops, accompanied by the mouthwatering scent of herbs and butter. As the waiter set the plate on the table, Kimmie rose. "We'll leave when you're done eating. In the meantime, I have work to do."

I picked up my fork, ready to dive into the scallops. With the invitation to poke around Invisible Prints, I had to lecture myself to eat slowly and savor the meal. Still, I was anxious to get to the office. The police lacked the evidence right now, but maybe the killer had made a mistake. And I could find it.

34

After I'd devoured each scallop morsel and sopped up every drop of sauce with bread, I finished my iced tea and signaled to Kimmie. She excused herself from her conversation with a waiter and came to my table.

"All finished?" she asked.

I patted my belly. "I might not be able to stand up from this table! I'm so full."

"Well, try. We need to get over to Invisible Prints. I don't want to be gone from the restaurant too long."

"After that meal, accompanying you is the least I can do." I rose. "Let's take separate cars, so I don't have to double back."

"Fine. Are you parked out front?" When I nodded, she said, "My car's in back. We can meet at Invisible Prints."

I walked past the tables full of diners and out the front door of the restaurant. The rain fell steadily as I rushed to my car. Once inside, I ran my fingers through my wet hair and got out my phone. Mom and Ashlee were probably still on their dates, but I felt the need to call someone and let them know my plans. This weather was looking more treacherous every minute, and I wasn't crazy about driving in it.

After I left messages for them, I called Jason. "Hi, I just wanted to touch base. I'm over here in Mendocino and had the most amazing scallop dish of my life at Kimmie's restaurant."

"Are you gloating?" he asked. I could hear the teasing in his voice.

"Maybe a little."

"If you're done eating, does that mean you're about to drive home in this storm?"

"Afraid so, after a quick trip to Invisible Prints. Kimmie has to find some tickets she and Wendy purchased together, and she's too chicken to go by herself."

"Sounds like Kimmie. Drive carefully and call me as soon as you get home."

"Will do." I stuck the phone back into my pocket, started the engine, and followed the highway along the coastline. My headlights illuminated the bent eucalyptus trees, which bordered the road, looking like specters reaching down to pluck my car into the air. I almost missed the turnoff to Invisible Prints, the driveway nothing more than an extra dark shadow off to one side. Through the rain, the building itself was barely discernible.

I pulled into the driveway, parked as close to the front door as possible, and killed my headlights. Darkness fell over the car like a heavy blanket, making me feel all alone in the world. I listened to the rain drumming on my car roof until headlights swept up the drive. Kimmie pulled in next to me.

I took a moment to enjoy the dryness of my car, then stepped out and darted for cover under the eaves, motioning for Kimmie to join me as I ran by. While I shivered beneath the overhang, I watched as her car door opened and a large umbrella popped into view. She stepped out, as if on a Sunday stroll through the park, and walked to where I waited.

"Dana, you're going to get soaked. Why on earth don't you have an umbrella?"

I already was soaked, but she probably realized that. "I forgot to grab one on my way out the door."

"I always carry an umbrella with me. This type of foresight has helped me so much in life."

"Great. Let's get this over with." I moved to the side while she opened her purse. She pulled out a key and inserted it into the lock. Moments later, we were inside the building.

Even with so many windows, the interior was pitch-black on this dark night. I shuddered, wishing I didn't watch so many horror films. Kimmie hit the switch on the wall. A soft glow bathed the lobby. "I'm sure Wendy left the gala tickets in her office." She climbed the stairs, and I followed. She stopped at the first door and turned on the light inside the room.

I hadn't been inside Wendy's office on my earlier visits. While Kimmie rummaged through the desk drawers, I studied the room. The furniture was mostly glass and metal, its stark appearance reminiscent of Wendy's living room. The walls held pale prints of pink orchids and white daisies. On the desk, an eight-by-ten photo in a sterling silver frame showed Wendy and Preston laughing together. I looked away, and my gaze fell on the shredder. What had Drew said? That the scraps of paper were in the wrong shredder?

"Found them!" Kimmie held two tickets aloft for me to see before she stuffed them into her purse. "Thanks for coming with me. Now let's go. I need to get back to the restaurant." She hustled toward the door, but I didn't move.

"Can't you wait a few minutes?" I asked. "As long as we're here, let's look around."

Kimmie turned back. "What for?"

"Anything. I might find information that will help me figure out the motive for these murders."

She inched closer to the door. "I'm sure the police already have everything. Besides, what you're suggesting doesn't seem quite legal."

I gestured toward the desk. "We're here for a perfectly valid reason. You even used a key."

"Sounds sketchy to me. Do you have any idea what my friends would say if I got arrested for trespassing? They'd kick me right out of my Women of High Morals Club."

I wouldn't mind getting kicked out of a club with a name like that, but Kimmie seemed troubled by the idea. "No one's getting arrested. All you have to do is stand here. Come on, Kimmie. You're the one who insisted I find out who killed Wendy. The least you can do is spare a few minutes."

She yanked on her jacket lapels. "You might not care about your reputation, but I do. Make sure you close the door all the way when you leave. It locks automatically." She turned on her heel and strode out. All I could do was watch her, mouth agape, as she clomped down the stairs and out the door.

Now, what was I supposed to do? I was already here. It would be silly to leave without looking around, but I wasn't crazy about staying here alone.

Kimmie was probably right. The police must have found anything that might be important by now. But as I moved toward the door, I glanced again at the shredder. What had Drew meant when she said she would have found the evidence sooner, except it was in the wrong shredder? Had Drew's remark been the ramblings of a drunk, or did she have important information that she would have explained if Kurt hadn't shown up right then? It was definitely an odd comment. I'd take two minutes to call her about it, and then I was out of here.

I pulled out my phone, glad I'd stored Drew's

contact information on it. I tried to ignore the silent office and the dark outside as I waited for the call to connect. Drew answered on the second ring, sounding more sober than the last time we'd talked.

"Drew, it's Dana. I wanted to ask you about something you told me yesterday."

She interrupted me before I could ask. "Ignore everything I said. I was drunk. Kurt's a nice guy, and I don't want you to think he isn't."

"I don't want to talk about Kurt. It's those shredded documents you found."

Drew exhaled loudly into the phone. "I'm not an accountant. Who knows what I found? I only thought they were suspicious, but Marvin realized right away it was proof that Wendy stole all that money."

"But you said you found them in the wrong shredder. What did you mean?"

"Oh, that. I never found anything in Wendy's shredder, at least nothing I could piece together. But I figured as long as I was snooping, I might as well open all the shredders. Kurt just knew Wendy was up to no good. I found the documents in Helen's office. I guess Wendy figured she'd be doubly careful by using someone else's shredder to get rid of everything."

Or Wendy wasn't the one shredding the papers.

A chill ran through me.

Through the phone, I heard a voice in the background, and Drew said, "I gotta go." She hung up.

That was fine with me. I was too busy thinking about the implications of Drew finding the evidence in Helen's shredder. Was Helen shredding the documents to hide Wendy's illegal activities until Helen could line up a job? Or was Wendy really so crafty that she'd use Helen's shredder to point the finger elsewhere? She might be that smart, considering she'd embezzled two million dollars.

But who said Wendy had embezzled the money? We'd all assumed that the disappearing funds had led to her murder, but that didn't mean she was the guilty party. Wendy was terrible at math. She'd traded favors in high school so someone else would do her homework, and Preston had mentioned that he'd been the one to balance the checkbook at home. Hadn't Drew said that Wendy met with clients and lined up new customers, while Helen ran the back office? Which meant Helen was in charge of the books. How easy would it be to blame a dead woman for embezzling and send the police off in the wrong direction? Pretty darn brilliant, as a matter of fact.

Mind whirring, I realized I was still holding my phone and stuck it back into my pocket. Was Wendy's death a matter of convenience for Helen, or had she helped it along? Perhaps Wendy had found out about the embezzlement and realized Helen was responsible. Had she confronted Helen, and Helen killed her so she couldn't tell anyone? Or was I jumping to conclusions?

Still, if Helen was sloppy enough to shred incriminating documents in her own office, maybe more pieces were waiting for me to find. I might as well check, considering her office was next door. After that, I was definitely on my way.

I walked down the hall, listening to the rain pelt the windows. I saw the headlights of a car as it drove past on the highway, reminding me how far back from the road the building was set. I wondered if anyone could see the lights in the office as they drove by. I needed to leave before someone called the cops and I really did get cited for trespassing. Kimmie would have a field day.

The door to Helen's office was closed. I flinched at the cool metal of the knob as I opened the door. The room smelled faintly of musty air and stale perfume. Eyeing the shadows in the corners, I turned on the light, illuminating Helen's vast array of trophies on the bookcase across the room. The woman clearly liked to win. Even her trophy for her fifth-grade citizenship award was on display, for crying out loud.

Not wasting any time, I stepped behind Helen's desk. Her shredder was tucked to one side in the kneehole, within easy reach while she worked. I dragged it out and popped off the lid. Fresh papers lay curled at the bottom like a bird's nest. I grabbed a handful and tried to make sense of the scraps.

Drew was right. You could easily read entire words or sets of numbers on the short strips.

Wendy must have bought the shredder at a discount store. I tried to make sense of all the bits and pieces, but I couldn't get a clear picture of what I was looking at. These pieces probably meant nothing. Still, maybe I'd take them home and assemble them like pieces in a Tetris game.

But I couldn't take the entire shredder with me. Helen would notice. I needed a bag. I poked through Helen's drawers, moving aside paper clips and boxes of staples, trying to hurry. As I moved to the other side of the desk, my foot bumped the trash can. The can had been emptied recently, and a fresh, empty bag waited. Perfect. I stuffed the shreddings inside, tied off the top, and pulled the bag out of the can.

The bag was thin and flimsy. One snag on a corner of the desk and it would rip. It reminded me of the bags the one guy had used to sell his dog poop at the festival. We definitely couldn't let him return next year, not after the complaints. My mind flashed back to opening day of the festival.

My mouth went dry.

Helen had been at the festival first thing in the morning and then supposedly left. I'd seen her walk off with Drew. The poop guy had arrived hours later, thanks to his dog's constipation. How did Helen even know about him if she'd already gone? As far as I knew, she'd never returned to the festival, yet she'd seen the so-called fertilizer booth. I started shaking as I realized what that meant.

Helen *had* to be the killer.

And I was standing in her office like an idiot.

Still clutching the bag, I yanked out my phone and called Detective Palmer. Once more, I got his voice mail. I left a hasty message, then hung up and called Jason. He'd barely gotten his "hello" out before I started babbling.

"Jason, Helen is the killer. It was the dog poop. The dog poop! How did she know about the dog poop guy at the festival? She mentioned him when she was talking to Preston at the funeral, but she'd already left the festival before that guy even showed up."

"Dana, slow down. I can't understand you. Did you just say that Helen killed Wendy and Preston?"

I was walking around in circles, heart racing, and forced myself to stand still. "I'm not sure about Preston, but definitely Wendy. I think Helen's the one who embezzled the money and then murdered Wendy to keep her quiet."

I heard Jason's sharp intake of breath. "You're not still at Invisible Prints, are you?"

"I'm leaving right now." As if proving my words, I moved to the door. I looked out the large glass windows and saw a pair of headlights swing into the driveway. I almost wet my pants at the sight. "Oh no, Jason. Someone just drove up," I whispered.

"Get out of there, Dana. Get out now! I'll call 911."

"Okay," I whimpered. I ended the call and hit the wall switch, plunging the room into darkness, but the lights remained on in the main part of the building, like a beacon to my location.

I darted down the hall and flipped the switch at the top of the stairs. The rest of the lights went out. Whoever had pulled up must have noticed my car out front and the lights on, but at least they couldn't see me inside the now-dark building. Maybe I could escape through a back door, if this place even had one.

Mostly blind, I gingerly stuck out a foot and felt for where the stairs started, grabbing the banister with one hand. The cheap plastic of the shredder bag made a slapping sound on the wood. After the first couple of steps, I worked my way up to a trot.

I was almost to the bottom when I heard the front door open and froze. I stared at the figure barely outlined in the doorway. Then the lights came on.

Helen.

Crap.

I am screwed.

35

Water ran in rivulets down Helen's jacket and pooled on the welcome mat. She squinted at me. "Dana?"

"Hi, Helen." My voice squeaked, and I cleared my throat. I shifted the hand with the bag of shreddings behind my back and forced myself to chuckle, though it sounded more like I was choking on a chicken bone. "Kimmie needed to retrieve fund-raising tickets from Wendy's office, and I offered to come with her."

Helen's head swiveled as she took in the room. "Kimmie was that friend of Wendy's, right? So where is she?"

I knew she was going to ask that. "She had to get back to her restaurant. I was on my way, too, but I had to use the facilities. Too much iced tea at dinner." I chuckled again, but Helen didn't.

Instead, she craned her neck to look upstairs. "I thought I saw the light on in my office."

So she *had* noticed the light. "You must have seen me in Wendy's office. I wanted to double-check that we hadn't left a mess."

Her gaze strayed to the front door. "How did you and Kimmie even get in here?"

I didn't want to answer more questions. All I wanted was to find a way out of here. But Helen blocked the only exit and didn't seem eager to move. "Kimmie has a spare key." I tried to keep my focus on Helen, but she must have noticed my attention continually returning to the open door, my one chance at escape.

"Oh, for heaven's sake, I'm letting in the rain," she said. She turned and slammed the door shut. The noise of the latch clicking into the slot reminded me of the sound of a cell door slamming shut in a prison movie.

I crossed the room to where Helen stood, but she made no move to get out of my way. "I think the rain's letting up a little. Now would be a good time for me to drive home," I hinted.

"Before you go, perhaps you could tell me what's in the bag."

My fingers convulsed on the plastic. "Bag?" I asked, trying to sound innocent, but only managing to sound guilty. I lifted the bag up like it held a goldfish that I'd won at the fair. "It's nothing."

Helen pursed her lips. Her gaze never left my face. "Since you're removing it from this office, I'd say it's something."

"Just the trash," I said. "I wasn't sure Kimmie

and I should let ourselves in, so I figured I'd at least take out the trash while I was here." I was a bad liar. I knew I was a bad liar. But in all my years of lying, I'd never come up with a dumber lie than that.

Before I could move, Helen swung an arm out and snatched the bag from my hand, untying the top in one swift motion. She peeked inside, then reached in and pulled out a clump of shredded paper.

As she studied it, her expression changed from mild curiosity to outright rage. When she raised her eyes to glare at me, I felt my insides shrivel.

"These are from *my* office!" She was seething.

I took two steps back. "I'm sure they're from Wendy's office."

She dropped the bag on the floor. "I knew you were trouble the moment you came here after Wendy was killed, snooping around. I answered your questions. I tried to convince you everything was fine. Still, you kept digging. Do you think you're going to blackmail me like Preston did?"

Aha! Blackmailing Helen must have been Preston's big plan to get more money. "Is that why you killed him?"

Helen sneered at me. "He knew Wendy was an idiot when it came to math. He realized I'd been handling the books, so I must be the one who stole the money. He thought he was entitled to it." Helen let out a laugh. "As if."

I backed up again, banging my spine against the

staircase post. My heel bumped the bottom step. "What now? Run off to your new company and start over?"

"Exactly." Helen reached into her inside coat pocket and pulled out a black object, which she gripped in her hand. She unfolded it to reveal the long blade of a knife. "As soon as I get rid of you, of course."

A gust of wind rattled the windows, and Helen jerked around to look. I used the precious seconds to grab a figurine from the end table and strike at Helen. We were far enough apart that I only managed to brush the blade, but the movement startled Helen. She jumped back and lost her footing, falling to one knee.

Even partly kneeling, she could easily grab me if I tried for the door. Instead, I turned and ran up the stairs, huffing and puffing in a panic. All I could picture was getting into an office and locking the door. It was my best chance while I waited for help to arrive. If help was even coming . . .

As I neared the top, I felt fingers wrap around my ankle. I fell forward into the hallway, automatically kicking my leg out behind me. My foot hit air, but Helen loosened her grip. I kicked my leg again, and she let go. I rose to my feet and risked a look behind me. Helen was rising to her feet. Her face was set with determination, and the knife was still clutched in her hand.

I rushed into Wendy's office and slammed the door shut, pushing the lock in the knob. As I turned on the lights, I saw the knob twist as Helen tried to open it from the other side. The sound of metal grating on metal filled my ears as she rotated it first one way and then the other.

I looked around the room for a weapon. My gaze roamed over the shelves and desktop, spotting a stapler, a phone, and a three-hole punch. Not much against a knife of that size, probably the same knife Helen used to kill Wendy and Preston. I pulled out my cell and tried Detective Palmer once more.

Before the call could connect, I heard the scraping of a key against the lock. I felt as if my entire body had turned into a block of ice. I should have realized Helen would have a key to every door in the building. I jerked my head around, hoping I'd see a potential weapon I'd missed the first time.

Nothing.

I shoved my phone in my pocket and turned off the lights, knowing the darkness would slow Helen down only for a couple of seconds. But it was better than nothing.

I crouched behind the desk and heard the lock disengage as the key found its home. The door swung open. The hallway lights created a perfect outline of Helen, knife in hand.

"It's no use running," she said.

Almost blind with panic, I leapt out from behind the desk, felt along the top of the desk, and snatched up the three-hole punch. I ran at Helen and swung the long metal tool at her head. It whacked into her temple. In the dim light, I saw her fall and the knife slipped from her hands. She made a grab at my pants as I moved toward the door, but I squeezed past her and ran for the stairs.

Slipping and skidding my way down the steps, I somehow managed not to break any bones. I darted across the lobby and yanked on the door-knob. Nothing happened. Fresh panic coursed through me.

I jerked the knob again, and the door flew open. Rain slapped my face as I lurched outside and stumbled to my car. Before I could open the door, Helen slammed into me from behind. I felt something scrape my side as I fell against my car. I swiveled around. In the feeble light cast from the building, I could just make out the knife back in Helen's upraised hand.

As she brought the knife down in an arc, I threw myself to one side and pivoted around. The knife clanked against my car door. With a grunt, I grabbed the back of Helen's head and shoved it toward the door. Her face connected with the top of the door frame, and she staggered back, clutch-ing her forehead. Dark lines of what I could only assume were blood streamed down her face, inter-mingling with the rain. The hand with the knife hung at her side.

I rushed forward and shoved her down, then turned and ran. I headed for the highway, water spraying up as my feet pounded the wet ground. The soggy moss beneath my shoes was making squishing sounds, slowing me down as if slogging through mud.

Willing my legs to obey me, I forged ahead. My muscles shrieked in protest. Just when I thought they'd fail completely, I reached solid pavement. I turned in the direction of Mendocino and spotted flashing red-and-blue lights up ahead, coming closer. Jason must have reached the cops. Help was almost here.

I risked a look behind me and saw Helen still at her car. As I watched, she opened her driver's-side door. Relief flooded through me as I realized she was no longer chasing me, too focused on her own escape.

With my last bit of strength, I raised my arms and waved as the cruiser approached. The car slowed as it neared me, and the driver's-side window lowered. "Need help, ma'am?" the officer asked.

Sides heaving, I nodded and pointed toward Helen's car. "That woman killed two people," I gasped out. Then I bent down to catch my breath. All I wanted now was a hot bath and dry clothes. And to be wrapped in Jason's warm embrace.

36

Two days later, I set the last moving box in the middle of my new living room. Well, Ashlee and my new living room, but I kept ignoring that part. I placed my hands on the small of my back and stretched out the muscles. I'd worry about the actual unpacking later.

The front door opened, and Ashlee bounded in, a scruffy-haired, leather-jacket-clad stranger in tow.

"Dana, this is Chip. We hung out together at a friend's party last weekend, and it turns out he lives on the other side of the complex. Isn't that a trip?"

We'd only moved in this morning, and Ashlee already had a new boy over? Oh, Lord, what had I been thinking when I agreed to move in with her?

"Come on, Chip, let me show you my room." She took his hand and pulled him across the floor.

He mimed a hat tip on his way by and muttered, "Later."

They disappeared into Ashlee's room, and she shut the door. Thank goodness I'd insisted on the two-bedroom place.

I shook my head at my sister's antics as I sank down onto the new couch, which had arrived this morning. The smell of chemicals and new material drifted up. I stood and opened the nearest window, thinking about everything that had happened in the last week. Lily had called this morning on the advice of her therapist to apologize officially for scratching my hood. She was also going to report herself to the police. I didn't want to see her go to jail, but maybe confessing to the cops would help curb her anger issues.

Someone knocked at the door. I crossed the room and found Jason standing there, a bouquet of red roses in his hand. Mom stood next to him, holding a toilet brush and a basket of cleaning supplies.

"Look who I found at your door," Mom said.

I swung the door wider so they could both enter, then took the bouquet from Jason. I inhaled the sweet fragrance of the flowers. "You sure spoil me."

"I'd bring you every rose in the store if they'd fit in my car," he whispered into my ear as I gave him a peck on the cheek.

I dug through a box marked *Kitchen* and unearthed a large glass shaped like a parrot, which I'd picked up on a trip to Vegas a few years ago. I filled it with tap water and set the flowers inside. I'd have to add a vase to my list of household items Ashlee and I needed to purchase.

Mom glanced toward the closed bedroom doors. "Where's your sister?"

"Ashlee?" As if I had more than one sister. "She's, um, in her room. She'll be out in a minute."

Mom raised her eyebrows, as if she knew I was leaving out part of the story, but I hustled her and Jason to the couch before she could ask.

"Have a seat, you two." I perched on the coffee table, my knees jutting between Mom and Jason. "I bet you've been swamped at work covering Helen's arrest," I said to Jason.

"The people of Blossom Valley can't get enough," he said.

Mom patted his knee. "You write such wonderful articles. I can't believe that woman was responsible for two murders."

"I'm just glad Dana was able to get away." He took my hand and squeezed it. Out of the corner of my eye, I saw Mom smile.

I squeezed his hand in return. "Well, I did have to hit her in the head with a hole punch."

"You always seem to hit someone in the head when you're in danger," Jason said with a smirk.

"It's my specialty." I released his hand. "But tell us more about the murders. What else have you found out?"

"Well, Wendy's death was completely spur-of-the-moment," Jason said. "Once Drew told Marvin about the missing money, Marvin confronted Wendy at the festival."

"That was the yelling I heard from her booth next door," I interjected.

"Right," Jason said. "Wendy had no idea what Marvin was talking about, so she called Helen, who had already headed back to Invisible Prints. Helen returned, the two argued, and Helen killed her. She told the cops she carried that knife in her purse for muggers."

"Has there ever been a mugging around here?" I shook my head in disgust. "Helen must have known she couldn't hide the embezzlement forever. She may have considered killing Wendy all along."

"Hard to say. She wouldn't admit that, even if it were true."

"What about that miniature turbine I saw next to Wendy's body? Did Helen say anything about that?"

"Total accident," Jason said. "Wendy was holding it when Helen attacked her."

I was almost disappointed that the windmill hadn't meant something profound. But at least the police had arrested Helen. "What about Preston's death?"

Jason grimaced. "He immediately knew Wendy didn't embezzle, because she would have never agreed to handle the money end of the business to start with. He decided to cash in with a little blackmail and set up a meeting with Helen at his house. She figured she'd already killed once, so what difference did a second person make?"

Mom shivered and I rubbed her shoulder.

"Poor Preston," she said.

"What's going to happen to Invisible Prints?" I asked.

"It'll be shut down. Marvin's company might be able to recoup some of the money through a sale of the assets, but Helen won't say where the rest is."

Here she'd killed two people, and she still wouldn't give up the location of the money. "Selfish to the end," I said. I thought about how off base I'd been about Helen. "What happens with Drew and Kurt now?"

"Now that Drew's unemployed, she can use the extra time to plan her wedding. Kurt popped the question."

I smiled. "I had no idea those two were so serious."

Mom looked pointedly at Jason and me. "I love when two young people fall in love and get married."

I tried to choke back a laugh at her blatancy and ended up coughing. Mom patted me on the back, and Jason jumped up.

"Let me get you some water," he said.

As he moved to the kitchenette, Ashlee came out of her room. Chip was right behind, with her lip gloss smeared all over his face.

"Hi, everyone," Ashlee said. "I'm going to walk Chip back to his apartment."

"Leaving so soon?" I managed to say, still coughing a bit.

"Chip has things to do." She half pushed him out the door, then turned back and whispered, "I have to finish unpacking before my next date gets here for dinner." She winked and pulled the door shut behind her.

Another date? Already? I gripped Mom's knee. "Please, I've made a terrible mistake. I don't belong here. I belong at home with you."

Mom laughed. "Nonsense. I'm ready for you girls to move out, and you, young lady, need to get on with your life."

I looked over at Jason as he dug through boxes to find me a glass. He must have felt my gaze, because he glanced up and smiled. A rush of warmth cascaded from my hair roots to my toenails.

I turned back to Mom. "You know, Mom, I think you're right. It is time to move on." Even if it meant living with my boy-crazy sister. At least it was a start.

Tips from the O'Connell Organic Farm and Spa

Here are a few easy and healthy tips from the spa's daily blogs:

Controlling Garden Pests Naturally

Pests can frustrate the best gardeners. Luckily, there are several natural methods to keep down the pest population. You can attract beneficial bugs, such as ladybugs, to your garden to eat less beneficial ones, such as aphids. Another option is to lay a porous fabric over the rows of plants that will still allow sunlight through for healthy growth. In addition, organic pest control products without harsh chemicals are widely available in garden stores. Be consistent in your applications. Before you know it, your garden will be free of pests.

Whipping up a
Banana-and-Yogurt Smoothie

Smoothies are easy to make and often include items that are readily available in your kitchen. Plain yogurt (or vanilla, if you prefer a sweeter smoothie) and ripe fruit are really all you need. Just put half a cup of yogurt and one medium banana in a blender, add a few ice cubes and a dollop of honey, and blend. You can also mix in a handful of ripe strawberries or peach slices for even more fruit flavor and health benefits.

Making Your Own Facial Mask

If you can't visit the new spa here at Esther's place, you can easily create a facial mask by using ingredients left over from your yogurt-and-banana smoothie. The lactic acids and milk proteins of yogurt provide a perfect treatment for your skin, while the banana provides added moisture. To make the mask, mash up half a banana and combine with two tablespoons of yogurt. Bring the mixture to room temperature and then slather it on your clean face. Let it sit for five minutes and then wipe everything off with a warm washcloth. Splash your face with water to remove any lingering residue and pat dry with a soft towel.

Cleaning with Lemons

Lemons have countless uses around the house, particularly when it comes to cleaning. You can make your own furniture polish by mixing one part lemon juice to two parts olive oil. Rub it on your wood furniture with a soft cloth. To bring the shine back to your aluminum pots, simmer lemon slices in water in the pots for an hour. (Don't let the water boil away!) Lemons are also great for removing odors. Use the cut side of a lemon to wipe down your cutting board or grind up lemon peels in your garbage disposal for a fresh scent.

Cutting Your Sodium Intake

Almost every food contains at least trace amounts of sodium. Sodium is an important mineral for keeping a body healthy, but too much sodium can increase your risks of heart disease, stroke, and kidney disease. To limit your sodium intake, focus on eating natural foods, like vegetables and fish. Avoid processed foods, particularly canned soups, pizza, and cold cuts. Reading package labels is the first step toward cutting your sodium and improving your overall health.

Making Homemade Granola

Homemade granola is delicious and easy to make. Start with two parts rolled oats and one part each of sliced almonds and shredded coconut. Add a sprinkle of brown sugar and a pinch of salt. Drizzle the mixture with vegetable oil and honey, and toss everything to combine. Spread the mixture onto a cookie sheet and bake at 350 degrees for a few minutes until everything is a toasty brown. Once the mixture cools, you can add in more delicious ingredients, like raisins, diced dried apricots, or butterscotch chips.

Learning to Meditate

Zennia is convinced that more people would meditate if they knew how easy it is. Meditation requires only a few minutes and no equipment. In fact, all you need is a quiet place to sit comfortably. You can sit on the floor, in a chair, or on a pillow, as long as you can keep your back straight. Then close your eyes and breathe through your nose. Don't try to rush it. Just focus on your breathing. In and out. In and out. Keep your mind clear and push stray thoughts away. Continue focusing on your breathing. Gradually your thoughts will quiet down, and you will relax. That's it!

Please turn the page
for an exciting sneak peek of
Staci McLaughlin's next
Blossom Valley Mystery
coming soon from Kensington Publishing!

1

Esther O'Connell, owner of the O'Connell Organic Farm and Spa, burst through the kitchen door. Her gray curls were clinging to her forehead. Her plump cheeks were flushed. "We're ruined, Dana!" she cried. She flopped into the nearest chair and paused for breath.

I felt a flutter of concern as I set the rooster-shaped mug I'd been hand-drying on the counter. I hurried to where Esther sat, fanning herself. "What happened?"

"It's that new spa on Main Street. My friend Mary Beth stopped in the other day to see what all the fuss was about. She said it's fancier than beaded lace." Esther let her hand droop. "Who'll want to visit my boring old spa now?"

As the designated Jill-of-all-trades here at the farm, I knew it was time for some damage control. I pulled out the chair next to her and sat down.

"People rave about this place. I know for a fact we've been booked all week."

The worry lines in her face only deepened. Esther was a fairly recent widow who had plowed her life savings into the place, and she constantly fussed about the financial status of the farm and spa. I couldn't say I blamed her. "They come here because we're the only spa in town. At least we were. Who's to say they won't switch to the new place?"

I rested a hand on her knee. "I say."

"Say what?" Zennia, the spa's creative and health-minded cook, asked as she walked in from the hall.

I hadn't heard Zennia approach in her Birkenstocks, but I immediately roped her into the conversation, knowing her serene demeanor would help. "Esther's worried about that new spa on Main Street."

Zennia didn't even pause on her way to the refrigerator. She swung open the door and pulled out the lemonade pitcher. "People might try that place once or twice, but they'll come back here. Everyone loves Gretchen."

Gretchen, our newest employee, had started a few months back. Between her knot-melting massages and wrinkle-reducing facials, she'd quickly cemented her place at the spa.

"I hope you two are right," Esther said. "It seems like there's always something to worry about with this place." She rose from her chair and glanced down at her faded plaid shirt. "I'd better change. I have bunco in a bit." She trudged out of the kitchen, leaving Zennia and me alone.

I rose and picked up the dish towel before grabbing another mug from the rack. "Have you heard anything about the new place? It's called The Pampered Life, right?"

Zennia flicked her long black braid over her shoulder. The gray streaks were becoming more noticeable, but no way would Zennia dye her hair. Too many chemicals. "Right. I heard some woman from San Francisco moved up here to open it."

I set the dried mug on a cupboard shelf. "Well, I'm sure once the newness wears off, it won't impact Esther's place." Much, I added silently and mentally crossed my fingers. Our spa hadn't been open long, and while customers seemed happy here, a full-scale spa that offered all the services we couldn't might draw people away. But I kept that thought to myself.

I finished drying the dishes and hung the towel on the oven door handle. "Guess I'll run into town for my lunch break."

"We have plenty of left-over chickpea and seaweed salad, if you'd like some," Zennia offered. "It's chock full of iron and magnesium."

"And the guests didn't gobble it all up?" I said in mock surprise. "I'm stunned."

Zennia gave me a knowing smile. "You'll come around one day."

"Today's not that day, I'm afraid. I have my mind set on a BLT." I licked my lips. "With extra mayonnaise."

Zennia clapped her hands over her ears. "Stop. Don't say such things."

Laughing, I headed down the hall to grab my purse from the desk in the office. I spent most of my working hours in this room promoting the spa, although Esther occasionally asked me to serve meals, catch loose animals, and help with pretty much anything else that needed doing around the place.

I crossed the empty lobby and pushed open the front door. A breeze tickled my skin, and the chatter of birds greeted me on the cool spring day. A flock of ducks drifted on the surface of the small pond near the front.

I walked to my aging Civic, which was parked in the corner of the lot, and climbed inside. The door creaked as I pulled it closed. The engine had started to make a funny squealing sound on colder days, but I'd decided to ignore it. Having just moved from my mom's house into a barely furnished apartment with my younger sister, Ashlee, I couldn't afford any additional expenses right now.

After starting the engine, I pulled out of the lot.

The drive down the highway was quick, and within five minutes, I was cruising through Blossom Valley's downtown. I eyed the front of The Pampered Life as I passed by. If I hadn't known it used to be a hardware store, I'd have never guessed. The new owner had darkened all the windows, etching the words, "The Pampered Life" in cursive script across the glass. A pink-and-white-striped awning stretched across the front, and a redwood and wrought-iron park bench sat to one side of the door. A sandwich board on the sidewalk announced a Botox party next week, only ten dollars per filler. I reached up and felt the skin next to my mouth, wondering if twenty-nine was too young to worry about wrinkles. Still, even at ten dollars a pop, I wouldn't be getting Botox any time soon. Or ever.

I drove to the next block and pulled into the Breaking Bread Diner lot. I parked between a dusty pickup truck and a motorcycle and walked inside. The stools that lined the counter were empty, and I settled on the closest one.

A waitress was helping a customer at a nearby booth, and she nodded in my direction. "Be with you in a minute, hon."

I nodded back and pulled my phone from my pocket to check for messages. I'd been here enough times that I didn't need to study the menu. I sent a quick text to Ashlee to see if she'd had a chance to pick up any toilet cleaner, then stuffed the phone back in my pocket. We were still working out chore duties, even resorting to a chart on the fridge. Ashlee's plan seemed to be to ignore the dirty dishes and grime-covered counters until I broke down and cleaned them myself. Sometimes her plan worked, much to my self-loathing.

The waitress finished with her customer and made her way over to where I sat. With her short, pink uniform and her dark brown hair piled atop her head, I almost expected her to snap her gum and pull a pencil out of her hair like on an episode of *Alice.*

"What can I get you today?" she asked.

"BLT and iced tea, please."

"Extra mayo?"

"Absolutely." An idea popped to mind. "Say, make that to-go. I have to run an errand right now."

"Sure thing. Give me ten minutes." She finished scribbling on her pad and stuck it in an apron pocket.

"I'll be back by then," I told her and slid off the stool. I pushed through the door and out onto the street, taking quick strides toward my intended target: The Pampered Life.

Now that Esther had told me how fabulous her friend thought the place was, I wanted to see it for myself. Surely it couldn't be that much better than ours. And if this spa was the greatest thing since laser hair removal, then maybe I could collect ideas for Esther's place. While I loved our little spa, there was always room for improvement.

As I neared the building, I slowed to peer through the windows, but the tinted glass made it impossible to see inside. I pushed open the door and stepped in. A low-volume techno beat reverberated in the dimly-lit space. The scent of jasmine reached my nose. In the corner, a small water fountain burbled, with the large marble ball in the middle spinning merrily. Three overstuffed recliners, looking much more comfortable than the rattan furniture at our spa, filled the small lobby area, along with several potted ferns. Photos of trees and meadows lined the walls. I was about to take my phone from my pocket to sneak some pictures when an ultrathin girl stepped through the archway at the back of the lobby and moved behind the counter.

"Welcome to the Pampered Life," she said. Her rose-red lips shone brightly against her pale skin. "Do you have an appointment?"

"No," I said, my voice sounding unnaturally loud compared to her soft lilt. "I noticed you recently opened and thought I'd stop by." I approached the counter. "Oh good, a brochure." I picked one up from the stack, eager to see what they offered.

Before I could look over the glossy pages, the

girl started talking again. "We have a wide range of services here," she said. "We do all types of massage, including Swedish and deep tissue, plus facials."

Everything we offered at Esther's place. I felt myself relax a notch.

The girl picked up a pencil and tapped it in time with her words. "Then, we've got the extras like mud baths, Brazilians waxes, Botox injections . . ."

My muscles tensed again. So this place wasn't exactly like Esther's. "Sounds like you've got everything I could ever need," I interrupted as she rattled off more items.

The pencil-tapping stopped, and she nodded eagerly. "Yes, and we offer payment plans. The last thing you want to stress about is how to pay to relax."

"How convenient," I mumbled. Was that something we could afford to do at Esther's? At least the farm had animals, a unique plus for Esther's place. The guests always commented on how much they enjoyed our ducks, pigs, and chickens.

"Hey, let me tell you about our seaweed wrap treatment. You start with an all-over body exfoliation—"

The girl broke off her explanation as a woman in her mid-forties entered from the back. With her perfect posture and tall, willowy frame, she was the type who could make yoga pants and a T-shirt look like formal business attire.

She appraised me for a moment, and then turned toward the girl. "Jessica, do you know what we have here?"

Jessica shook her head, her eyes wide in anticipation.

The woman raised her hand and pointed her index finger at me. "A spy. She's a spy."

How had she known? I gulped as a wave of heat washed over me. I was in some deep seaweed.